How to Tackle Your Dreams

How to Tackle Your Dreams

Fiona Hardy

For Belinda and Michelle

First published by Affirm Press in 2022
Boon Wurrung Country
28 Thistlethwaite Street,
South Melbourne, VIC 3205
affirmpress.com.au
10 9 8 7 6 5 4 3 2 1

A catalogue record for this book is available from the National Library of Australia

ISBN: 9781922626684 (paperback)
Cover illustration by Jess Racklyeft © Affirm Press 2022
Typeset in Fournier MT Std 11.75 / 15.25 by J&M Typesetting
Proudly printed in Australia by McPherson's Printing Group

ROUND 1 STATS

Career Game Averages
Kicks: 8
Tackles: 3
Possessions: 9
Goals: 2

'You have to go up and tell him.'

I crossed my arms. 'Me? You were the one who did it!'

'But it's your turn to take the heat!'

'You're the one who kicks the ball onto his roof like ninety per cent of the time!'

'Come on! He yells at you less.'

'Hmm,' I said, 'maybe that's because he knows you're the one who's always kicking the ball onto his roof?'

'Ugh. Why are you such a jerk?'

'Blame my parents.'

Mum snorted. 'I am exceptionally good at that already.' She sighed and looked over at Mr Huber's roof. 'Do I *have* to?'

I raised my eyebrows and pointed to his house.

'Okay, but you have to be there as moral support.'

We went over and Mum knocked on the door. Mr Huber answered, in his usual outfit: a jumper way too warm for this weather was tucked into pants that were way too high for this world. When he saw us on the doorstep he pulled his pants up even higher, which he liked to do before telling somebody off.

'Mrs Schneider!' he hollered. 'Did your son kick a football onto my roof again?'

'Yes,' she said.

'Hey!' I yelled behind her.

She hissed without moving her lips, 'I'll give you five bucks to spend at Maker Acre if you wear this one.'

Dammit, she'd got me. 'I'm sorry, Mr Huber,' I said, in my Very Good Boy voice. 'I was just too excited about helping Mum train. You know it's her big game this weekend, right?'

'So I heard.' He crossed his arms and glared at her. 'Is your football team willing to pay for the damage to my roof?'

'I'm sure there's no damage,' Mum said. 'If there is, I promise they will.'

'This is the *last time*, Mrs Schneider,' he said, for the sixty-eighth time.

'Thank you,' she said, 'you are too generous.' She couldn't help herself, though, and added, 'but it's not Mrs Schneider, remember? It's Ms Falzon.'

'Hmph.' He grabbed at the door handle and said, 'You better win after all this practice on my property,' then slammed the door.

'Want me to get the ball down?' I asked, feeling a bit bad for her.

'No way. If anyone's going to fall through the roof and mess up Mr Huber's day, it's going to be me.'

I got the ladder from behind our place and held it for her while she climbed up and threw the ball back down. 'Mum,'

I called up, 'after this, can I go inside and finish up fixing my PE shirt? It's nearly done.'

'No way. You've got practice with your dad.'

'But I want to get it finished by tomorrow!'

'He only just knocked off work, remember?' She climbed back down and said, 'It's now or never, baby.'

'What if I'm already as good at football as I'll ever be and practice makes me go backwards?'

'I won't even pretend to answer that,' she said, putting the ladder back. 'So let's go.'

'Ten push-ups,' Dad said.

'But I just did twenty!'

'What's your point?'

'My point is that you're mean?'

He crossed his arms.

Mum said, 'Better do what he says. You know how he gets when he crosses him arms.'

I did the push-ups.

'Fifty star-jumps,' Dad said. When I'd finished those, he said, 'Ten squat-jumps.'

'Is he sweating enough?' Dad asked Mum.

She came up close and stared at my forehead. 'Doesn't look even slightly tired.'

'Mum!'

She grinned and punched me on the arm, then turned to Dad. 'Kick to kick, you reckon, Timo?'

'Dad usually asks me to do handballs now,' I put in.

'We can do handballs,' Mum said.

'Make him work for them,' Dad yelled.

We put the iPad up on a bench so Dad could watch us practise. Mum would punch the ball just out of reach, I'd run to it, and Dad would holler, 'Go harder, Homer! You call that a handball? Get in front of her!'

After a while I just fell on the ground in a heap. 'Get up,' Mum said, poking me with the toe of her shoe. 'This is practice for me too.'

Dad said something I couldn't hear and I rolled along the grass over to the iPad. 'Huh?'

'How's your Mum feeling about Saturday?' he asked.

'She's pretending not to be stressed,' I said, and she came over and sat on me while I yelled, 'Hey!'

'I hate it when he's right,' Mum told Dad, looking down at me. 'Luckily, it doesn't happen a lot.'

'Hey!' I said again.

'You'll be great,' Dad said to her. 'You've got the best coach.'

'Yeah, Doug's been really—'

'I mean me,' Dad said huffily.

She laughed. 'Actually, Homer's way more critical of my moves than you are. He's probably the meanest coach of all of you.'

'How do you think she's going to go, Homer?' Dad asked, giving me as much of a Meaningful Expression as you could hope for on a screen that kept making him go all blurry.

'She's going to be great,' I said.

'I feel sick,' Mum said, rolling off me onto the ground and moaning. I picked Dad up from the bench and held him up so he could see both of us sprawled on the ground.

'Why would you be nervous?' Dad asked her. 'It's football, and you're an expert at it.'

'True,' Mum said.

'Except it'll be on television and everyone will be watching you,' I said helpfully.

'Your whole life has worked towards this,' Dad said. 'All those years running and working out and learning to be a physio and playing sports, and now you're here.'

'Neither of you are helping,' Mum said, covering her face with her hands. 'What if I'm too old?'

'You're not,' Dad said firmly. 'And remember, you couldn't even play national football when you were a teenager because women's teams didn't exist yet. You are doing it now and the team is lucky to have you. I am so excited to come over on Friday and watch you destroy the opposition.'

'What if my shoulder isn't up for it?'

'What did your doctor say today?'

'That it's fine.' Mum crossed her arms.

'And how did it feel after your last training session?'

'Completely normal.'

'Hmm,' Dad said. 'Sounds like you're going to kill it on Saturday. Unless, of course, you spend all your time lying around moping instead of practising.'

'What if it turns out I'm better at moping than I am at football?'

I got up. 'Then you'd have been drafted into the Australian Moping League,' I said, 'But you were actually drafted into the Australian *Football* League, so I guess you must be really amazing at it?'

'Stop being so encouraging,' she said. 'You'll make me want

to start practising again. A few kicks?'

'Dad would've said to do some running bounces,' I said.

'Homer,' Dad said, 'you can listen to what your mum says, you know?'

'It's okay,' Mum said. 'I can do some running bounces. And way faster than Homer can too.'

'What?!' I said, pretending to be super offended even though, obviously, she was way better than me.

Later, when we were both completely wrecked and Dad's voice was hoarse from yelling loud enough that we could hear him, he croaked out a goodbye.

'See you Friday,' I said. 'Nanna's going to drive me to the airport to pick you up.'

'When she buys you a muffin while you're waiting for me to disembark, don't eat the entire thing,' he said. 'They're full of unnecessary sugars and you need to stay health—'

'BORING,' I yelled.

He sighed, then looked at Mum. 'I can't wait,' he told her. 'You're going to be spectacular.'

She grinned. We hung up, packed up the iPad and the footballs and all the other stuff and trudged back home again. While we walked, I watched Mum weighed down with all the gear and was about to tell her to stand up straight before I realised that's exactly what Dad would say. He hadn't walked next to me after training and told me off for slouching for so long that I almost missed it. I definitely missed him not helping lug all the gear home. Mostly, I missed him actually being at the home we got back to.

'You really are going to be great on Saturday,' I told Mum so I'd stop thinking about Dad.

'I hope so.' She bounced a ball in front of her. 'I'm not usually a nervous person. But I'm feeling nervous about this.'

'You don't have to be nervous. You're going to kill it. Remember all the years you spent ignoring me and playing sports? This is what that was for.'

Mum froze. 'What?! I didn't ignore you. Oh god, did I ignore you?'

She looked so devastated that I felt bad and said, 'I'm joking! I didn't feel ignored. I had Dad to help me out when you were at games or practice. And now ...' I stopped for a second and adjusted the bag of gear on my back. 'Well, now Nanna and Pa can.'

'While I still ignore you,' she whispered.

This was all getting way more serious than I wanted, so I took out a cone from the bag, put it on my head like a hat and said, 'I'll cast a spell on you for your team to win on Saturday.' I got out the skipping rope, stared at it in horror, and said, 'Oh no, my wand is broken!'

'You're a goose,' she said, but at least now she was smiling and not pulling her Sad Parent Face, which I'd seen a lot on both her and Dad since they split up. (But fifty per cent less now that Dad moved away, which is, you know, good and bad.)

I whipped my skipping wand on the ground to distract myself from Sad Dad Thoughts and told her, 'If you can make it home in four minutes, I guarantee you'll win on Saturday.'

'Four minutes?!'

I looked at my watch. 'You're losing precious time by complaining.'

She bolted. I strolled after her, lugging the bag of stuff and thinking that if Dad had been here, he'd have made me run after her. Instead, I got home to find Mum doing push-ups and saying smugly, 'Three minutes and forty seconds, thank you very much.'

Later that night, in bed, I sent Dad a goodnight text. Back when he was trying to convince me that him getting a job interstate would be fine, he explained that I should be glad because he and Mum would give me a phone so I could call him whenever I wanted. Even though I'd been whining for a phone for years, I still looked at it sometimes and remembered that feeling in my stomach when he said that. Like moving two and a half thousand kilometres away from me wasn't a big thing. Like he could buy me off with a phone.

Especially when I would've way preferred to have been bought off with a Switch.

Night, he wrote back. *Hope the rest of practice was ok.*

Pretty good, I said.

Check this out, he wrote, then sent a link for an hour-long video of some guy in a banana costume called HANK SHOWS YOU SOME AFL SKILLZ. There was no way I was going to watch it, but I wrote: *Thnx, I'll look at it in the morning*.

Love you, he wrote.

You too.

I got back out of bed and checked my uniform was ready for the morning. Usually I didn't care and just threw on whatever was in the mound of clean laundry on the couch, but I had big plans for tomorrow. The PE shirt was done, and my least ancient shorts were folded underneath it. I even had my cleanest white socks out for effect, and I'd rubbed my runners with a bench wipe so they were slightly less gross than usual.

Tomorrow was my day. And I was going to impress *everyone*.

ROUND 2 STATS

Hours Until Dad's Plane: 57

Every morning I rode my bike to meet Mario and Ng on the corner opposite school. We called it The Bad Corner, because it wasn't on school property and we were allowed to do as many illegal things there as we wanted. We hadn't actually come up with anything illegal to do yet, but we still had, like, nine months of grade six left to figure something out.

Ng was always late, but Mario was there when I rolled up on my bike. He was eating all the best parts of his lunchbox so that he could pretend his Mum hadn't packed anything nice and steal somebody else's chips later. He wiped biscuit crumbs off his face and said, 'Why are you standing like that?'

'Like what?'

'Like you're trying to be on a movie poster or something.'

'This is completely normal for me,' I said, with one foot up on my schoolbag, my hands on my hips and my chest puffed out like a superhero.

'What gives?'

'Haven't you noticed?'

He squinted. 'Did you cut your hair?'

'No.'

He stroked his chin. 'Does ... does your shirt look different?'

'Yes! Look.' I jumped up and down and ran on the spot, then pointed at my neck.

'Mate! Your shirt isn't even strangling you.'

'I know! I fixed it!'

He reached over and pulled at my neck and investigated my sleeves and said, 'How?'

'I altered it! I fixed the shoulders so they'd stop falling backwards.'

'Why didn't you do mine too?' he whined.

'I literally just finished mine on the weekend. I didn't even know if it worked. But it feels great, and I'll know for sure at the end of PE.'

Ng turned up, out of breath from running. His mum always dropped him off two minutes before the bell rang, no matter how early or late they left their house, even if there was traffic or roadworks. It was her superpower, even though I don't think the Avengers will be calling about it.

'What's up with your shirt?' Ng asked me. 'Why is it different?'

'I was sick of it always choking me, so I fixed it.'

'How?'

'Magic,' I said.

'Sewing,' Mario added. 'His Pa is a tailor, remember? I bet he did it.'

'Nope.' I shook my head. 'It was all me. Well, ninety-six

per cent me.'

'Rad,' Ng said. 'Can I wear it?'

'What? No!'

'Why not?'

'It's mine!'

'Ugh, whatever,' Ng said. 'When are you going to do ours?'

'Exactly,' Mario said.

I crossed my arms. 'What's in it for me?'

Ng gasped. 'How could you?' he said dramatically. 'Your very best friends? And you wouldn't just *help* us?'

'Remember that time you said your mum packed too many Tim Tams in your lunch box and I helpfully ate them all?' Mario said. 'And this is how you repay me?'

'That is *not* how I remember that day going down,' I said.

The bell rang and we bolted over the road to class after another morning of not using The Bad Corner to its full potential. Mr Skia, clutching a coffee and wearing a blue shirt he hadn't ironed, black jeans and a pair of Converse sneakers, said, 'Boys, have you considered turning up to class *before* the bell rings?'

'All the time,' Mario said breezily, walking past him into the room.

Mario and I got into trouble a lot. It was hard to explain why, but it was probably because we didn't listen or pay attention and never stopped talking and always deliberately did the wrong things because they were funny. (Ng did all these things too but was way better at not getting caught.) I'd been extra awful last year when Mum and Dad were splitting up, and a real jerkjack over the summer when Dad had moved away and I was Working Through Things (as my psychologist said), but now I was just back to being a normal low-level rascal who stole pencils from the people on my table and blamed whoever I was sitting next to whenever I farted. This month, I was sitting on a table with Tom, K., and Thi, and they loved it when I did those kinds of things.

'I got you a book for free reading,' Thi said, pushing a copy of *Salvatore Rocco: Full Tilt Forward* at me. She held up *Left of Centre*, one of the other Sal Rocco books, and said, 'Race ya.'

'No fair! You already started.'

'Should've got here early then, huh?'

Everything with Thi was a competition and she was annoyingly good at heaps of things I was also good at, like PE, so I didn't even get to win all the time. One lunchtime last year we made a bet about who could kick the most football goals in a row. It took all lunchtime and still ended up in a tie, which was probably a good thing since we'd bet fifty bucks on it, and I only had the handful of money I'd been trying to save towards plane tickets for Dad to come over, and Thi probably didn't have fifty bucks either.

When it came to reading she was definitely going to beat me, but the Sal Rocco books were my favourites and I'd already read *Full Tilt Forward* a bunch of times, so I kind of zoned out of this race until Mr Skia was suddenly beside me hollering, 'Homer!'

I jumped. 'Skia!'

'Homer. Did you turn a single page in that book this whole time?'

'A single page? Definitely.'

'More than one?'

'You'll have to ask my lawyer,' I said, pointing at Tom, who spent about ninety-five per cent of his time telling everybody that his dad was a lawyer and that he was going to sue them for things like stealing his pencils or blaming him for their farts.

'I'm not asking Tom. I'm asking you. Can you make any text-to-self connections with your book today?'

'Sure,' I said, 'like this?' I picked up my book and smashed myself in the face with it.

Everyone cracked up laughing. Skia raised one eyebrow very slowly and then pointed at it. 'You see this?' he said. 'I couldn't do that before this year. You alone have given me so many reasons to raise one eyebrow that I have become amazing at it.'

'You're welcome,' I said politely.

'Homer,' he said again, in his This Is The Last Straw voice. 'Can you. Make any. Connections. With your. Book.'

'Yes. I think Sal from my book would have found that pretty funny.'

'Well done,' he said. 'And do you need to go to the sick bay after that stunt?'

My face actually hurt a lot but I couldn't say that out loud, obviously. 'I'm fine.'

'Thi, can you make any text-to-self connections with your book?'

'Yes. In *Left of Centre*, Sal's friend Rhys joins the team halfway through the year and he's nervous, and it made me think of Homer's mum, who's playing her first game this weekend even though the season's already started.'

Skia said, 'Homer, is it really this weekend?'

I nodded. 'You going to watch?'

'I am going to sleep all weekend,' he said, 'but I will be watching in spirit.'

'I'm going to the game,' Thi blurted out. 'I can't wait.'

'Good text-to-self connection,' Skia told her. 'Or, as usual, good text-to-football connection.'

Thi beamed at me, and I smiled back at her. I was glad she was pumped about Mum's game. I mean, generally, anything that made people pay attention to me was a good thing.

As long as they all stopped talking about Mum for long enough to notice how amazing my shirt was, then I would be blisteringly famous in no time. Posters. Storefronts. People everywhere talking about me for outfit reasons instead of about that time I headbutted an apple between two teachers giving a speech about respect and hollered 'GOAL!'

Fame was only one PE lesson away. I knew it.

ROUND 3 STATS

Hourly Shirt-Compliment Average: 2

When PE rolled around after lunch, I was ready.

Our year level got sports uniforms on the first day of grade five, and we'd all been suffering ever since. The shirts looked great, but they extremely sucked to wear. The collars fell down at the back and the front bit went right up to your throat and then the whole thing stuck to your sweat, so every PE lesson was spent trying to yank it down so you could breathe. The only way to get less strangled was if you tucked it into your shorts, but if you tucked it into your shorts then Taylor, one of the two worst people in our class, would straight up murder you with insults. So our choices were, basically, *maybe* die from the shirts or *definitely* die from Taylor, which meant we all just took our chances with the collars.

But this year I was sick of it. After hanging out in Pa's tailor shop over the summer holidays and asking him for advice, then drawing up some sketches that looked maybe thirty per cent like a shirt at first, I'd done it: come up with a plan to make them better. First, I fixed the shoulder seams so the collar sat in the right place, and since I'd already found the right shade of thread I took the shirt in around the sides so it fit me better, then I hemmed it so it didn't hang so low that it made me look stumpy. I thought I looked pretty good, at least for somebody who was wearing the exact same clothes as everybody else in my class. More importantly, I *felt* amazing, and free, like I could take on anything.

We were doing athletics for PE this term and Ms Honeybone had set up for high jump. Tom was the tallest kid in our class and loved to show off about being naturally good at this just because his legs were longer, which was mostly cheating. He was my friend, kind of, but he was also the other worst person in our class, so watching him yank uncomfortably at his collar the whole time he was waiting in line was pretty satisfying. I might even have laughed a bit when he yanked it again as he was running up to the bar, which distracted him, made him leap short, and then just smack straight into the pole. I'm not tall, but I am bouncy, and I sprinted up to the bar, my whole body feeling completely loose, and sprang right over it.

'Excellent job, Homer,' Ms Honeybone said. She was my favourite teacher because she never told me off, because I actually listened, because sport was the most interesting thing about school. 'I hope everyone else has noted your form.'

Tom was rubbing his back and looking at me with his eyes narrowed. 'There's something different about you,' he said.

'Is it that I look like a winner?' I said, flexing.

'Definitely not,' he said. He stared harder and said, 'It's your shirt! It's better!'

'I fixed it,' I said smugly.

'Give it to me,' he said, putting out his hand.

'Nah.'

'Come on. You're cheating.'

'It's not going to work on you. I made it to fit me, not you,' I explained. 'You're, like, a whole different shape.'

'You mean since I'm taller and better looking?'

'Uh, I didn't measure it for my face?'

'Just give it to me.'

I knew he wouldn't shut up about it, so I said, 'Fine,' and we swapped shirts. His smelled like dad perfume and not much running. Mine smelled like a sweaty dude who'd just rolled in the grass. Tom's face looked like he agreed.

'This better be worth it,' he said.

'What, worth all of us having to see your belly button?' Ng said from behind me.

Tom looked down and growled. 'Why is it so short?'

'Like I said, we're two different shapes. It was too long on me before. I have a shorter body than you, so now you look like you're wearing a crop top.'

He took it off and threw it back at me. 'It was gross anyway.'

I put it on over the top of his shirt and he yelled, 'Homer!'

'What?'

He ran at me and I bolted while he chased me around the oval. Usually I would've won, but I was wearing his stupid shirt that pulled my shoulders and annoyed me, so I just dove into the grass and rolled out of his reach until he got a hold of my shoe.

'Boys!'

Ms Honeybone looked dangerously close to finally telling me off. I took off both shirts and gave Tom his useless one back.

'Sorry, Ms Honeybone,' I said. 'Just getting in some extra fitness.'

She rolled her eyes. Like my mum, she wore workout gear all the time, except for during winter when she wore the exact same thing but with a giant basketball hoodie over the top, so I thought she'd appreciate the fitness line. Apparently not.

She lifted the bar and we went around again. I cleared it with no problem and added a somersault on landing for effect. A few other kids made it too, like Thi, who tucked her shirt in before she ran to show she was serious but untucked it straight after the landing so Taylor wouldn't notice. Thi was out the next round, but I flew over the bar like it wasn't even there and when I landed I did two somersaults for double effect. After that round, it was down to me, Henry, who was good at basically everything, and Jhyll, who spent all her time rollerskating everywhere and was enjoying how springy she could be without wheels attached to her feet. Ms Honeybone raised the bar again. Henry knocked it off, but Jhyll made it over. I shook out my shoulders, took a few breaths and ran for it. I pushed off, and I soared. I couldn't even feel my shirt. I was just the air.

I flew over the bar, landed in a roll, and did three somersaults off the mat.

It was, it turned out, too many somersaults.

I fell off the side of the mat straight onto one foot, my ankle giving way underneath me. I yelped in pain, and Ms Honeybone ran over.

'Homer, you okay?'

'I landed weird on my ankle,' I said from the ground. 'It hurts.'

'What have I told you about showing off?'

'That it'll get me sponsorships when I'm famous?'

'Homer!' she laughed. 'I probably do say that. Anyway, I'll get you some ice.'

'Nah, I'm okay,' I said, getting up and testing my foot gently on the ground. 'I'll walk it off.'

I watched from the side of the oval while Tom destroyed everyone in long jump and Thi conquered the triple jump then made sure to come past where I was sitting to say, 'When you're better, I'll still beat you.' When I got up and chased her down, I only limped a little, and after Ms Honeybone finished pretending to be mad at me she said I was going to smash it on Athletics Day next term. She was probably right, though I wasn't as good at the other stuff, like javelin, which Taylor usually won because she was always throwing tantrums (at least that was Ms Honeybone's theory), or long-distance running, where K. slayed everyone because they'd had a lot of practice running away from their one million brothers and sisters.

I felt so good when I left school after the bell rang that I wasn't even mad when Tom ran past, threw his shirt at my face, then kept running in just his shorts and hollered, 'Don't take it up like yours, and you better wash it too!'

ROUND 4 STATS

New Shirts to Fix: 1
Season Average Injuries: 1

At training, our coach, Crabtree, lined us all up straight, walked up the line like we were soldiers and stopped at me to say, 'How's your mum, Falzon Schneider?'

He always did this and I hated it. I cleared my throat and didn't make eye contact, instead staring at his grey-and-yellow LaFontaine kicks, which were primo footwear even when you wore them with fishing rod-print socks like he did. 'She's over there in the stands if you want to ask her.'

'I'm asking you. You two been practising?'

'Yeah.'

'We'll see.'

We ran five laps of the oval, stretched, and practised our footwork and tackling. I was still wearing my PE shirt, still feeling great and still flying. We worked on contesting marks and I sprang right off Ng's back for one that was so epic that Crabtree made me sit in time out for a bit to Think About Being More

Careful. I powered through the burpees he loved to torment us with and weaved all over the field doing handball drills. After Crabtree had worn us down into the ground, he called a scratch match and it was absolutely on.

Tom was on the other side, and he was good. It annoyed me that he got to be naturally athletic as well as tall, because if he bothered to practise more or care about football more than he cared about his face, he'd be incredible.

I was thinking about this now because I'd decided that today I was going to target Tom. I was going to play against him, and I was going to win. I was going to remember all the times he didn't bother turning up to practice because he'd washed his hair and it had dried in the right direction. I was going to remember all the times he'd stolen my muesli bars in grade two. I was going to remember that time I wore a shirt he said looked rad and when I told him I made it he called me a liar. I was going to kick his ass.

Crabtree blew the whistle and I bolted away from Jerome, who Crabtree'd paired me up against, and towards Tom. Everyone was trying to get the ball to him, since his long arms meant he had good reach, but I used my t-shirt super-strength and bounced up like the grass was a trampoline to snatch it right out of his hands. I landed, rolled on the ground, then sprang up and kept going while Tom yelled, 'Hey!' without moving, and Crabtree shouted at him, 'Tom, go get the ball back!'

It was too late. I was running through the centre square, bouncing the ball cleanly, feeling the sun on my back and the breeze on my face. Right inside the 50-metre line I had a crack at a goal, smashing it through the posts while everyone on my team cheered and Tom finally turned up, out of breath, to say, 'Uh, I thought we were supposed to be friends?'

‘We are,’ I said, smiling at him with all of my teeth. ‘Isn’t this us spending quality time together?’

Crabtree came up and said, ‘Listen, you’ve got to stay on your player.’

‘Or I could just win instead?’ I said.

He pointed at me. ‘Don’t think I won’t put you on the bench for your first match.’

He totally wouldn’t, but I rolled it back anyway. ‘Yes, sir.’

We started again. While we scrapped around waiting for the bounce, Jerome whispered, with his elbow in my face, ‘That was fun to watch. I know Tom’s on my side but feel free to make him suffer again.’

‘I’ll do my very best.’

The ball went up again. Aaron leapt up and tapped it over towards us. Jerome grabbed it out of my hands and kicked it straight towards Bucky, who pelted away with it while I ran after him, feeling like the football oval was half the size it usually was and like I could have run the length of it forever. Bucky couldn’t outrun me, but I saw Tom charging in from the side and knew Jerome was hot on our tail, so I made a calculated risk and leapt for Bucky, tackling him to the ground then springing back up with the ball in my hands. Tom was right in front of me, looking pleased with himself for purposely getting in the mix instead of waiting by the sideline for the ball to come to him like usual, and I couldn’t avoid him. I did the second-best thing: fell into a roll, smacked into his legs, knocked him over, and spun the ball along the ground to Aaron, who bolted off with Jerome in pursuit while Tom tried to untangle from my legs and said, ‘What the hell?’

‘It was an accident,’ I said, widening my eyes innocently.

'Get up,' Crabtree said, kicking grass at us both. 'Aaron got another goal, so Tom, you better kick your game into gear.' He backed away. 'You,' he said, pointing at me, 'better stop mucking around. Didn't your mum say your dad was coming over from Perth for your first game? You want to make sure I put you on the ground then, huh?'

I hauled myself up and put my hand out to help Tom, who slapped it away. I went back to Jerome, who said, 'Are you okay?'

'Fine,' I said, rearranging my face to look calm. When the ball went up again, I pulled myself together. I wasn't designed for the bench. I was made to be out on the ground, like now, letting that afternoon sun get all over my skin like I was solar-powered, like it was charging me up to run around the ground, chase after the ball, pass it to whoever was open, make sure we won, make sure I didn't wreck my chances of Dad seeing me play for the first time in—

I'd forgotten completely about my ankle. But I'd turned to punch the ball to Jay and twisted around all wrong. I fell over and howled.

Crabtree jogged over. 'What happened?'

I could see Mum standing up from her seat and watching me. 'It's my ankle,' I said to him. 'I wrecked it in PE today but I thought I'd be all right for this afternoon.'

'He fell after high jump,' Ng explained.

'I'll be okay,' I said, standing up, then falling over straight away.

I ended up in the stands with my mum, with ice on my ankle. She'd been sitting up beside Thi and some other girls I half-knew, and they'd all been watching because next year, finally, we were getting a girls' team. Sometimes, if my team hadn't annoyed Crabtree so much that he needed a break, he'd give the girls that had rocked up a little training session for the twenty minutes between when we finished and when the seniors got started. He'd seemed pretty cranky today, but now that I was sitting here it was up to the rest of the guys to put him back in a good mood.

'You all right?' Mum asked, checking in. She'd already gone over all the usual things as soon as I hobbled up there, making me move my ankle left and right, poking it and rolling it around and asking where it hurt and deciding that I'd recover before slapping my other foot so it didn't feel neglected.

'Sure, I'm fine,' I said. 'I guess I need a break for today to rest it.'

'Poor thing. Lucky training's picking up from next week, huh? Then you get two sessions a week. It won't matter that you've missed out today.'

'Yeah,' I said, watching the rest of the guys on the oval running around getting goals perfectly well without me. Our team this season was a great one. We'd smashed the ladder last year and only missed out on the grand final by two goals even though we'd been down by fifty at half-time. This year we had a chance at the premiership, and I knew this because nobody ever shut up about it.

'We're definitely in for a chance this year,' Thi said.

I rolled my eyes. 'You're not even playing until next year!'

'We. The club. It's a team effort,' she said. 'Do you need lessons about what football is again?'

'Ha ha. Shut up.'

'You shut up.'

'No, you.'

Mum said, 'I can hear you, you know. Homer, don't tell people to shut up.'

'She started it!'

Thi poked her tongue out me and I tried to grab it while she laughed.

'Angela,' Thi said, slapping me away and suddenly getting serious, 'what was it like when you got drafted last year?'

Mum put her hands behind her head and leaned back. 'I honestly don't have the words for it. It was kind of like when Homer was born – like a part of me I didn't realise I'd been missing suddenly arrived. As if … I don't know. As if I'd grown wings and suddenly I could fly.'

'That's amazing,' Thi breathed.

'Billions of birds think it's pretty normal,' I said, and Mum poked me in the ribs.

I thought we could head off early so I could get started on Tom's shirt, but Mum refused to leave. 'You're part of a team, remember? Like Thi said.'

'Observation is important too,' Thi said.

'She's smart,' Mum said.

Thi blushed and looked away. I liked Thi, but she couldn't talk about anything but footy. Of course, Mum thought that was the best, and the two of them went on and on for the rest of training about the importance of teamwork and how Mum was feeling about her upcoming game while I died of boredom and also frozen ankles.

When it was finally over and I got up to leave, Thi stood too and leaned in to say something.

'Yeah, yeah,' I said, interrupting her before she started telling me off again. 'I was *watching* and *observing* and *being part of a team*. And Mum'll make me train at home.'

'I'm not telling you off. I'm just saying,' she said, leaning in closer, 'I *know*.'

'Know what?'

She gave me a very long look. 'Nothing, I guess,' she said, stepping away. 'I hope you feel better tomorrow, okay?'

'What were you guys talking about?' Mum asked as Thi made her way down the stairs.

I stared after her.

'I have no idea,' I said.

ROUND 5 STATS

New Shirts to Fix: 1
Last Year's Daily Parent Fight Tally: 4

At home I got to lie dramatically on the couch all night, with my foot up on a chair and Mum fussing over me. She even brought me a bowl of tinned spaghetti with a tender kiss on the forehead and a whispered threat that if I got any sauce on the couch she'd roll me into a ball and punt me into space. We put on *Night at the Museum* and I whined at Mum to bring down my sewing kit from my bedroom so I could fix Tom's shirt while we watched.

I'd already spent one million hours on my own shirt figuring out how to make it work, so fixing Tom's wasn't so hard. Once I'd redone the shoulders I thought about the fact that he liked shorter sleeves, so I took them up a little too, though I knew he'd really only be happy if I turned it into an open-side tank top, which I absolutely did not want him to wear at school because once he'd told me 'I just like feeling the breeze on my nipples' and it ruined tank tops for me forever. I thought about hemming his shirt too high to annoy him, especially since he was always annoying *me*, but, sadly, I mostly wanted him to look good, like my Pa's clients did.

Pa had run his tailor shop in the city for longer than I'd been alive, and I'd always loved it in there. It was warm, and smelled like vanilla, and everybody left the shop looking super sharp. I'd go there sometimes in the school holidays and spin in the chair behind his desk while he'd fit people for suits or dresses or help them make their favourite shirts and pants sit better on their bodies. All that time with him had made me think a lot about what people were wearing, and how when you saw somebody in something that fit them right, they seemed so much happier, which made them look great. I liked thinking about that, but it wasn't until last year that I realised it was something I could actually do myself.

It was when Mum and Dad had been fighting a lot, and I'd gone to Nanna and Pa's house to give them some time to 'work things out', which I was pretty sure was code for 'fighting but with swears Homer isn't supposed to hear'. I've always been pretty good at being just enough of a general clown for people to roll their eyes when I said or did something ridiculous without getting super mad at me, but when Mum and Dad were going through all this I was actually a straight-up pain in the butt.

That day, Pa had made meatballs in sauce and I'd told him they looked like brains and I wouldn't eat them, and then I slurped all the sauce up with a straw while Nanna watched me with her arms crossed and Pa shook his head in a very theatrically disappointed way. Then I refused to wash the dishes because, as I pointed out, I never got *any* free time to just *be a kid*, etc, and then I ignored their exchange of pointed looks and stormed off into the lounge room to watch Netflix.

After they'd done the dishes and cleaned up the mess from my straw, they came into the lounge and sat next to each other and started working on something with a piece of material. I didn't look at them because eye contact would be nice, and nice was not my style anymore, but after a while my mouth said anyway, 'What are you doing?'

'We're making a training t-shirt for your mum,' Nanna said. 'She's getting so strong that the arms on the shirt she was wearing today looked too small for her. So we're making her a new one.'

'Why not one for Dad?' I said. 'Is it because you don't like him?'

'Of course we like your dad,' Pa said. 'But *his* shirt looked fine.'

The material they were using was sea green, covered in paler green triangles and shiny gold lines like sprinkles. 'Do you think she'll like it?' Nanna asked.

'Green's her favourite colour,' I said.

'Do *you* like it?'

I went up close and touched the material. 'Yeah, it's nice. But I don't want it as a whole shirt for me.'

'Nobody was offering,' Pa said.

'Not a whole shirt, huh?' Nanna said. 'But maybe part of a shirt?'

'What do you mean?'

She shrugged. 'Well, I guess I don't know.'

I watched them a little longer and thought about how maybe it'd be cool on me as just, like, the sleeves on an otherwise black t-shirt, and maybe on the pocket too. I picked up the offcuts that had fallen on the ground and said, 'Can I have these?'

'Go for your life,' Pa said.

Mum came to pick me up the next day, and she looked tired. When Pa handed the shirt over, she smiled and hugged it to her chest.

'This material is so beautiful,' she said. 'I could look at it all day.'

That night, I'd found a black t-shirt of mine and carefully stitched the material I'd picked off Nanna and Pa's floor over the top of the sleeves and the pockets. Pa had taught me how to do basic sewing when I was little and given me a box of needles and threads and buttons, so I had kind of an idea about what I was doing, but it was pretty scrappy. Still, when I put it on, it changed a boring three-dollar shirt into one that looked way better, and when Mum saw me she said, 'That material!' and then hugged me and said, 'I could look at you all day.'

'If you ever wear your shirt at the same time I wear mine I will never forgive you,' I told her.

Anyway, after that, it was like I'd discovered I was a wizard with magical clothes-healing powers. I could take up all my annoying shorts that hit the back of my knees and turn all my other three-dollar Target shirts into better versions of themselves. Dad popped a button on his shirt one day when he was already running late and looked like he was about to explode into either tears or fire, and I had it stitched back on before he'd even finished brushing his teeth. Pa started helping me out making shorts and shirts from scratch, and suddenly my wardrobe expanded and I felt good all the time in whatever I was wearing because it fit my actual shape instead of the general not-always-right kid shape the shops designed it for.

For a long time, while I'd been figuring it all out, I hadn't really talked about making clothes much with any of my friends – not even Mario and Ng. It was hard to explain why. I kind of wanted it for a thing that was all my own, that I was going to get good at without everybody seeing me mess up all the time. When I'd learned to play football it was with all of my friends, and we'd all sucked equally at first – missing goals and punching ourselves in the faces when we were learning to handball. But it was just me making clothes. If I had turned up to hang out in a pair of shorts where I'd accidentally made one leg shorter than the other, it would just be me looking like a goof, and everyone would be like, 'I knew you'd never be good at anything but football.' And if they'd said that, then maybe I'd have believed them.

After all this practise, though, and after making a few shirts for the weekend, I was starting to feel like I had a grip on it – like every outfit I made was kicking another goal. When I finished Tom's school shirt, I held it up and showed Mum.

'I still remember all those times he stole your shoes in grade one for laughs,' she said. 'He doesn't deserve you. I hope you filled it with itching powder.'

'I'm telling Mr Skia you said that,' I said.

'Pfft. He's met Tom. I bet he'd tell you to listen to your mother.' She stretched out. 'You looking forward to seeing your dad tomorrow?'

'Who?'

She rolled her eyes. 'Don't joke like that around him – he's already emotional enough about it. He was getting choked up on the phone when we were organising who was coming to get him from the airport.'

'Good,' I said, trying not to imagine my dad almost-crying

about seeing me because it kind of made my eyes want to rain in sympathy.

'Better get a good night's sleep,' she said. 'You'll have a lot to talk about tomorrow.'

'Like all the reasons I'm amazing?'

'That sounds like a pretty short conversation,' she said, flicking me in the toe as she got up. 'How's the ankle?'

'It's okay.'

'I told your dad about it today. He said you had to look after it. Then he told me to look after you. Then he said he'd come and look after you himself. Then I think he got all choked up *again* because he started coughing a lot and changed the subject.' She looked me up and down. 'Need me to carry you up the stairs?'

I put on some Please eyes and she said, 'That was a *joke*.' Then she sighed and said, 'It would be good training though.'

'Bet you can't,' I said, to get it over the line.

'Excuse *me*,' she said.

And as it turned out, my Mum *could* still carry me up the stairs.

The next day, I handed Tom's PE shirt over as we lined up for class. Without blinking, he took his regular school shirt off and put the new one straight on while Taylor said 'Tom!' in an encouraging tone and her horrible friends Olivia J and Olivia R giggled and swooned, which was a word I'd read but had never witnessed until right now. Tom jogged on the spot, did some star jumps, then shook his shoulders out and said, 'Sweet.'

He struck a pose and the Olivias sighed even louder, and Mr Skia behind them said, 'Girls, please stop encouraging Tom when he's not wearing his school uniform.'

'Actually,' Tom said, putting on his annoying My Dad Is A Lawyer voice, 'I think you'll find this is an official school uniform, so you are incorrect.'

'Actually,' Skia said, putting on his Not Taking Crap voice, 'I think you'll find that you know perfectly well that PE uniforms are only to be worn on PE days, which I think you also know was yesterday, and that the punishment is going back home to get changed?'

'That seems contrary to the learning environment you're trying to shape,' Tom said. 'Besides, Homer fixed it up for me and I was just showing everybody the great job he did.' He put his hand on my shoulder and I shrugged it off. 'I have my other uniform right here.'

'Interesting that you'd defend the sanctity of learning so much while putting off doing the exact thing that will get class started,' Skia told him. 'You've got until everyone sits down to get changed or you can take your law-speak to the principal. AND,' he added, as Tom got prepared for another lecture, 'Hien is *not* in one of her good moods today, so I'd not if I was you.'

I knew he was right because I'd seen Hien, our principal, walking into school today wearing the red blazer she always wore when she'd scheduled a meeting with someone's parents, which I recognised because she'd worn it all the times she'd met with mine. Tom muttered law words I didn't understand as we all headed into class, and I could tell when he'd stripped off to change because I heard the Olivias sigh again and it made me want to rip my ears off.

After recess, when I sat down at our table, K. whispered 'Homer!' really loud and then looked around furtively. I stared at them, confused, as they looked out the window while pushing an envelope towards me. I opened it and saw three crisp five-dollar notes.

'Can you do mine?' K. hissed.

I looked at the money, confused. 'What?'

'The shirts. I don't know how much you charge to fix them so I just guessed.'

'Huh? And why are you whispering?'

'I told Thi I liked your shirt and she said you'd probably fix mine for money, but she didn't know how much, so I just guessed. And I'm whispering because I don't want Skia to confiscate my pocket money.'

I took the envelope and put it in my pencil case. 'Uh, okay.'

'You can do the shoulder thing to my shirt too, right?'

'Yeah, for sure.' I was starting to feel a strange tingle in the back of my neck at K.'s enthusiasm, and at those dollars in my pencil case. 'Do you want your sleeves shorter too?'

'You can do that? Could I have them like …' K. put their hand on an angle near their shoulder.

'Like a cap sleeve?'

'Yeah?'

'Sure. I can try that.'

K. beamed. I felt kind of weird taking their money, but obviously not weird enough to hand it back over or anything.

Skia started talking about writing a persuasive piece on a topic I immediately forgot about because I was thinking about the cash right there on my desk. Fifteen dollars was a lot and also not much. It could get you an epic lunch order at school, or five

Dope Ropes from the milk bar, or some Pokémon cards since everybody was back into them again. But it couldn't get you, like, a plane ticket to Perth if your dad had moved there last year and couldn't afford to come over much. For example.

I looked up at K., who looked back at me and grinned. They'd noticed my shirt. And they'd thought it was good enough to pay for.

'Thanks,' I said, and I'd never meant it as much as I did then.

ROUND 6 STATS

Hours Until Dad's Flight: 9
Shirts Made Better: 2
New Shirts to Fix: 1

I spent the rest of the day super hyped, bouncing off the walls (something, it turned out, I could do literally, which Skia wasn't real impressed with), and thinking about this afternoon. It was Friday, the sky was clear and Mum's game was tomorrow. Mum was staying at her teammate Polly Rocket's place tonight so they could *talk tactics* and *get into the game mindset*. This completely missed the point that having a sleepover at the league's most famous player's house was absolutely epic, and when I'd told Thi about it, she'd genuinely cried from jealousy. After school, Nanna was going to pick me up, and then we were going to drive to the airport to collect Dad where she would definitely let me get a blueberry muffin and also a milkshake, and if she got weepy enough about all the people reuniting at the gates I'd probably get a souvenir too.

At lunchtime, as we headed to the oval, Mario said, 'What's up with everyone?'

'What?'

'They're pointing at me.'

I looked around. K. and their friends, who usually hung out under the big tree with the hanging branches, were looking at us and pointing. 'Huh. What did you do?'

Mario sputtered. 'Me? I didn't do anything! I'm innocent!'

Ng said, 'The more you say that, the more I don't believe you.'

'I'm sure I haven't done anything wrong today,' Mario said, tapping his chin in deep thought. 'I have plans to tie Tom's shoelaces together this afternoon, but that's it.'

'Classic,' Ng said. 'Nobody would be mad at you for that.'

We played a footy game against the grade fives, which was unfair since there was an extra grade five class and we were always outnumbered, but not *too* unfair since we were all way better than they were. While I was shoving away some kid I was pretty sure was called Roman to take a mark, he said, 'Hey, you're that shirt kid, right?'

I missed the catch. 'What?'

'I heard you can fix sports shirts. Can you fix mine? Last week we were doing javelin and usually I'm really good at it but that time I just threw it on the ground in front of me and then James in my class laughed at me and—'

'Yeah, I get it,' I said, grabbing the ball out of the air and booting it without looking. 'I don't know. Like, yeah, but I'm doing some for my friends this weekend, and I'm busy with my mum's … I mean, with other stuff. Maybe come ask me next week?'

'Thanks!' he said, and ran off after the ball.

I stayed by the goals and thought to myself: *you're that shirt kid, right?*

I'd been called a lot of names at school, but this one – this was my favourite by far.

Sometimes I got bad feelings I couldn't explain. Like when I got home from school one day last year and Mum and Dad were both home and sitting in front of a cake, but as soon as I sat down with them I didn't feel hungry. Turned out, it was a '... and that's why we're splitting up' cake, and now I don't like red velvet anymore.

I got that feeling again when I saw Nanna and Pa's car waiting for me out the front. I walked up to it slowly, like it was going to bite me. I knew it was their van because it had FALZON DRESSMAKING all over the side, but when I got in and sat down, something still felt wrong.

'Hey, kid,' Pa said, turning around in his seat, 'I'm sorry, but there's some bad news.'

That's when I realised why I had the bad feeling. Pa was here, instead of at work like he was supposed to be. We hadn't immediately started driving, which meant we weren't immediately heading to the airport, and the car was off, which meant we had to talk before going anywhere. Worse still, my Pa, who always wore an Italian linen suit, a shirt in a contrasting colour, and a hat with a matching band, had forgotten his hat.

'Not *bad* bad,' Nanna said. 'Everyone's all right. But your dad ...'

I stared at the floor of the van. Pa kept it real clean for when he was transporting clothes, but I always ruined it when I got in there with my muddy shoes. There was a tiny stone in the carpet, probably brought in by me, and I kicked it around with my toe, trying not to listen while Nanna said things like, 'He had a client that he couldn't say no to … he tried to make the flight … it's hard for both of you … you know he wants to be there for Angela too … this is what his job is now …'

'So we're not going to the airport?' I asked, even though I knew the answer.

'No,' Pa said. 'I'm sorry.'

'We can go to Maker Acre, if you want?' Nanna said. 'Pa will buy you some fabric for a shirt.'

'Excuse me, I will *what*?' said Pa.

'Okay,' I said, after a while.

'Maybe Nanna will buy us both milkshakes from the place next door too,' Pa said.

'I'm sorry,' Nanna said, 'I will *what*?'

I left them to their bickering while Nanna started the car. I kept looking down at the stone in the carpet, kicking it around, thinking, *so I'm not seeing Dad after all.*

He wasn't coming to Mum's game, even though it was super important to her. He wasn't coming to see me, even though I hadn't seen him for eleven weeks. Not that I was counting or had a calendar with the days marked down to today or anything.

It had been heavy when Mum and Dad split up. In the middle of all of it, when Dad was looking for a new place to rent, he lost his job and had to stay living with us after all. He'd got a part-time job working night shifts in a supermarket, and even though he'd liked it, he was sad that he couldn't find another engineering job and do what made him happy. But then an old work friend of his in Perth had found a position for him over there that he'd always dreamed of having, and the company would help pay for him to move out west. Dad had this whole plan where after he'd impressed everybody he'd transfer back to their Melbourne offices as soon as he could, and then we'd be together again. But not this year. He said the pay was okay, so he would be able fly back to Melbourne to visit all the time, and everything would be normal and great. But then he ended up having to buy a car to get around, and then he had to spend his wages trying to pay off his car loan. And he was always busy with work. And then it had been months since I'd seen him on anything but video calls, and I had to pretend that was okay because it wasn't like being mad about it made it not happen, and I know Dad felt bad because I heard him and Mum Facetiming about me sometimes when they thought I was asleep.

Maker Acre wasn't as great as usual. I usually loved it here, the way it was filled with all the making stuff you'd ever need and some you'd never even heard of. They'd designed it like the inside of a toy house, so there were things like walls all covered in different wallpaper, poles that looked like matchsticks and seats that looked like spools of thread. All over the place were displays of things their customers had made, like tiny clay animal sculptures, resin lamps, cardboard lion masks and epic costumes that looked like real armour or something out of a sci-fi book. The staff knew all of us by name and when I was little they always gave me free buttons and told me it was money you could use if you ever met an elf.

I didn't believe in Maker Acre magic today. I followed Pa around while he picked out some new material, then I followed Nanna while she went and got some more clay to make the jewellery she sold at Pa's shop, and eventually I half-heartedly looked through all the rolls of material to make my new shirt out of. I saw some little kids carefully examining some really shiny fabric while their dad waited patiently for them to decide between gold or silver. He gave them little pats on the head and looked down at them and smiled. I dropped what I'd been holding, went over to Nanna and said, 'I'm going to go sit outside for a while.'

It was even harder outside. I wasn't very good at just kind of hanging out with my feelings, because they were boring and there wasn't anything useful to do with them. But this was really heavy, like when Dad left and everybody had told me he'd be there whenever he could and that he wasn't leaving forever and sometimes I believed them but today I really couldn't.

My phone rang in my pocket. I wiped my nose and got it out.

'Hi, Dad.'

'Homer,' he said in a rush. 'I'm so sorry. It was … I tried so hard to make the flight. There was this client, and they wanted all these last minute changes, and I tried to fix everything they wanted, and they just kept changing things, and I'm so new and they are really important to our company, so I couldn't just leave. My team leader tried to help and managed to get me out of the office forty-five minutes before the flight was supposed to leave, but then there was an accident on the highway and the traffic was banked up so far.' He sighed. 'I was hoping the flight would be delayed, you know? Or they'd hold it for me. But they didn't. I wasn't even in the carpark when it took off. I watched the plane go up without me.'

I couldn't say anything. Imagining what he was describing was hurting my chest.

'I'm so sorry,' he said again. 'I couldn't leave. I'm so new, and I worried that if I didn't help out then they'd let me go … do you know what probation is?'

I panicked and found my voice again. 'Are you going to jail?!'

'What? No! Not that kind of probation. It's where you start a new job and they give you six months to prove you're good enough to work for them, and if they don't think you are then they can fire you and they don't have to pay out your contract. While you're *in* probation, like I am, you have to do everything they say.'

'Sounds like school,' I said.

He laughed. 'Yeah, I guess it does. Is your mum there?'

'I'm out with Nanna and Pa. Mum's staying at Polly's tonight.'

'So you won't see her before the game?'

'Nah.'

'Oh. Well, I'm going in to work tomorrow to make up for the hours I missed today, and I'm going to play it in the background the whole time, okay? Know that I'm there with you in spirit even if I can't be there in person.'

'Okay.' I picked at the grain on the wall of the building. 'Can't you take a plane now, or something?'

'I wish I could, but because I missed the plane I can't get my money back. They might give me a little bit of flight credit if I ask, but I don't know for sure. By your game, though, I'll have the money for a return ticket again, I'm sure.' He paused. 'Are you all right?'

NO, I yelled in my mind. 'Yeah,' I said out loud. 'I get it.'

'I'll still be down there when I can. I absolutely promise I'll be there for your first game of the season, right?'

I'd seen enough movies to know that dads who promise anything are almost always lying, but I let him keep talking. 'I've been looking forward to watching you again so much,' he went on. 'Seeing how all your training is paying off, and seeing how you play now that you're older and stronger – it's going to be amazing.' He sighed. 'This isn't me trying to stay away, you know that, right? This is me trying really hard to come.' He broke off for a second, then came back and said, 'Sorry, there's a work call coming in. I've got to go. I love you, okay?'

'Okay.'

I hung up.

'Was that your dad?'

I jumped and turned around. Zara, from my class, was behind me on the footpath, looking up at me with her head tilted.

'What are you doing here?' I asked, hiding my phone in my pocket like that'd make her unhear the conversation.

'Same thing you are, probably. Buying craft stuff.'

'You make clothes too?'

'Me? No way. I buy thick poster paper from here. It's the best for signs to take to rallies.'

'Rallies?'

'You know. Protests.'

'What are you protesting?'

'Everything,' she said. 'There's so much I want to change. There's one protesting the treatment of offshore refugees in a couple of weeks,' she said. 'I need time to think up a good slogan. You want it to be clever so people react, short so people can read it if it makes it onto the news, and you can't have swears otherwise they might censor it. Anyway, I also do some positive protesting. Is there a word for that?'

'You're asking the wrong person.'

'Attesting, maybe? Sometimes I make signs and take them to places where they do good stuff. Like there's this animal shelter not too far from me and they work so hard to adopt animals out.

So I make a sign saying "THIS PLACE IS GREAT!" and sit outside.'

'That seems like it might confuse people,' I said.

'Good. Anyway, you didn't answer my question. Was that your dad?'

'Maybe,' I said. Talking to Zara had confused me enough to make me forget everything for about ten whole seconds. 'Why?'

'You looked sad,' she said. 'Do I need to start a petition against dads?'

Zara's dad, who'd been leaning on the wall next to her this whole time, said, 'I'm right here, you know.'

She rolled her eyes. 'He says he's only going to buy me two poster sheets today. He deserves it.'

'We don't have to protest dads,' I said. 'Mine is just ... he can't come down this weekend like he said.'

'That blows,' Zara said. 'Do you miss him?'

I didn't really know what to say, so I ran up the wall of the store and did a flip. Zara and her dad applauded politely.

The distraction must've worked because Zara said, 'I guess you need to buy some stuff for your whole tailoring business.'

'My what?'

'Aren't you setting up some kind of shirt-fixing shop? At school?'

'No? Who told you that?'

'Homer, I don't need to be told things. I just know what's going on. Also, Thi told me about it. You've got a skill, and people are interested, so I just assumed that you were doing something about it. Like how everyone comes to me when they need somebody yelled at.' She paused. 'Do you need me to yell at your dad? I can probably make that happen for, like, five bucks.'

'Zara!' Her dad glared at her. 'You are not yelling at other people's parents for five dollars.'

'You're right,' she said. 'It's probably worth more like ten.'

He snorted, then straightened up. 'Hey, Homer, I'm sorry about your dad. I know this kind of stuff is hard – my parents got divorced when I was around your age too.'

'Yeah,' I said. 'Thanks.'

They headed inside, and as Zara rolled away, she whispered, 'If you get me some extra poster paper I'll call up your dad and yell at him for free.'

After she left, I thought a little about what she'd said. When Nanna and Pa came outside lugging some bags, I'd lost the edge of my bad mood and was ready to milk their sympathy for all it was worth.

'Nanna,' I said, putting on my best Big Sad eyes, 'I really wouldn't mind a thickshake, if that's okay.'

'Oh, you poor thing,' she said. 'Of course. Any flavour you want.'

'Can I have one of those ones with all the lollies and stuff on top? Please?'

'I don't see why not.'

'Can I have one too?' Pa asked her.

'You made me carry the heavy bag,' she sniffed. 'You can have a glass of tap water and be glad for it.'

'Is it okay if we go back to Maker Acre again afterwards?' I asked. 'There was something I wanted to get.'

'Of course. Did you see some good shirt fabric?'

'Not really,' I said. 'I need some poster paper.'

'What for?'

'It's a surprise.'

ROUND 7 STATS

Angela's Career Game Averages
Kicks: 0
Tackles: 0
Possessions: 0
Goals: 0

The morning of Mum's game, I woke up, pulled on my footy jersey with Mum's number 18 stitched on the back, and headed downstairs. Nanna and Pa were in the kitchen already, and they both smiled when they saw me. Then Pa looked at me closely and said, 'Are you okay?'

'I feel sick,' I said. 'My stomach hurts.'

'I told you you'd had too much macaroni for dinner last night,' Nanna said.

'You're just excited for your mother,' Pa said. 'It's the game she's been waiting for her whole life.'

'Yeah,' I said, 'it's probably that.'

My psychologist always said I spent so much time pretending I didn't have feelings that I'd prefer to learn how to breakdance or something instead of talking about what was on my mind. When I thought about that, I guessed Pa was probably right. It was my mum's biggest life moment, apart from the day

I was born (I assumed), so I was probably just worried for her. What if it didn't go well? Then she'd be sad. I didn't want my mum to be sad. Though, when I thought about it, I always got to watch more TV when she was.

Pa slid a pancake onto my plate with a slice of lemon and a little dish of sugar. I took it to the table and saw that he'd made it into the shape of a shirt, and I stared at it for a long and even more confused time, like I'd forgotten how to eat.

While we spent the morning packing the cooler full of snacks and checking that Pa's camera was working and that he'd put the lens on right and that we had all of our scarves and beanies even though it was way too hot for woolly clothes, I kept checking my phone to see if Dad had called to say he was coming after all. In case he'd tripped over a wad of cash and been able to hire a private jet, or something. He was supposed to be *here*, telling me off for whining about wearing a beanie when it was twenty-eight degrees outside, comparing notes on the other team with Nanna and Pa, or yelling 'Schnell, schnell!' to make me hurry up when I wasn't getting in the car fast enough.

But he wasn't here. I looked up plane tickets for today on my phone, and they were three hundred and fifty dollars, not the two hundred dollars he'd paid for the flight he was supposed to be on yesterday. It was too expensive, and too late.

'Chin up,' Nanna said, looking over my shoulder. 'We've just got to scream so hard your Papa can hear us all the way over in Perth.'

We got to the ground early enough for Pa to spend twenty entire minutes deciding on the best place for us to sit so that Mum could see the sign they'd made the night before with some of the poster paper we'd picked up at Maker Acre, which read:

'#18 is #1!' Once we'd settled in, Pa shuffled his chair over to me and said, 'How did your PE shirt go down?'

'It was so good,' I said. 'Smashed the high jump. Tom was so impressed he gave me his shirt to fix too.'

'Do we have to?' Pa said. 'Isn't he the boy who stomped on all of Nanna's flowers when he came over that time?'

'Maybe,' I said.

'I'm sure he's matured since then.'

'Definitely not, but I already fixed it for him anyway.' I sighed. 'Pa, my shirt felt *so* good. Everything was easy, and I could just *move*.'

He patted me on the head. 'Very good,' he said. 'Very good.'

The weather was perfect for football. Warm, though not too hot. A small cool breeze, but not so strong it'd send your kicks flying off in the wrong direction. Cloudy enough so that the sun wasn't beating down on your face, and with enough blue sky to feel like it was bright and summery. As it got more crowded, I sat there thinking how nice it was being there with Nanna and Pa and their extensive snack selection, and definitely not thinking about all the times I'd gone to the footy with Dad just because he'd let me scream really low-level swear words like 'bloody' and we'd jump and cheer and then talk about the game for days.

Nanna kept finding my hand and patting it, and Pa couldn't stop smiling. People kept turning up and then Thi was there and Mario with his family and suddenly that buzz – that incredible feeling you got at a game, that feeling of all of us there and everything happening and excitement so intense you could almost see it – that buzz was everywhere, and my stomach wasn't so bad anymore because my heart was starting to beat frantically in my chest, because behind one of those gates beside the oval, my mum, my own mum, MY MUM, was waiting to come out and play in front of thousands of people. Nanna was still patting my hand and Pa was wiping his eyes a lot and then the gates opened and my mum came out leading the pack and she looked so nervous that I almost ran out to give her a hug. Instead I just started to scream her name, and everyone around me screamed her name too, and then she smiled and the siren rang out and the feeling was just so good and so big that I didn't think I'd ever feel sick in my life again.

Watching my Mum play was like watching somebody speedrun a video game they'd played a thousand times. She knew where to be and where to go. She was running so fast that she was everywhere, leaping like it was a dance. She tackled and soared but she was also there in the dirt, grappling for the ball, kicking, fighting. My whole life she'd never been afraid of anything, and she was definitely not afraid of anything on that field. Not the other players, who were bigger and younger and running at her, and not of the ball, which she'd try to smother no matter how hard it was being kicked.

When Mum booted a goal from behind the 50-metre line the crowd roared. I flew out of my seat like it was a catapult and Nanna burst into tears. Pa screamed, 'GO FALZON!' and the rest of the crowd started chanting her name. It's my name too, one of them, and I was hearing it around me in surround sound. My friends nearby were calling it out along with Mum's friends from work and the families of all the most famous people on her team, like Polly Rocket's dad, who'd played two hundred games for Collingwood and was screaming 'POL-LY!' and 'AN-GEL-A!' because Polly and Mum were there at every goal, in everybody's faces, and it was so, so good, seeing Mum duck in behind people with a grin that felt exactly like the one I do when I sneak the same move and I wondered if she'd learned that from me or if she'd taught me in the first place.

The game was so tight I could hardly breathe the whole time. We were up, then they were up; I blinked and we were two goals ahead; then suddenly the ball was all theirs for ten minutes.

I remembered Mum crying at the hospital when she'd hurt her shoulder and the doctor told her she couldn't play for months. I remembered her face when her coach sat by her bed and said that meant she'd be out for the first few games. I remembered how she thought her chance was over before it even started.

But now we were here, in game three, and someone behind me said there were only four minutes left in the game. Mum was running, the ball in her hands, everyone left for dead behind her. The coast was clear. She ran past the 50-metre mark and kicked. It hit the post, and everyone fell quiet.

The ball was booted back into play, but it was a mess of people in front of the goals. The other team's halfback was tall – too tall for Mum – and grabbed it off the pack. The halfback bolted, then kicked it low to the ground. Their wing grabbed it but suddenly Polly was there, wrapping her arms around the wing and getting her to the ground while the crowd around me went completely wild. Somehow Mum, who was miles away three seconds ago, was right there in it all, picking up the loose ball. There were seconds to go now and the crowd knew it, and from their screaming the players did too. And Mum spun around, snapped a kick towards the goals, and the siren sounded.

Two points down, and the ball was flying.

ROUND 8 STATS

Angela's Career Game Averages
Kicks: 7
Tackles: 3
Possessions: 8
Goals: 2

I'd always thought nobody else had noticed The Bad Corner. I mean, you can't get up to bad stuff if everyone knows about it, right? Just like I didn't know where to find Zara in the mornings (I guessed she just raged into the school grounds on her way from a protest), or Thi, or K., I didn't think anybody knew where to find me.

Turns out they do, because if you've ever seen twenty people crammed into a street corner designed for two people to walk along, you know they're not there accidentally.

'There he is!'

A squeal came from somewhere in the pack and the whole pile of kids came barrelling towards me. I'd done an assignment on avalanches when we'd learned about natural disasters last year, and I knew you could survive by making a pocket of air as the snow hit, but before I could figure out how, the avalanche was already on top of me and it was *loud*.

'Can we get your mum's autograph?'

'Is it true that the opposition cried?'

'I heard that she got offered a million dollars to join Adelaide!'

'Are you really going to join the seniors when you turn fourteen? They're changing the age just for you, right?'

'I can't believe you didn't tell me you're moving to America for the NFL season!'

That last one was from Mario, who burst out of the crowd looking angry.

'I probably didn't tell you because it's not true!' I yelled.

'But Tom told me!' He crossed his arms.

'Tom?' I said. 'Like, Tom who lies all the time about everything? That Tom?'

'I'll sue you for defamation,' Tom yelled from somewhere in the crowd.

'I'll sue you for making stuff up!' I yelled back. 'I bet that's a thing!'

'It's totally a thing,' hollered Zara.

Everyone started talking at me again and my stomach filled up with something that was either a pile of gravel or this morning's cereal or both of them having some kind of war. I backed away from everybody until a car honked right behind me and I jumped. Ng's mum leaned out of the window, yelling, 'You kids hop off the road before you get killed!' while Ng covered his face in the back seat and presumably died of embarrassment.

I stormed over to the school, partly to save everybody's life and partly because I wanted to get away from this weird pile of people yelling at me. They followed me across like a cloud of dust and excitement, but broke apart at the playground when everyone realised the monkey bars, A.K.A the official school throne, were free. While I watched the fight for victory, Mario stomped over and said, 'I still can't believe I had to hear it from Tom.'

'Mario, he's full of it. I'm not going to the US. Mum played *one game*. I mean, she was brilliant, but, you know, I don't think that's how it works. Is there even a women's NFL in America?'

'Sure there is,' he said, in the really loud voice he used when he didn't know something.

'Look, if she gets drafted, I promise I'll tell you and Ng first, right?'

Like I'd summoned him, Ng came running over, panting. 'Oh man, your mum! I've never seen my family shout so loud at someone who wasn't me. I thought my mum was going to cry. My dad *did* cry. When we got petrol on the way home he told the person behind the counter he was friends with your mum.'

I cringed. 'That's embarrassing. They probably didn't know what you were talking about.'

'Are you kidding? He'd had it playing on his phone the whole afternoon. He gave me a free KitKat for being your mum's friend!'

I blinked. I knew that Mum had played an incredible game – I'd been there when everyone in the stadium was screaming, and I'd seen her final kick at the siren on the news again last night. But hearing that even a random guy in a petrol station knew who she was? *Now* it seemed real.

'Did you save the KitKat for me?' I asked.

'Ha! No way. I ate it before Dad could ask me to share with Lily and Daniel.'

'Legit.'

'So if you're not moving to America,' Mario said, 'does that mean you're moving to Adelaide instead?'

'I'm telling you, she wasn't asked.'

'Hasn't been asked,' Ng said, 'or hasn't told you yet?'

'She's not moving! I mean, *we're* not moving.'

'What about you joining the senior club at fourteen?' Ng asked.

'You weren't even there when somebody yelled that! How did you hear about it?'

'It was all over the group chat.'

'But I didn't see any messages?'

'You're not in it,' Mario said.

'What? Why?'

'Homer,' Ng said, 'it's much easier to talk about somebody when they're not there. Like, right now, you're making this conversation take way longer than it should by asking all these unimportant questions.'

'I think it's pretty important to know why you're having a group chat without me but also entirely about me?'

'It's not entirely about you,' Mario said. 'We also talked about your mum.'

'Zara's starting a campaign to get your mum to come do a talk at the school,' Ng said.

'A campaign? Why doesn't she just … ask?'

Mario leaned into Ng and whispered loudly, 'Did you notice how he didn't answer the question about joining the seniors?'

'I am not joining the seniors!'

'He must be sworn to secrecy,' Ng said.

The bell rang, and we headed to line up where I was swamped again by everybody and their questions. Movie-obsessed Hayley said the game had too good an ending and was obviously staged; witchy Marcie asked if it was true that my mum sold my soul to win the game and if I felt different now I didn't have a soul; and Ava, who knew everything about things that no one else cared about and nothing about the things they do, asked, 'Why is everyone talking to Homer?'

'Because his mum just saved an entire AFLW game!' Ng shouted at her.

'AFLW?' she asked, puzzled.

'Yes! AFLW! The Australian … Football …' he stopped, furrowing his eyebrows. 'Legends?'

'Ladder!' someone shouted from nearby.

'List?' another voice suggested.

'Squad,' somebody yelled.

'That doesn't even start with L,' I yelled back. '*League*, Ng. My mum's in the Australian. Football. League. Women's. That last bit's weird to say out loud.'

'That's very impressive,' Ava said. 'I'm impressed. Are you proud of her?'

'Of course I am,' I said, annoyed.

'I am too,' Ava said.

'She's not your mum!'

'Once in grade three I fell over in the car park and she gave me a bandaid,' Ava said. 'That's a pretty mum thing to do.'

'Okay, everybody calm down,' Skia shouted from the front. 'You're embarrassing yourselves. He's still the same Homer, okay? It's time to go inside and do work.'

Everyone groaned and headed inside. Skia motioned for me to stay back and then whispered to me, 'Can I get your autograph, though? In case you eventually get famous and I can brag about being your favourite teacher?'

'Who says you're my favourite teacher?' I asked, but when I saw his face I said in a hurry, 'I'm only kidding, obviously,' and signed the piece of paper he was holding out.

It was a weird morning. Skia didn't call on me for any questions, and everybody kept staring at me. When we finally had a chance to talk to each other, I leaned over to K. and said, 'Did you bring your shirt? I can start working on it if you need.'

'Nah,' K. said. 'I talked about it with my mum and she was like, "He's got more important things on his mind than fixing his friend's perfectly fine shirt." And I mean, it's true, you're famous now!'

'I'm not famous!' I yelled.

'Homer!' Skia yelled from the other side of the room. 'Stop thinking you can be disruptive just because you're famous.'

'I'm not famous,' I hissed to K. 'I can still do your shirt.'

'Keep the money,' K. said. 'You can do it later, when the football season's over.'

'Surely you've got to help your mum train,' said Thi, leaning over. 'You've got to look out for her.'

'But she trains at training!' I pointed out. 'And besides, we already train together heaps.'

'That was before she was a national legend,' Thi said. 'She's on the news now. Did you see the back page of the newspaper?'

'Pfft. Who reads the newspaper?' Tom said.

Thi rolled her eyes. 'Tom, you don't read *anything*.'

'I saw it,' I told her. Nanna had gone out on Sunday morning and returned with ten copies of the paper because on the back cover there was a great shot of Mum kicking the ball under the headline 'ALL EYEZ ON FALZON!' Pa had spent all Sunday building two frames so we could have copies of it up in each of our houses.

'Now that you're rich, can you give me ten bucks?' Tom asked. 'Or at least get me a sneaker sponsorship?'

I snorted. 'You know Mum still has to have another job, right? If we were rich then Dad could move back home.'

'But your parents split up. Your mum's not going to pay for him to come back.'

'Yes she would,' I said, feeling a different kind of weird in my stomach now.

'Anyway,' K. said, because they were always good at stopping Tom and me from murdering each other, 'you're busy with your mum now and training for the seniors for when you're fourteen and stuff. You can do my shirt later.'

'I'm not going to be in the seniors when I'm fourteen!'

'Homer!' Skia shouted. 'This is your last warning. Well, second-last, if you get your mum's autograph as well.'

I put my head in my hands and waited for recess to come.

It took me forever to get to the oval. I couldn't move for all the prep kids who'd spent their morning watching highlights of the game with Mr Golding, my old teacher. They'd all drawn pictures of my mum's game-winning kick (which surely wasn't actual work), and they all wanted to show me. Then I had to tell each of them they were really good, even though they were terrible, because you have to be nice to prep kids and pretend that primary school is full of nice people before they get older and realise the truth. By the time I finally made it to the oval, I knew the game being played wasn't a normal scrappy one. Something was going on.

I saw Zara and K. watching from the boundary, so I went up to them and said, 'What's up?'

'They're re-enacting the end of your mum's game,' she said. 'Look, Thi is being your mum.'

'Thi?'

'Yeah. Mario tried but Thi bit him.'

'She *what*?'

'She didn't bite him,' K. said. 'It was more of a snarl. Either way, she won.'

I watched Thi take the final mark. Olivia J, who was the best in our class at impressions, made a loud sound like a siren as Thi did Mum's final kick. Thi missed and everyone booed while she shrugged and smiled.

'Again!' somebody yelled, and everyone shuffled back into position.

Thi didn't miss again. I watched them do the play three more times, and then while everyone was taking a breather, I went up to Roman, the kid who'd asked about his shirt on Friday, and said, 'Hey, I can do your shirt, if you want?'

He stared and said, 'YES! I knew it!'

'Knew what?'

'I knew you'd talked to me! My sister didn't believe me when I told her!'

'Okay? I mean, it was only like three days ago and—'

'I need your autograph or something. Can you write on my hand saying you talked to me last week?' He found a pen in his pocket and handed it over.

'Um, I guess so?'

I wrote 'SAW ROMAN FRIDAY' and signed my name.

'That hurt,' he said. 'You're the best.'

'So yeah,' I said, 'the shirt?'

'What shirt?'

'You said you wanted yours fixed on Friday? That's why we were talking?'

'Weren't we just playing a game?'

I looked at his blank face and thought maybe I'd time-travelled, or landed in somebody else's body, and last week hadn't even happened. 'Yeah, and you came up to me and asked about your shirt?' I said slowly. 'You said you were losing at javelin and—'

'What? I'm not a loser!'

I sighed and gave up. 'Your sister's gonna think you just wrote that on your own hand,' I yelled as I walked away.

'What? Hey, wait! You're right! I'll make somebody take a picture! Get back here!'

'Sorry! I'm too famous for pictures!' I hollered, breaking into a run. 'See ya another day to kick your ass!'

If I hadn't been so busy shouting I'd have probably noticed Skia standing right nearby.

'All right,' he growled. '*That* was your last chance. No swearing without a permission slip. Now get back to class.'

ROUND 9 STATS

Shirts Fixed Already: 2
New Shirts to Fix: ~~K.'s Roman's~~ 0???

The next morning, while I pedalled to school, I thought that everyone would probably be over the whole thing already. But as I got closer to The Bad Corner, I heard someone yell, 'There he is!' and I realised a bunch of kids were there again, but since I could actually see the footpath through the crowd now I guessed it was a smaller group than yesterday. I squealed my tyres to a stop in front of them and then Roman appeared at the front of the pack and said, 'Is it true?'

'I don't know what you're going to say,' I said, 'but probably not.'

The whole crowd sighed sadly. 'You're not friends with Polly Rocket?' Roman said.

'Oh! Well, actually, yeah.'

Everyone flooded around me. Someone called out, 'Is it true that she's the tallest person in Melbourne?'

'I don't think so?' I said. 'She is super tall, though.'

Someone else asked, 'Is it true that if she doesn't like somebody she kidnaps them and uses them for tackling practice?'

'No! Who does that?'

'He just hasn't seen where she hides them,' somebody else announced. 'I heard it on the news.'

'No you didn't!' I yelled.

'Is it true that she can kick two footballs at once and make them both hit the poles?'

'I don't ... think so?'

Someone sighed. 'Do you know *anything* about her?'

'Her favourite food is Pringles,' I said.

'Oh my god,' someone yelled. 'That's *my* favourite food too!'

I slowly eased out of the crowd while everyone started arguing about Pringles flavours (which is stupid, because original is obviously the best) and rode across the road to school. I was locking up my bike in the shed when Thi came in too, hauling her scooter behind her.

'Hey, Homer,' she said. 'How's your mum?'

'She's good,' I said.

When I looked at Thi stretching her arms around her scooter lock, I suddenly thought about her arms in her PE shirt, and how I didn't like to think about her being uncomfortable, so I asked, 'Hey, so, your PE shirt. Is it annoying?'

'What? I mean, sure, they all are. About your mum, though, I took heaps of notes on Saturday.' She unzipped her bag and brought out a notepad striped with blue and white stickytape so it looked like a Geelong jumper. 'For her next game I'll bring something to record my voice. I think I'll become a footy commentator for my part-time job when I'm a player.'

We walked out together. 'For sure,' I told her. 'You always pay attention to everything that's happening *and* you can't ever shut up about football. You'd be great.'

'Yeah,' she said, and grinned. 'I would be.'

'And you're so modest,' I added.

'The best at being modest.'

I'd already asked once, but I had another try. 'So about your shirt …'

'Oh, that reminds me! I forgot to show you something yesterday, but I bet they'll be doing it again today. Ask me about it at recess.'

'Ask you … what?'

'I'll show you then. It's great, trust me.'

I didn't try a third time. Instead, we headed over to Science, where Oates did a probably cool chemical reaction experiment at his desk, but I'll never know for sure because I was sitting too far away. While I was attempting to fill in an Observation and Reflection worksheet about something I couldn't see properly, I thought that maybe if I was particularly quiet, I could grab some bicarb soda from his desk and helpfully replicate the experiment for everyone at the back of the class. So when he went into the storage room for something – probably for some scissors so he could make his pants, which were always too short for him, even shorter – I raced up the front to grab it while Olivia R, who lives to dob, tried desperately hard not to yell out. I got back in my chair the exact same second that Oates came back, looked around at everyone and said, 'You're all being too quiet. Who took it and what was it?'

'Nothing,' Olivia R squeaked.

He looked at her and she said, 'Not Homer!'

She'd kind of tried, so I couldn't even be mad at her. Oates stormed up to me and put his hand out for the bicarb. 'I was just trying to helpfully replicate the experiment for everyone at the back of the class,' I told him.

He glared. 'I'm not impressed with you like all the other teachers are, you know.'

'The other teachers are impressed with me?' I said. 'Sweet.'

'NO,' he shouted. 'And you can spend the rest of the class outside.'

'Awesome,' I said. 'Maybe one of the other teachers will come by and we can talk about how great I am.'

It was only slightly more boring being outside than inside. I kind of hoped that Skia would come past, because I bet he was one of those impressed teachers. I was also kind of impressed by him, since I'd heard once that the reason all the kids at our school called each other 'jerkjack' when they were being annoying was because Skia had made up the nickname years ago when Oates – whose first name was Jack – once threw out his soy milk from the staffroom fridge. If I hadn't heard that rumour and been so impressed by Skia's immaturity I'd probably be in trouble in class way more than I was.

Thi launched herself at me when the bell rang for recess. 'Come on,' she said, yanking my sleeve. 'I'll show you what I was talking about.'

She dragged me over to the school oval and pointed at a bunch of grade three kids at the picnic table. I hadn't really paid attention to them yesterday, since they were always there trading Pokémon cards or highlighters or whatever thing they were into this week, but they weren't doing trades today. Instead, some determined-looking kid with her tongue sticking out was drawing the number 18 on sheets of paper in thick black texta. When she'd written it, she'd pass the paper over to Artie, from my club's under-10s team, who was standing in front of a line of kids from all different grades. He'd get them to turn around, then pin the numbers onto their shirt backs before they sprinted onto the oval, yelling something I couldn't hear.

I turned to Thi. 'Are kids allowed to bring safety pins to school?'

'I feel like you're missing the point of what's happening here,' she said.

'What do you—' and then it hit me. The number 18. It was my mum's number.

There were kids everywhere running around with my mother's number on their backs.

I stared. And when I listened, I could hear what they were yelling: 'FALZOOOOOON!'

'Pretty cool, huh?' Thi said.

I didn't know what to say.

All I could do was grin.

ROUND 10 STATS

Days Until I See Dad Again: 1,000,000

Dad rang that afternoon while we were in the car. 'Hallo, mein Junge. How's tricks?'

'Hey Papa,' I said. 'I'm on the way to training right now.'

'Why do you think I called? Somebody's got to motivate you!'

'Hey!' Mum shouted. 'Not that I'm listening in, but hey!'

'Tell me how many motivating words your mum has said, and I'll double it.'

'She hasn't said *any*,' I told him, and Mum poked me in the leg while I squealed.

'Well, that's easy, because what's double nothing?'

'Ugh, are you trying to do maths on me? School's finished for the day!'

'I'm waiting,' he said.

'I don't know! Double nothing? Is it one?'

There was silence.

'Okay, okay! Is it nothing?'

Still silence.

'Dad?'

There was a fuzzy sound. '—mer?'

'Dad?'

'You cut out! I'm in the printer room where it's quiet, but the reception i—'

'Dad?'

He was quiet again. Then he came back, super loud: 'Okay, I think we should be good now. What were we talking about? Double nothing.'

'Nothing?'

'Good job, squirt.'

'I'm not really a squirt.'

'What?'

Mum said, 'I mean, compared to him you are.'

'What did she say?'

'She's sticking up for you!'

'We're a team,' he said smugly.

'Weren't you just telling her off for not being enough of a motivator?'

'Moving along,' Dad said, 'how was school today?'

'Good. All the kids are just replaying Mum's match.'

'HEYOOOO!' Mum yelled, honking the horn.

'Oh my god, Mum, stop,' I said, cringing.

'Sorry,' Dad said, 'what was happening at school?'

'Nothing,' I said, afraid Mum would scare everyone around us again. 'Oh! And I forgot to tell you because I was going to show you, but I fixed my shirt!'

'Oh, did you get one with your Mum's number on it?'

'No – but actually there's a whole other story there with all these kids at my school who put her number on their shirts – I'm talking about our PE shirts. You know, the ones we wear on PE days?'

'Like your school shirt?'

'Our sports one.'

'For footy training?'

'No. Dad. Like for PE.'

'Oh, yeah,' he said in that same voice he used when he didn't understand something, like when I made him listen to hip-hop or explained the differences between LaFontaine kicks. 'Shirts.'

'Anyway, so I fixed mine the other day.'

'Like, with your numbers?'

'No, that's another story – forget I said that. No, I fixed—'

'What? I can't hear you.'

'I fixed—'

'Sorry, it's always a pain to call anyone here.'

But you called me anyway, I thought. 'It's okay, Dad. Anyway, so I was talking about the shirts. Remember how we have these ones we wear only for PE? And how I always complained that they were made really badly and said I'd fix it? So I finally did it! I made it so the shoulders are better and it doesn't pull or strangle me or anything. Pa helped, but it was mostly me. Anyway, if you've got any shirts that don't fit, bring them next time you're down and maybe I could fix them too, okay?'

He didn't say anything. Maybe his shirts didn't need fixing.

'Dad?'

I checked my phone and saw it was dark. He'd been cut off altogether. I had no idea how much he'd heard. Maybe none of it.

'Aw,' Mum said. 'Did he cut out?'

‘Yeah,’ I said, looking at my watch. ‘We’re going to be late.’

‘Ah, it’s fine,’ she said.

I didn’t say it out loud, but we were never late when Dad drove me to training. My phone beeped and I looked down to see a text from Dad: *I’ll call you tonight. Good luck at training.*

When we pulled up, it looked like there were a lot more people around than usual. There was probably some Eastern Cockatoos team meeting or something, I thought, until we got out of the car and someone yelled, ‘There she is!’

Within seconds we were surrounded by what was probably thousands of under-10s and under-8s and Littlefoot Footy Squad toddlers, who were all staring at Mum. She beamed back and said, ‘Well, hello, everybody! I should let you know that now that I’m famous, it costs ten dollars to look at me.’

Everybody squealed and ran away while she took off after them, laughing and shouting, ‘I’m kidding! It costs a high five.’

Ng came up to me, a football tucked under his arm. ‘Wow.’

‘Right?’

‘Do you reckon that’ll be us someday?’ he asked. ‘Like, when we’re famous and trying to casually walk down the street, people will yell “there he is!” and we’ll be mobbed?’

‘It’s going to be exhausting,’ I said. ‘We should probably make the most out of it while we’re still everyday people.’

‘Not sure if you are everyday anymore,’ he said, pointing at the five or six kids who’d stayed behind from Mum’s crowd to stare at me.

‘Mister,’ one of them said, ‘can your mum be my mum?’

‘You’ll have to ask her,’ I said. ‘I think she’s too busy for more kids, though.’

‘Can she marry my dad?’ some other kid said. ‘He said she

was the best when he was watching the game the other day.'

'Abby, your parents aren't even divorced,' Ng said.

'So? You can have two mums. Can't you, Mr Homer?'

'Well, of course, but I don't think you can have *my* mum as one of them …' I tried to leave but they were like tiny fierce gnomes that I was afraid of tripping over.

'BOYS!' Crabtree hollered from across the oval. 'STOP MUCKING AROUND AND GET OVER HERE! You can do push-ups while I'm talking if you've got so much time to waste!'

The kids bolted and we headed over. Halfway through the team's twenty squat-jumps, I realised Crabtree wasn't even watching. He was off talking to the club president, Cassie, who wore flowery dresses, big earrings and crisp white sneakers everywhere she went but would always smash a kick into any ball that came her way. Thi was standing near them, jumping from foot to foot and looking excited.

'All right,' Crabtree called, coming over. 'I've got some news for you all. As you know, the girls have been hard at work building enough members to field a team for next season. You could all learn a thing or two about motivation from them, to be honest.'

'Especially our own ex-Cockatoo, Angela Falzon,' Cassie said, and I secretly glowed. 'And it's thanks to her, and her new club's community outreach program, that we're holding a drawing competition to celebrate our new girls' team!'

'Drawing is for babies,' yelled Bucky.

'Great,' Crabtree said. 'So don't enter. Then you won't get to see your jersey design on all the girls' teams next year, and you won't get the two-hundred-dollar cash prize either. Too bad.'

Two hundred dollars?

'Two hundred dollars?' yelped Bucky. 'I'm going to win.'

'Sorry, Liam, but I'll have to take your first answer,' Crabtree said.

Bucky growled.

'After training's over, I'll hand out flyers that'll give you all the information you need,' Cassie said. 'I can't wait to see your entries.'

'Two hundred bucks!' Mario said. 'I'm going to buy …' he started counting on his fingers and then gave up. '*So many* Dope Ropes.'

'I'm going to put half in my savings,' Ng said. 'And then I'm going to buy a video game on the day of release. Not pre-owned. Not when my cousin's finished with it. The *day* it comes out.'

'What game?' asked Jones, who somehow knew more about the internet than any of us even though his parents didn't allow screens in the house.

'I don't even know yet,' Ng said dreamily.

Thi ran up to me. 'Homer, you must be dying right now,' she said. 'This competition is *made* for you, right? Clothes *and* football? Oh my god. What are you going to spend the money on?'

'Excuse me?' Jay said. 'Who says he's going to win? I'm a *great* drawer.'

I ignored him. 'I don't know,' I said to Thi, but I was lying. The first thing I'd thought of was being able to surprise Dad with a plane ticket to Melbourne. It wasn't enough to get him back to Perth again, but I didn't want him to go back anyway.

'Stop the chitchat!' Crabtree yelled. 'It's time to get moving. Anybody who hasn't done ten push-ups by the time I've had a drink of water gets to do more laps.'

We dropped to the ground. Thi ran back to the fence then dropped to the ground too, while Mario panted, 'Who would *voluntarily* do extra training?'

My dad, I remembered. When he took me to training, he'd sit on the sideline and yell encouragement and do star-jumps at the same time as us while I faced away from him and pretended he wasn't there. Now there was my mum, who'd done the same at first, but these days she just sat on the side talking to the other parents or put her baseball cap over her face and had a nap.

'Do you reckon I can win?' I asked Mario.

'Course,' he said.

'No way,' Jay said. 'What about the seniors? They're, like, professional adult drawers.'

'I dunno,' Jones said. 'Adults have, like, zero imagination.'

While we practised kicking with each other, I thought about our uniforms. At the moment, they were just yellow and black with a white cockatoo head over the heart. I was more about making clothes fit properly than designing them, but the more I ran around the oval the more I *knew* I could do it. So many ideas sprang into my mind that I couldn't keep hold of them, and every time Crabtree was in my ear yelling about pacing or reflex drills or whatever, it'd knock an idea out of my head. I tried to ignore him and just picture myself in a new, better, winning shirt. I imagined wearing it at the airport to meet Dad when he came over, and how he'd see it and smile.

'You all right?' Ng said, jostling me in the scratch match I hadn't even realised I was in.

'Distracted,' I said.

'I mean your ankle,' he said.

'What?' I looked down, and the ball hit the ground in front of me.

'HOMER!'

'Sorry,' I yelled to Crabtree. 'It was my ankle.'

'Go sit out the rest of training,' he grouched. 'You've been hobbling around on that for the last five minutes. Give it a break. Get your mum to have another look at it, if she can fit it into her busy schedule.'

I limped to the sideline and waited out the rest of the game until Crabtree dismissed everyone, saying he'd see them on Thursday. I waved my friends goodbye and went to wake up Mum, who was drooling onto her shoulder.

'Mum, it's over. Home time.'

'How'd it go?'

'Yeah, fine. My ankle went weird at the end.'

'Oh no, I'm sorry, I didn't see!' She wiped her mouth. 'Are you okay? I'll check it when we get home.'

'It was only for a minute. I'll be fine.'

It wasn't until after dinner when I was sitting in front of my sketchpad and icing my ankle again that I realised I hadn't picked up the flyer from Crabtree. I knew Mario wasn't allowed online until after he'd done his homework, and I also knew that he never did his homework, so I dropped Ng a message.

Homerun: *hey i forgot to get the flyer*
NotDave: *The wha?*
Homerun: *the stuff about the new uniforms*
NotDave: *Oh yeah! What do you want to know*
Homerun: *all of it*
NotDave: *OK hang on*

NotDave: *So*

NotDave: *Just says it's due on the 29th. And you gotta use the same colours and a cockatoo head. And there's like an image of the shirt you can draw on.*

Homerun: *can you send it to me*

NotDave: *For sure*

NotDave: *Wait. What's in it for me*

Homerun: *if i win the two hundred i'll give you ten bucks*

NotDave: *Hmmm but if I don't send it to you then you can't enter and I'll win???*

Homerun: *or i'll ask Mario and give him the ten bucks*

NotDave: *OK FINE I'LL EMAIL IT. Jeez*

Homerun: *thaaaaaaanks dave*

NotDave: *DO NOT CALL ME DAVE*

Homerun: *then why did you make it your screen name if you don't want to remind people about your first name being david*

NotDave: *YOU KNOW IT'S BECAUSE WHEN WE FIRST CAME UP WITH THESE NAMES WE WERE IN GRADE FOUR AND MRS LOO WOULD ONLY SAY DAVE. This was grade four me being a REBEL*

NotDave: *ANYWAY I REGRET HELPING YOU*

Homerun: *byeeeeeee*

Homerun: *ng*

NotDave: *That's better.*

I'd print out the t-shirt template tomorrow at school. For now, I flipped to a blank page in my sketchbook, drew a version of what Ng had emailed to me, found my green and yellow textas, and got to work.

ROUND 11 STATS

Jersey Competition Prize: $200
Yellow & Black Textas Used Up: 2

I had my best Nicest Student face on when I went up to Mr Hamilton's desk in the library.

'Homer!' he said. 'I don't think I've ever seen you here outside of class hours. This is a nice surprise. Looking to see what new footy books we've got in? I'm sure we've got last year's AFL almanac somewhere …'

I sighed, but only on the inside, since I was being Very Polite Homer. 'Thanks! But actually I wondered if I could print out some templates for a drawing competition?'

'A competition! Well, that's exciting. How many? Two, three?'

'… Fifty?'

He put on the expression he gets when he sees kids putting books they'd just picked out back in the wrong section. 'You mean five, correct?'

I took my five templates to a spare seat, where Ava was

sitting at a table in front of something that looked like blueprints. 'What's that?' I asked, chucking my stuff down beside it.

'I'm drawing up all the tunnels underneath the school,' she said without looking up. 'Did you know there's a trapdoor in the art room floor, underneath the rug? I think maybe that's where Lin went missing.'

'Wait, what? Lin who moved away last year?' I stared at her. 'Lin who wrote a whole-class postcard to us like last week?'

'The school wants you to think she moved away,' Ava said mysteriously. 'I think the postcard was faked.'

This was all my fault for trying to have a conversation with somebody who never made any sense. I looked down at the paper in front of me, at the outline of the shirt, and suddenly all the ideas I'd been storing in my head poured out of me. I drew cockatoos flying and standing and then I drew stripes and circles and then I made everything bigger and smaller and all over the place. I didn't even hear the bell go until Ava walked past me and said, 'I'll tell Skia you're in a deep meditation.'

'What? No, I'm not,' I said, dazed.

I spent all of class drawing cockatoo heads in the margins of my exercise book while half paying attention. I wasn't actually that great at drawing, so they all just looked like really angry ducks. Maybe I'd try and ask Willow for advice. She was so great at art that one time for Halloween free-dress day she used puff paint to make my shirt look like open-heart surgery was happening in my chest and she did such a great job that we both got detention.

When the bell rang for lunch, I cornered Mario and Ng before they could sprint to the oval.

'Guys! Instead of footy today, come to the library with me.'

'Nah, I've got enough to read,' Ng said.

'I don't know what books are,' Mario said.

'Not to *read*. To do the jersey competition.'

'The what?' Mario said.

'Dude. It only happened yesterday. Remember? The competition? To design a new jersey?'

'Oh, right.'

'You were going to buy, like, a million Dope Ropes?'

'Yeah, but then I had a Dope Rope yesterday and remembered how I get sick after only one,' Mario said.

'Ng!' I said, turning to him. 'You'll come draw with me, right?'

'I think I'm going to go play footy,' Ng said, shrugging. 'I mean, I had a go at the competition when I got home. I drew stripes that went up and down, I drew stripes that went sideways, then I ran out of ideas and played Mario Kart.'

'Guys,' I said, 'come on. You gotta come work with me.'

'Not today,' Ng said. 'Sorry, but we really have to destroy the grade fives. They're getting cocky since those twins with abs moved down from Darwin.'

'Whatever,' I said, crossing my arms. 'When I'm a hundredaire you'll be sorry.'

'Probably,' Ng said. 'You can buy new shoes and make us all jealous.'

'Nah, he'd use the money to see his dad, right?' Mario said.

They both looked at me and I wiped my nose. 'I mean, yeah.'

'So really, we're being good friends by not entering the competition, right? Because then it gives you a better chance of winning.' Ng folded his arms. 'Yes. We are, actually, amazing friends.'

'The best,' Mario agreed. 'Now get out of our way so we can go play without you while you go sit on your own.'

Ava wasn't in the library this time, which probably meant she was out digging up the grass and trying to find tunnels that didn't actually exist. I put down my pencil case and looked around at the people walking around the room, trying to shake my brain into having new ideas. It's tough when basically everyone is wearing a version of the exact same school clothes, but at least there was Hamilton, standing over in the corner. He was looking at the photocopier like it had sworn at him and was wearing, like always, black jeans and a t-shirt with a book cover on it. Today's: *The 13-Storey Treehouse*.

I tried drawing a cockatoo in a rectangular book shape. It didn't work. I tried writing 'SOUTHERN COCKATOOS' on it in big letters like it was a book cover. That didn't really work either. I thought of putting the cockatoo in a tree, but it felt too chaotic.

After I'd drawn and erased on one page so many times I'd ripped a hole in it and had to scrunch it up, somebody came and sat next to me.

'Your friends told me you were here,' Roman said. 'Your team sucks without you.'

'What? My team doesn't suck.'

'Sorry, but they do,' he said. 'I'm just leaving to give the grade sixes a fair chance. And because I want you to fix my shirt.'

I blinked. 'Didn't we have a whole discussion about how you'd forgotten that? And did your sister believe my note on your hand?'

'She totally did,' he grinned. 'And yeah, look, I had to wear my sports shirt yesterday, and in the middle of PE when I was being strangled again I was like, *oh, right, this is the reason I was talking to Homer that time*. So can you do it?'

I looked down at my jersey drawings. So far, they were a real mess. Nothing looked as good as it had in my head. 'I'm busy,' I said. 'I don't think I have time anymore.'

'I'll pay you, like that girl who's in charge of the footy said,' he added. 'I have five whole dollars.' He dumped a heap of twenty and fifty cent coins on the table in front of me.

'You can count it,' he said. 'I'm not great at maths.'

'I'm sure it's fine,' I said, staring at the pile. It looked like a lot of money when it was in small coins.

'Come on. My shirt sucked so much yesterday. I couldn't do anything. I hate it. I know you can fix it. I heard you were better than, like, Spider-Man or Black Widow or something in PE after you fixed yours.'

'Spider-Man and Black Widow *wish* they were me,' I said, secretly proud.

'Anyway, I need it by next Tuesday,' he said. 'Cheers. See ya.'

I picked up the coins, which were only mostly sticky, and put them in my pocket. They felt heavy.

My jersey ideas currently sucked, and now I'd thrown a grenade in the time I could spend working on them by fixing another shirt. But it'd be fine. I had a month before the competition was decided. I could perfect the jersey by then, make two hundred dollars, then see my dad.

I jingled the coins in my pocket, and thought. Sure, winning the jersey competition would buy a one-way ticket from Perth to Melbourne. But I knew Dad wouldn't come unless he had the money to fly back again. If I fixed a bunch of shirts as well as winning the comp then maybe I could get enough money to buy Dad a return ticket, which would mean he'd definitely come, because he could go back again. Or I could fly myself there and then back home. Either way, extra money would mean the other side of the country wouldn't seem so far away.

The more I thought about it, the more it seemed actually achievable. Maybe I could make it happen: fix everyone's shirts, make heaps of money. But how could I convince more kids to give me their shirts?

I needed help.

I needed Zara.

ROUND 12 STATS

Shirts Made Better: 2
New Shirts to Fix: 2
Shirt Money Earned: $20
Jersey Ideas: 13
Good Jersey Ideas: 0

Just like how people don't react if Ava says she's investigating hidden tunnels, everyone walked right on past without blinking when I stood next to the classroom the next morning holding a giant sign that said 'ZARA, I NEED YOU! PLEAES HELP ME'.

I didn't really know what time Zara got to school, so I'd had to get here early enough to be here before her. Standing in one place for ten minutes wasn't really one of my best skills, and I was about ready to faint from boredom when Zara finally rolled up, looked me up and down and said, 'Do you need help with your spelling?'

'What? No!'

'You got your S and E the wrong way round.'

I turned the poster around and sighed. 'I was too busy trying to make the O in YOU look like the tyres on your wheelchair,' I said.

'Well, you did a good enough job to attract my attention. What do you need my help for if it's not about your spelling?'

'My shirt-fixing business.'

Her eyes sparked. 'Ha! I wondered when you'd take my advice.'

I bowed. 'You are the queen of all wisdom and knowledge. An oracle. A smart person ... who ... I'm running out of words.'

'All right, let me save you. I'm the best, yes. And now you want my help. What if I don't want to give it to you?'

'There are four more sheets of poster paper behind here that are all yours if you help me out,' I said, raising my eyebrows.

She drummed her fingernails on the arm of her chair. 'I mean, that's a good opening bid. What about all the times you were a jerkjack last year, though?'

'I was never!'

'What about when you farted in my school hat?'

'That doesn't sound like me,' I said, trying really hard to not laugh now that I'd been reminded about doing it. 'What about when I helped you out with all that Murphy stuff earlier this year?'

'I paid you in candy!'

'But I still did it,' I pointed out. 'I'm a changed man. Maybe I did some things last year that weren't great, or maybe your memory is just fuzzy and it wasn't me at all. The point is that I'm great *now*.' I put on my best Nicest Classmate face. 'I'm just trying to start a small business, Zara. All I want to do is make people more comfortable.'

She gave me a hard stare. 'What's your real motivation?'

'I promise it's that!' I said. 'Well, and money.'

'What's the money for?'

‘This is a lot of questions.’

She sat back and folded her arms.

‘Okay, okay. To pay for a plane ticket to see my dad.’

‘I love it!’ she yelled. ‘A feel-good story. A young entrepreneur wants to save up and see his father that he desperately misses. We can get some real juicy news stories about this. I’ll be famous.’

‘Aren’t we talking about me here?’

‘Yes, but I need to have more volunteer work on my resume. Imagine how great this will sound in the future when I’m campaigning to be Prime Minister.’

‘So ... you’re saying yes?’

‘Will you give me fifty per cent off when you fix my shirt later?’

‘Sure.’

‘Then it’s a deal. Also, my first piece of advice: stop being such a pushover.’

‘What?’

‘You immediately caved on giving me a discount without even fighting me for it!’

‘I’m sorry! You can’t have the discount!’

‘My second piece of advice: never back out on a deal. It makes you look untrustworthy. It’s too late now, Homer, the discount is mine.’

We had our first business meeting at recess. Zara and her friends hung out at the stumps, which was what we called this little square made by a bunch of portables that had all been dumped together, leaving a space behind them all. Someone had painted cricket stumps on the back wall of one of them, which was helpful, and then immediately put a bench in front of it, which was not. Anyway, it was like the only secret nook in the whole school, and teachers totally ignored it because they knew it was Zara's spot and they were afraid of her always writing up petitions to get them fired, like when they didn't let her go on an anti-Oates strike for a whole term of Science.

Zara was there already with Murphy and Avery, her usual crew. Thi was there as well, holding a clipboard and looking important.

'So what's your company called?' Zara asked. 'That's the first thing we need for the business plan.'

'Business plan?'

'Yes. Obviously. It's not like you can just start *fixing clothes*.'

'Why not?' I asked.

'Well, how many shirts do you have to fix so far?'

'Well, there's Roman, from grade five, who's gonna bring his soon, and K., if I can convince them to let me do theirs. They've both already paid. And Mario and Ng asked me to do theirs too, but they haven't actually remembered to bring them yet so I haven't been counting them.'

'Two people have already paid? That's excellent! Though that's not the point. I'm saying that you've already said you'd do four. So what happens if all the other kids give you theirs at once? You'd lose track of them all.' She narrowed her eyes at me. 'Do you have room for sixty shirts in your house?'

'Maybe?' I said. 'Shirts aren't that big, right?'

'And how are you going to keep track of them?'

'I don't know.'

'Exactly,' Zara said with satisfaction. 'You have to take it slow, make sure you communicate with the people, make sure they understand the wait time, stuff like that. But first, a name. Something catchy, like "Sew What".'

I was annoyed that she'd come up with something good straight away. 'Why does it need a name?'

'So something like "Homer's Alterations"?' she asked, rubbing her chin. 'It's boring, but if you insist.'

'I'm not insisting!'

'Pretty insistent voice for someone who's not insisting,' Avery said.

'I think it's going to be harder to rhyme the word "alterations",' Murphy said. 'It's easy to rhyme "what", though.'

I was lost. 'Rhyme …?'

'Avery and Murphy will be writing the jingle for your shop,' Zara said. 'Keep up.'

I was so far behind, it was like keeping up with a marathon happening in a different country ten years ago. 'Sorry, why a jingle?'

'We can play it during recess radio as an ad,' Zara said. 'Avery and Murphy have volunteered to do this for free.'

'Thanks?' I said, still a bit confused. They both waved at me.

'You're lucky with your timing,' Zara said. 'Avery got a new synth last week and they both want an excuse to try it out. Also, I brokered a discount on their shirts when you get around to fixing theirs too.'

'No,' I said firmly.

'Yes,' Zara said, more firmly. 'It's the discount, or you pay them actual dollars.'

I shut up.

'And we'll need posters,' she added. 'I spoke to Willow this morning and she's on board, but only if she gets fresh pens as payment, which Thi says she will take care of.'

I smiled at Thi, but she was staring at the ground. 'Thanks, Thi, but do you need … wait, Zara, when did you speak to Willow? I only asked you this morning.'

'Homer. That was *ages* ago. *Tens* of minutes ago.'

'And we were in class for all of it?'

'That type of narrow thinking is bad for your company,' Zara said. 'If you want to take Sew What to the next level, you're going to have to think of every class as an opportunity to get the people onside.'

'Not that I don't agree with you,' Thi said, chewing on the end of her highlighter, 'but doesn't Homer get into trouble in class enough without talking to everyone while we're supposed to be working?'

'*Fine*,' Zara said, sighing as the bell rang. 'I guess we'll only work during recess and lunch, then.'

At lunch, I headed back over to the stumps. The moment Zara caught sight of me coming through the gap, she stopped talking to the others and pointed at me so hard I almost felt it from five metres away. 'So,' she said, 'how long do you think it will take you to do the shirts you've already got?'

'I dunno. I can maybe do one a night, but not when I've got training, which is twice a week.'

'And you'll want weekends off.'

'No, I won't. Why?'

'Activists from the olden days campaigned *hard* for the right to a five-day working week. I can't make you give up your weekends.'

'But I want to see my father,' I said, walking over and making the Sad Abandoned Child face that Mum had banned last year.

'That is very mean,' she said, frowning. 'Now I feel bad for you. You can do *one* each weekend. So, what, four a week?'

'I can do six,' I said. 'I'm sure.'

'We'll start with four,' she said. 'How about you finish all the ones you're doing and we can start taking the first orders for your tailoring shop next Tuesday?'

There was this slow, good, bubbly feeling washing over me. Like when you're in a crowd at a game watching the match turn in your favour and everybody starts to get excited, and there's this buzz that builds up, knowing that maybe, just maybe, you can win this.

'That sounds awesome,' I said, my smile so big it started to hurt. 'Thank you.'

'Did you hear that?' Avery said, putting his hand to his ear. 'Did Homer just say "thank you"? Homer *Falzon Schneider*? I didn't even know he could.'

'Hey!' I said indignantly. 'I'm nice.'

'Remember when you kicked a soccer ball into my face in PE and laughed so hard that *both* of us had to go to sick bay for nosebleeds?' Thi asked.

'I'm sure that's not how that went,' I said.

'Remember how you copied all of my maths work for the whole of grade four when we sat together?' Avery said.

'Not *all of* it,' I said. 'That's an exaggeration.'

'Once you stuck a tadpole in my wheelchair bag and it died,' Zara said.

'That was like five years ago! I thought it'd be okay because I put water in there too! I didn't know the water would leak out!'

'Last year you said I was a nobody,' Murphy said quietly.

I didn't really have a comeback for that one. I looked down on the ground and felt bad. I didn't even remember saying it, but Murphy had always been so quiet, so under-the-radar, that I probably said something like that without even thinking. I imagined for a moment what it felt like to hear someone say that.

'I'm sorry,' I said. 'There was a bit last year where I ... I was going through some things. But that's not an excuse. I know you've gone through things too and you didn't call me a nobody. And you're not even a nobody,' I pointed out. 'After everybody heard all those amazing songs you wrote at the start of the year you basically became the most famous person in the school.'

'Thanks,' Murphy said, with something that was almost a smile.

'Well, that was some heavy stuff,' Zara said, after a minute. 'The point is, you're a jerkjack, but you're not actually evil, like some people I could mention but won't but actually I mean Tom and Taylor.'

'Agreed,' I said.

'Well, good. Then it's time to get to work.'

ROUND 13 STATS

Sew What Meetings: 2
Shirt Discounts Given: 3
Days Until Shop Opens: 5

Ms Honeybone was looking way too pleased with herself when we got to PE that afternoon. She had a lot of footballs out, and a lot of equipment that looked exactly like the equipment we have all the time at footy training. 'Homer!' she said, running up when she saw me. 'My little helper!'

Tom snorted. I said, 'Huh?'

'Well, in honour of your mother's *incredible* game, guess what we're doing? A fourteen-week AFL focus for PE!'

'Whoa,' I said, while Thi and Ng high-fived next to me.

Jhyll said, 'You mean four weeks, right?'

'I said what I said.' Ms Honeybone grinned at her.

'But when do we get a rollerskating unit?' Jhyll said crankily.

'When the school gets more insurance funding for all the broken bones that would happen?'

'What? I've only broken my arm twice and had three concussions! It's not that many!'

'Man,' I said to Mario, 'my PE report is going to be *so* good this year.'

'Um, when is it not?'

It was true – Ms Honeybone was the one teacher who never told me off or sent me to Hien's office. Once I'd even heard her telling my grade four teacher, Mrs Loo, that she must be blaming the wrong kid when she complained about me always eating her plants. (Which was *completely* untrue – I just hid them and then put a leaf out of the corner of my mouth in a suspicious way.) Still, my next report would be so good it might even make my parents not notice the results for all my other classes.

'What did you mean by helper?' Thi asked.

'I mean that he's had training by a professional AFL player,' Ms Honeybone said. 'So he's going to help me run the class. What warm-up should we do, Homer?'

I went to the front of the class, scooped up a football and stood next to Ms Honeybone. This should be the easiest class I'd ever done, but for a moment my brain was stuck on coming up with something, like all the thinking I'd been doing at the stumps had stretched my brain out too loose.

'Go Homer!' Zara yelled. Then, even louder, 'WOW, YOU LOOK SO RELAXED IN YOUR TAILORED SHIRT THERE! IF ONLY OTHERS COULD HAVE THE SAME.'

'BOY, I SURE WISH I COULD HAVE A SHIRT LIKE HOMER'S,' Avery hollered.

I wasn't sure if I was embarrassed or stoked. I spun the ball forward in my hands, then backwards, like I did before a kick, and between that and my shirt feeling so good on my shoulders it was like I somehow got back into my body again. I put the ball back down and did an elbow stretch above my head. Everyone copied me, and I grinned. The grass was freshly mowed, the balls had been pumped, and everybody was listening.

'All right,' I said. 'We'll start with some fitness. Zara, twenty spins. Everyone else, ten burpees. Ms Honeybone, twelve burpees.'

Everyone groaned, and Ms Honeybone said, 'What? That wasn't part of the deal!'

'I've changed my mind,' I said. 'Everybody do the chicken until Ms Honeybone caves.' I made my arms like wings and started bok-bok-ing until Ms Honeybone dropped into a push-up, then leapt up and growled, 'Just you wait until I'm in control again.'

I was exhausted when I got home from school, even more tired after Mum reminded me it was my night to vacuum the floors, and I was completely wrecked that evening by the time I got in the car on the way to training. Mum wasn't in the mood to listen to my dramatic moans this time – usually I could count on her to join in until we were one big wail about life being 'TOO HARRRRD' – and said, 'Maybe if you stopped complaining and helped me out we could get to training on time?'

I kept whining, but the truth was that I did actually want to go. I felt like today I'd trained for a week already, but at least there I'd be able to ask everyone about their jersey designs and, once I'd found out, I could work on how to annihilate them. I pulled on my boots and dragged my overworked brain and the legs attached to it to the car, then, for dramatic effect, pretended to sleep the whole seven-minute drive to training. When Mum caught me opening one eye to see if she was watching me be definitely asleep, she said, 'You know, every single day of our week has training in it. This is what we've chosen to do with our days. Are you really going to be annoying about it?'

'I just had a big day at school.'

'Classes were hard?'

'*Classes*? I don't know, I wasn't listening! PE was just extra physical today.'

'You don't think PE is a class?'

'It's not supposed to be! Anyway, mostly I was tired out by this other thing I've got going on with Zara. She's helping me figure out how I can fix everyone else's shirts like I did to mine.'

'You sure that's a good idea? Aren't you going to be tired like you are now, except every day, if you do that as well as training as well as school as well as your punishing schedule of messaging your friends to talk about training and school?'

'It's fine!' I yelled.

'I can tell you're right because of how calm you are,' she said, and laughed.

Training was a bust. I mean, the football part was exactly what it usually is – we did heaps of reflex training, so I copped a ball in the side of the head more than once – but nobody really wanted to talk about the jersey comp at all. Jones said his sister had stolen his t-shirt template, cut the shape out and superglued it to her teddy bear. Bucky said he'd drawn a picture of my face covered in boogers and already submitted it. Jay said he'd done a really good one but he'd forgotten about the cockatoo part and just drawn a phoenix instead. I told him if he put a cockatoo beak on the phoenix then it'd probably be fine, but I don't know what he said after that because I got another ball in the side of the head and then Crabtree yelled at me for not paying attention.

Part of me was annoyed that so many of the others weren't taking it seriously, but then part of me was like: *then maybe there won't be any competition, and the two hundred dollars will be mine?*

When Crabtree made us do Superman exercises – lying flat on our stomachs with our legs and arms straight out – I was glad I was already on the ground, because they were Dad's favourite exercise and thinking about that made me feel weak in a strange kind of way. Everything was way too distracting all day, really, and I was already barely focusing when Ng came up to me after training was done and said, 'Hey, you want to catch up tomorrow?'

I was thinking about working on the jerseys, or maybe the shirts. 'I've got something on at home,' I told him. 'Sorry.'

'Um, no you don't,' Mario said, pinging a ball off my head. 'You're coming over to my place after school because your mum's at training, remember?'

'Oh yeah,' I said, pretending I definitely remembered that. 'I guess that's the thing I've got on at home.'

'What, not being there?'

'Exactly.'

'You can come over too if you want to bring your Switch,' Mario told Ng.

'Nah, Dad says I can't take it anywhere. Too expensive to replace, he says, all because of that time when I threw the controller through the open balcony window when we were playing Just Dance and it smashed all over the car park.'

'Well, if you're not bringing it you can't come over,' Mario said, and then Mum had to come over and break up their giant mostly-pretend fight while trying not to laugh.

Dad called that night while I was working on some more jersey ideas. Instead of saying hello, he said, 'Mum said you were limping at training. Are you going to go to a doctor to see about your ankle?'

'When did you speak to Mum?'

'She texted me while you were at training.'

'Oh. And no, I'm fine. It's fine.' I didn't like thinking about my ankle. 'How's work?'

'Eh, it's okay. I made a new friend, though! I'm going to start going to the gym with him. He's real hardcore. I reckon he'll give me great tips for workouts for you.'

'Great,' I said, wedging the phone between my ear and my shoulder so I could draw my millionth cockatoo head. 'Hey, did I tell you I'm going to enter into a competition to win two hundred bucks?'

'Whoa, that'd be so great! Imagine what you could spend that on. I wish I had two hundred bucks – I just had to use the hundred dollars from the partial refund of my flights for an emergency trip to the dentist after my filling fell out.'

I sat up. 'But don't you need to use it on the flight here for my game?'

'Ach Jungchen, don't worry. I'll have the money again by then.'

'But what if another filling falls out?'

'That won't happen.'

'But if it *does*, it'll be okay, because I can spend my two hundred dollars on your ticket. Or on a ticket to see you.'

He laughed, and it felt weird. 'Yeah! That'd be so great. Fingers crossed. Is this competition through school or something?'

'Through the club.'

'Oh, what? Is it like a most handballs or goals type of thing? Or most hours spent working out? Because I can write up some boot camp plans for you if—'

'No, Dad, it's to design a new jersey.'

'We only just bought you that one!'

'For the girls' team! Though we'll probably have it on ours in a couple of years too. I've been drawing heaps of designs. Can I send them to you and you can tell me which is the best?'

'Sure, Freundchen. But I don't know – clothes aren't really my thing. Don't you think Pa would be a better person to ask? Is the competition just for the under-13s?'

'Nah, all the levels.'

'Oh. So the seniors too?'

'Yeah.'

'I mean, no offence, but … don't you think one of them will probably win?'

I looked down at my sketches. They were getting better, apart from the whole angry duck thing.

'Not all the seniors are into clothes, though,' I said, but my voice sounded weird. 'I know Bucky's older brother is obsessed with trucks and wears flannel all the time. And whenever I've seen Jay's sister she only ever wears plain black clothes to go with all that eyeliner. And Saanvi only wears shorts and band t-shirts. And—'

'Tell me you're not about to name every single person over thirteen that you know?'

I shut the list in my head down. 'All I'm saying is that maybe I'm the *only* person who's into fashion stuff. I can win.'

'I'm only saying, Homer. Keep your expectations … realistic.'

I felt heavy, and turned all my sketches over so I didn't have to look at them. 'In PE today Ms Honeybone said we were having a fourteen-week footy program.'

'Fourteen? What? That's amazing! What did you do today?'

It was like I was now talking to a whole different Dad. 'She asked me to help her with the class today since I trained with "a professional".'

He whistled. 'Wow. All right, tell me everything you did. Wait – I've gotta go, but I want to hear everything about your class, okay? Next time we'll start with that.'

'Sure.' I hadn't even noticed, but I was still drawing cockatoo heads all over the back of the page. 'What are you doing?'

'I'm meeting up with Han, that new friend I was talking about. We'll come up with a good training plan for you.'

'It's okay,' I said. 'You can just, like, hang out instead.'

'Nah, it'll be great. I'll send it to you soon.'

When he hung up, I turned my sketches back over, took a picture of each one of them, and sent them to Dad. Then I stared at them for a while, and went downstairs to watch TV with Mum.

Just before I went to sleep that night, my phone pinged. I got up to check.

Heya squirt! Love your drawings. Made up a good plan for you.

Then he sent a picture of a new boot camp workout he'd drawn up on a napkin. But nothing about which sketch he'd liked the most.

I didn't know if he was right about me winning or not, but I did know one thing.

Talking to my dad on the phone sucked.

ROUND 14 STATS

Dad's Plane Credit: $0
Days Until Shop Opens: 4
Good Jersey Ideas: ~~2~~ 0

Zara wasn't at school on Friday.

'But I thought we were going to work on my shop thing,' I whined at Avery when I cornered him outside class at recess.

'Well, first of all, she's in the hospital today, which maybe you'd know if you were her friend instead of her, uh, co-worker. And second, maybe she wanted to just hang out today anyway instead of doing work for you?' Avery crossed his arms.

'Well, first of all to *you*, Zara *is* my friend, probably, and is she okay? And also don't pretend that Zara wants to do anything else once she has an idea. I don't even hang out with her and I know that.'

'He's got a point,' Murphy said. 'And yeah, she's okay. She spends a lot of time at hospitals, but she never makes it seem like a big deal.' She tapped her chin. 'Which, I guess, doesn't mean it isn't.'

'So what now?'

'We're going to write Zara a get-well-soon sea shanty,' Avery said.

'You can help if you want,' Murphy said, but when she saw my face she laughed and added, 'Or not.'

Mario and Ng had already headed towards the oval, and I started shuffling towards it as well before ducking back into the classroom, waving at a surprised-looking Mr Skia, grabbing my notebook and pencil case, then rushing back outside and heading to the library. I saw a free chair, sat down, opened my notebook, drew a shirt-shaped pattern, and got started.

'Ahem,' a voice said right in front of me.

I yelped and looked up. It was Thi, covering her mouth and trying not to laugh.

'Shh!' Mr Hamilton hissed from his desk. 'No shrieking in the library.'

'It wasn't a shriek,' I hissed back.

'It was totally a shriek,' Thi said.

'Why did you creep up on me like that?'

'Why did *I* creep up on you? You're the one who sat at my desk!'

'No I didn't! It was empty!'

'Was not!'

'Was too!'

Mr Hamilton called out, 'Look, this isn't the type of library where I want you to be *super* quiet, but really, you need to at least not get into a shouting match.'

'But she—'

'And for the record, you sat at *her* desk.'

'Told ya,' Thi said.

I sat back in my chair. 'Really?'

'You were very focused,' Thi said. 'You weren't paying attention.' She leaned over and looked at my notebook. 'You're really determined to win this shirt competition, huh?'

'I'm definitely going to win,' I said.

'You're definitely going to come second,' she said. 'I'm going to win.'

'What?!'

She held up the clipboard she'd been leaning on, which had one of the templates from the jersey competition on it. She'd drawn what looked like waves from a beach and was colouring them in yellow, white and black.

'I don't like this idea,' she said, putting her board back down, 'but I'm still going to come up with the perfect one before you do.'

'No way!' I frantically started drawing cockatoo heads all over the shirt outline while Thi laid into her picture with her yellow pencil. After a few minutes of both of us scratching violently away at the paper in front of us, Thi's pencil broke and she squealed.

'That was definitely a shriek,' I said.

'Whatever,' she said, laughing. 'At least I'm not drawing ducks all over my shirt.'

'Hey! Don't make fun of my poor terrible ducks. It's not their fault I can't draw cockatoos.' I got out a new sheet of paper. 'Why are you here, anyway? I thought you'd be out playing on the oval.'

'Eh, I'm already way better than all of them. If I train too hard they'll never stand a chance.'

I snorted and Thi kicked me under the table.

'How's your mum feeling about the game tomorrow?' she asked.

'I don't know. Nervous, I think. She was a bit cranky yesterday. She's been training so hard, though. She's like, "last time we faced them we lost", and I keep telling her it's a different team now, with her on it, and Polly Rocket was off injured last time they played too.'

'And they got Tehan and Hermosilla in the trades,' Thi said, leaning in. 'I reckon they'll have a tough match tomorrow, but they might be in with a chance.'

I leaned in too, getting pumped up thinking about the game. 'Mum's been working on her strength training as well. It's going to be hard against their tall players, though.'

'Oh yeah – I mean, Henny is massive, and so good, and that's who your mum's up against.' She shivered. 'I honestly can't believe we get to talk about a football player that we *know*. Who lives in your *house*. How does it feel?'

'You know,' I said, going back to my paper. 'Weird. Fine. I mean, she still tells me off when I get toothpaste on the bathroom mirror, and even if I say that I'm just helping her build up some rage to use in her football games, somehow *I'm* the bad guy. So. You know. She's still being a mum.'

We worked on our drawings, much more calmly this time. I gave up on the duck heads and experimented with patterns and colours.

'Hey,' Thi said, 'can I borrow your yellow pen?'

'Hmm, I dunno,' I said, tapping it on my teeth. 'It's not like you've ever given *me* one of your pens, except for once a week since grade one.' I rolled it across the table to her.

She picked it up with a slightly horrified expression and said, 'Do I really want a tooth pen? I don't know.'

I watched her colour in with it way more neatly than I've

ever coloured anything and realised, for the first time, that maybe somebody else *could* win the jersey competition. Then I wouldn't get the two hundred dollars. And I wouldn't be able to fly Dad over. Which means I wouldn't get to see him.

I didn't like that thought, but I didn't know how to shut it down. I drew a spiral on the paper in front of me and kept circling and circling like it would never end.

'Homer?'

I looked up. Roman was standing next to me with a plastic bag.

'I've got that shirt you said you'd fix,' he said, holding it towards me. 'Dad washed it and stuff. Tuesday, yeah?'

'Yeah,' I said. 'No problem.'

He waved and said, 'We're beating you again. Remember how I said the grade sixes sucked before?' He pointed at Thi. 'Without her they're even worse.'

'Good,' Thi said smugly.

I still had all the coins Roman gave me the other day in my pencil case, and I poked it with my pen to hear them tinkle reassuringly. I was still thinking about Dad using his plane money to fix his teeth and about how my first game was only a few weeks away and how he might not be able to come any more.

Unless I helped him.

'Thi?'

'Yeah?'

'Do you think my shirt business is a good one?'

'Hell yeah,' she said. 'I saw how you dominated PE when you were wearing it. It's going to be awesome for everybody. Why do you think I told Zara to ask you to do it?'

'You what?'

She shrugged.

I learned in towards her. 'But what if I mess Roman's up?'

'Why would you do that?'

'I don't even know what he wants. I should've asked. He's shorter than me.' I looked at Thi. 'Like, your height.'

'Uh-huh.' She went back to drawing.

I looked at Thi. She was more Roman-shaped than me-shaped. It'd be good to have an idea of how a shirt would work on her. I knew Pa got people to come in for fittings all the time, but then I remembered the way he'd put his arms around people to get their measurements and then imagined myself doing it to Thi and something inside me went a little wonky.

'You okay?' Thi said.

'Eurgh,' I replied.

'Riiiiight,' she said. 'Anyway, did you hear the bell or were you drifting off again?'

'I don't drift!'

'You're a race car in a human body,' she said. 'Come on.'

I'm usually pretty good at asking questions. I'm not embarrassed when I don't know something in class, because there's nothing wrong with not knowing everything. And I told people what I thought of them all the time, including Tom (who didn't ever listen). What I mean is that it was weird that I couldn't just *ask* Thi if she could come for a fitting. Instead of just saying something, my brain decided it had to think about it first.

I thought about it for so long that K. had to poke me with their ruler and hiss, 'Homer! You've got to fill in your maths sheet.' They tapped the sheet I hadn't even realised was in front of me and said, 'You've been asleep with your eyes open for like ten minutes, buddy.'

I looked at K. with appreciation for the way they didn't want me to get in trouble with Mr Skia. (Or, maybe, they didn't want to lose table points yet again this year because of me not entirely paying attention.)

Then I looked at them a little harder. They were taller and leaner than me, and had a different body shape from Thi's too. If I had K.'s measurements, and Thi's, and mine … well, that obviously wasn't all the bodies in the world or anything, but it was a pretty good start.

'K.,' I said. 'Could you come over for a fitting for your shirt?'

'A what? And you don't have to worry about doing my—'

'Yes, I do,' I said, using my best Cranky Mr Skia voice, and they shut up. 'I want to do your shirt. Bring it to my house next week. You'll be doing me a favour if I can take your measurements.'

'Uh, I guess that's okay.'

'And you,' I said to Thi, pointing a bit more angrily than I meant. 'You too.'

'I haven't even asked you to do my shirt!' she said.

The table went quiet.

'I mean, you do want me to though, right?' I said, trying to keep my voice normal.

'Well, obviously.'

'He did mine first,' Tom put in.

I ignored him. 'You can come do a fitting too,' I said to Thi. 'You and K. can both come. At the same time. Definitely.'

I wished I could pull out my own tongue to shut myself up.

'I mean, I can't come until Wednesday,' K. said. 'Maybe Thi can come on an earlier day? In case you want to—'

'THAT'S FINE,' I said. 'WEDNESDAY IS FINE.'

'Really?' Mr Skia said in my ear while I jumped. 'Because I don't think that's the answer to any of the questions on the maths sheet you're diligently not filling out.'

'Sorry,' I squeaked.

He stood over me while I ticked some boxes that said: 8, 1/12, 0, 258. When he finally left to tell off somebody else, I whispered, 'Wednesday, right?'

K. nodded. Thi whispered back, 'I'll check, but sure.'

I was going to say 'thanks', but for some reason, I couldn't. Instead I went for 'fine', but then halfway through decided to go with 'cool', and instead I said, 'Fool,' and then they both stared at me, and I was just glad it was Friday so it would be two days before I had to look either of them in the eye again.

ROUND 15 STATS

Shirts Made Better: 2
New Shirts to Fix According to Zara: 4
Upcoming Fittings: 2
Days Until Shop Opens: 3

If you'd told me a year ago that I'd enjoy a quiet Saturday morning sitting around with my grandparents voluntarily sewing something, I'd have howled with laughter. I mean, my grandparents were great and I liked seeing Pa making clothes, but back then Saturdays were for ball sports, and nothing else was more fun than that.

Turns out, fixing clothes was *exactly* as fun as that.

Today, we were watching Marvel movies in the background while Pa said, 'Who's that?' and 'Wait, didn't he die?' a million times and Nanna, who was way more into comics than either of us, patiently explained over and over what was going on. Ng and Mario had finally stuffed their shirts in my bag yesterday, so I was working on them now, starting with Ng's. I was attempting to get a little faster than I had on the last few shirts, while also doing a better job, and it was, well, not easy.

'Gah!' I yelled, when I'd pricked my finger for the one

millionth time.

'Use a thimble,' Pa said. 'There's one in my suitcase.'

'What's a thimble?'

'How have we not had this discussion yet? It's like a tiny metal glove for your index or middle finger to stop you stabbing yourself in it.'

'What if I keep stabbing myself in all my fingers and also my leg?'

'Then you need a suit of armour.'

'Do you have one of those in your suitcase?'

'I think I might've left it back at the shop.'

I sighed. 'I think I'm getting a little faster, at least. I can't believe I spent so much time on Tom's. Now that I've done his shirt he's stopped speaking to me again until the next time I'm useful.'

'Should've sewn a curse into his shirt,' Nanna said.

'You mean, like shi—'

'No!' she yelped. 'I mean sewing in some words like "a plague on your house"! What do they *teach* you at school?'

'To be fair, I don't think they teach either kind of curse at school,' Pa said.

'Wait! I know what you mean. Marcie from my class is a witch or something. When she's mad at you she doesn't just call you a jerkjack like everyone else does – she says stuff like, "may your curtains never close all the way so the sun wakes you up too early" or "may your eraser only rub out the lines you meant to keep".'

'Wow. She sounds terrifying,' Pa said. 'Do you think I could hire her to write curses for my mean clients?'

'Should I write a good one, for Mario and Ng?' I asked. 'Like, so good things happen?'

'That seems nice,' Pa said. 'And it'd be good practice for getting them small enough so you're good at hiding them when they're mean.'

While Pa carefully sewed thousands of sparkling beads into a wedding veil, Nanna hemmed pants for the shop and I very slowly embroidered some nice curses onto fabric to hide in Mario and Ng's shirts. Once I'd finished Ng's shirt and showed it proudly to Pa ('Good improvement,' he said, 'but your stitch lengths are uneven and you need to work on your knots'), we packed the cooler and headed across town to Mum's game. I was feeling pretty chilled out. I was one shirt down and Mum was about to smash another game. I'd make a bunch of money, she'd get more famous and we'd live happily ever after. As long as this game was just like the last one.

The game was not like the last one.

It felt like half the kids from my school and almost everyone from the Cockatoos had turned up. I recognised heaps of people, and there was one whole row of grade one kids who kept staring at me while Ng said, 'You're so famous they can't even watch the game.'

'What?'

'Hello, your mum is out there playing in a massive stadium, and there's some complete stranger over there with a flag that says FALZON AND ON!! Because of your *mum*. Because she's a *celebrity*. That means you're a celebrity *kid*.'

'Do you reckon that means I'll get a free pie at the stall?'

'Oh, definitely. Just go up and yell, "I'm Angela's son!

Give me a pie!" Actually, make that three pies.'

I stood up and Thi pulled me down again from the row behind. 'Absolutely do not listen to your awful friends,' she said. 'You will not get a free pie that way. The way you do get one is to tell your friends to buy one for you or you won't be their friend anymore.'

'She's onto us,' Mario yelled. 'We've been busted!'

Having so many people I knew here made it way, way more fun. We hollered Mum's name whenever she went near the ball, and the whole crowd around us started to get into it too, realising we knew *the* Angela Falzon, until the whole section had become a super hyper pocket of excitement every time Mum kicked the ball.

Which ... wasn't a lot.

The opposition was too strong. Mum had started last week on the forward line, where she was powerful and fast and could kick all the goals, but this week the ball barely made it down to her. She kicked one goal over her shoulder and everyone went wild, but despite all the yelling and the screaming and Mario accidentally losing his scarf into the crowd from spinning it too hard, we lost by thirty-three points.

It was quiet in Ng's family's van on the way back to their place. There'd been so much noise back at the stadium, but now nobody really knew what to say. Mr Ng said the team needed to pick up their game and get the ball to Mum more often. Mrs Ng said that the other team probably ate more for breakfast. Ng's brother Daniel said the other team were secretly superheroes and that's the only way they could've won. His sister Lily said the other team was made of boogers. Ng just patted me on the back.

Mrs Ng, who always wore pants even when it was over forty

degrees, gave me a container of curry from her freezer and said if I didn't cook it for my exhausted mother for dinner tonight she would never let me in her house again, and Ng went pale enough that I took her word for it. Mr Ng, who always wore things with pockets so he could put his hands in them at all times, nodded with a serious face in the background.

'Hey, let's play a thousand rounds of Smash Bros,' Ng said, once I'd put the curry carefully by the front door.

'Can we do some more sketches for the jersey thing?' I asked.

'Homer, you're always doing that,' he said. 'I haven't kicked you off a ledge for ages. Come on, I'll never be a beta tester if I'm only ever competing against the little kids in my family.'

'But I really need to draw,' I said, in a Stern Mr Skia voice.

'But I really need to game,' Ng said, in a Sterner Hien voice.

'Actually,' Mr Ng said, leaning past the door, 'I think you both really need to play with Daniel.'

So I didn't get any drawing done after all, but we did build Daniel a giant Lego stable/garage for all of his ponies and Hot Wheels cars that was four storeys high by the time Mum came by, looking exactly as exhausted as Mrs Ng had predicted.

'That was an amazing game,' Mr Ng said to Mum. 'Not as many disposals as last week, though.'

'No,' Mum said, shaking her head. 'There were not. I'm glad you had fun, though.'

'You should have seen Lily,' Mrs Ng said while Lily stood behind her, staring at Mum in awe. 'She had this face on the whole time. She can't believe you are really on the field.'

Mum leaned in and smiled at her. 'Are you going to play footy when you're older too, Lil?'

Lily shrieked and ran away.

'I guess I should be flattered?' Mum said. 'Usually she loves to talk to me.'

'You're too famous now,' Mr Ng said. 'No more normal conversation.'

In the car, I was glad Lily had run away from Mum. Even after the loss, she had a little smile on her face the whole way home.

Once we got there, I sat her down on the couch and heated up her dinner. It was late, and she yawned fourteen times while eating it.

'Are you okay to go to work on Monday?' I asked.

'I can hardly call in tired. They already let me get away with having all this extra time off work to get to training and I've got next Friday off for the interstate game if they select me for the team.'

'Maybe you should go to bed now?'

'You're not my dad,' she said, yawning again. 'Rack off. I can stay up late if I want.'

'What is it you'd say to me if I was the one telling you this? "Fine, but I don't want to hear any whining tomorrow when I wake up."'

'I didn't raise you to be practical, I raised you to wreak havoc. Stop being sensible and get me a glass of water.'

'Ahem?'

'Ugh, who brought you up to care about manners? Get me a glass of water *please*, before I die.'

When I got back barely a minute later, she was already asleep. I turned off the TV, got her doona from her bed and put it over her.

'Hey, kiddo?' she said as she snuggled in.

'Yeah?'

'I'm sorry you don't get to go to school with a cool story this week.'

'Mum,' I said, 'I don't need you to be cool. I'm way too cool on my own.'

And my mother's final, loving words before she fell asleep,were: 'Sorry to tell you this, but saying you're cool means you're really, really not.'

ROUND 16 STATS

Shirts Made Better: 3
Shirts to Fix: 3
Days Until Shop Opens: 2

I was having this really great dream about running along bouncing a football and catching it smoothly on the cleanest, greenest grass you've ever seen, grass that just went on softly, forever, until I ran face-first into a cloud.

'GET UP!' the cloud yelled.

Turns out, it wasn't a cloud. It was a pillow. And it was coming towards my face.

'Ow!'

'Sorry,' Mum said, not looking sorry, 'but I tried to wake you up gently at first, whispering motherly loving things into your ear, then with smooches, but you didn't listen. So now it's the walloping with a pillow.'

'Is it late?'

'Very late,' Mum said. 'It's eight o'clock.'

'But it's Sunday, right?'

'Your point?'

'Don't we sleep in on Sundays since Dad moved out?'

'And look where that got us!' She flung her arms out. 'A massive loss in front of a huge crowd!'

'It wasn't that bad,' I said, covering my eyes.

'Point is, I've been too slack about training.'

'Mum. You train with your team three times a week and with me sixty times a week.'

'Listen up, bud. You've got three seconds to get up or I'm going to dump this tray of ice cubes over you,' she said, holding it up. 'I've been holding it in my hand this whole time and now I can't feel my fingers.'

'Why were you holding it this whole time? Doesn't seem very motherly loving-like to me.'

'And three,' she said, tipping it over me while I yelled and jumped out of bed.

Dad rang while we were in the middle of Mum's favourite training game, spin and kick, where you stand in the middle of the oval with your eyes closed, spin twice on the spot and then kick to the other person. It was fun for the person spinning, but not for the person chasing the ball when someone, who will remain nameless but is terrible at her own made-up game, kicks it literally behind her. I'd just come down from the tree she'd kicked it into when she held out her phone for me and said, 'It's your dad.'

'Hey, Papa,' I said. 'Good timing. I'm dying.'

'Angela said you were doing some early morning training. Good for you both.'

'Is it really?'

He laughed. 'I just wanted to check that you're okay, that your mum's okay.'

'She's fine. I think she might make us train all day, though.'

'Tell her to take a break.'

'I'm sorry? Who is this? My dad doesn't know anything about breaks.'

'I'll have you know I'm on one right at this moment. I'm at the beach with Han.'

'Who's Han?'

'My friend, you know? The one who helped me with those training ideas.'

'Are you training right now?'

'Nope. We went for a swim, threw a ball around, and then when I was sitting in the sun I thought, *oh, I should call my son*.'

'Oh, ha ha.'

'What's the weather like out east?'

'Bit soggy. It rained last night.'

'Ah, that's too bad. It's so nice over here. Sun's out, I'm feeling good.'

I wasn't really sure how to feel. I was a bit jealous, really. It'd be nice to sit on a beach right now with Dad and Han and not run after Mum's random kicks.

'Hopefully I can come over there soon.'

'I hope so too. Maybe in the spring school holidays.'

'Yeah.'

'How's that drawing you're doing going?'

I perked up. 'Good!'

'You know, I did like that one you did – the one with the big cockatoo head spots? I reckon that's the one to go with.'

'Really? I agree!'

'Yeah, you did great. Look, I'm sorry that I wasn't really listening the last time we talked – it had been a big day at work, and it was hard to pay attention. But I just really wanted to talk to you anyway, so I called. It's hard, you know? If you speak to me when I'm cranky you get me at my worst and that's it the whole day. If I'd been at home then I'd have eaten dinner and stopped being so hangry and then I'd be much nicer.'

'No, then you'd say we should go run some laps.'

'Ha! You're not wrong, sport.'

Mum had given up on waiting and was now kicking the ball for herself to chase after. Dad started telling me about how he'd had a great day at work last week because he had a new client that was a massive AFL fan and was super impressed that Dad knew 'THE Angela Falzon? With that mad goal at the end of last week's match!?', but halfway through his story he stopped and said, 'Oh my god, there's a Mr Whippy truck coming around! I have to go chase down an ice cream. I'll talk to you later.'

I hung up and stared at the phone. Mum came over and said, 'You all right? It was like your tail started wagging halfway through there.'

'I'm not a dog,' I said indignantly.

'I know,' she said kindly. 'If you were a dog you'd catch those stray kicks way faster. Was Dad okay?'

'Yeah. He asked after you. He was in … a good mood?'

She laughed. 'You sound shocked.'

'I guess he hasn't sounded super happy since he moved.'

'It was hard on him too,' she said, putting her hand on my back. 'You know, it was probably way harder than on us. He misses you like crazy, even if it doesn't always come across. Were you happy hearing him be happy?'

'Yes. No. I don't know.'

'Like, if he's having a nice time that's really great because you love him, but also how dare he enjoy his life without us?'

'Exactly! But just about me. You guys broke up.'

'Okay, jeez, all right. I can still miss him, can't I?'

'Nope,' I said, then took the football out of her hands, closed my eyes, and punted it into a tree.

'Fetch,' I told her.

She pointed a finger at me. 'Bad dog.'

That afternoon, Mum came up and watched me while I stitched the last of Mario's shirt together.

'You were good out there at training today,' she said.

'Uh-huh.'

'Not really limping either.'

'Cool.'

'Are you ignoring me?'

'I'm concentrating!'

'Booooring.'

'Mum, are you seriously trying to stop me working here?'

She watched me for a while until I finally looked up at her. 'What's up?'

'Was I good out there?' she asked, in a little voice.

'What do you mean?'

'At training. Was I good at training?'

'Oh my god, Mum. Of course you were. I was wrecked. Why do you think I can't even talk right now?'

'Because you're mean?'

'Because I'm tired!'

'But Homer,' she said, 'will we ever win again? What if last week was just a fluke?'

I put the shirt down for a second. Sometimes I forgot that Dad wasn't around to help with these kinds of questions – to have the grown-up types of conversations, like making my mum feel better about herself even though she was an incredible athlete and always had been.

'Mum,' I said sternly, 'you don't need to hear from me that you're good at this. You know you are. You got drafted into a *national team* last year because you're so good. You literally just won a match for them single-handedly a week ago, and, obviously, you can't win every single game. You know all this. What would you tell me if I'd said what you did?'

She crossed her arms and mumbled, 'Those things.'

'Exactly. You'd also make me a coke spider to drink to make me feel better, so you should probably go make yourself that too.'

'You know what?' she said. 'I think you might be right.'

'Good,' I said, getting back to my stitching. 'Great. I mean, while you're there, if you want to make me one too, I guess that's okay.'

I didn't look up, but I could hear her rolling her eyes anyway.

By the time she came back with my spider, I was done. I held the shirt up and looked at it, pleased, while Mum ruffled my hair, looked at my shirt with confusion and said, 'Great job at … uh … whatever it was that you did with that?'

'Thanks,' I said, beaming.

Because when I was finished with all these shirts, my whole school was going to *rock*.

ROUND 17 STATS

Shirts Made Better: 4
Shirts to Fix: 2
Days Until Shop Opens: 1 (!!!)

On Monday morning, while we glued facts about Australian history onto timeline posters, Zara rolled over to me and said, 'I'm pretending I need your glue.'

'Okay,' I said, passing mine over.

'Don't you know what pretending is?'

'I honestly don't know what level of pretending you need. Do you want me to pretend I don't have glue?'

'Forget it,' she said. 'It's an excuse to tell you that we're having a meeting at lunchtime. Clear your schedule.'

'My ...?'

'Just turn up,' she said, exasperated. 'We've got a lot to talk about.'

'Yes, ma'am,' I said, and saluted while she rolled her eyes.

I turned back to doing my project and said, 'Wait, where's my glue?'

'You pretend gave it to Zara,' K. said. 'Who actually took it.'

'Can't finish my work then,' I said, throwing up my hands.

Thi rolled her eyes. There seemed to be a lot of that happening. Maybe there was some kind of eye-rolling disease going around the school.

'Just shut up and use mine,' she said, handing hers over. 'And you've glued your Emu War bit upside down.'

By recess, after we'd got to the part where we had to glue the word 'Treaty' on the timeline and then found that we didn't actually have a treaty with the people who were here first and then we all got mad, I wasn't really in the mood to go kick a football around. I cornered Mario and Ng and said, 'I've got something for you.'

I went into my backpack and pulled out their shirts, all wrapped up in brown paper and tied with string, because Pa said good presentation is half the point.

'I'm still keeping this present, but I will also be honest and tell you that it's not my birthday,' Ng said.

'You goof. It's your shirt.'

They both ripped open the packages and Ng said, holding his up, 'It's beautiful. I'm going to win at everything. This will change my life.'

'I think I just became a better person by owning this,' Mario said. 'I can feel myself getting smarter.'

I snorted. 'Tell your friends how amazing it is, okay? Get my business out there.' I clicked my fingers in an impatient, businessy way like I'd seen Dad do at his office.

Mario turned to Ng. 'Hey, you should see how great my new Homer shirt is.'

'Oh really? I bet my new Homer shirt is better.'

'Nuh-uh!'

'Is too!'

They started to wrestle and Skia came over to kick us out of the classroom. Outside, I said, 'Let's head to the library.'

'The what?' Mario said.

'You already did that gag last week,' I said impatiently. 'Come on.'

Ng shrugged. 'I could read,' he said.

'Sure, maybe Hamilton's got new stuff in,' Mario said.

We found a whole free table in the library so I could work on my jersey drawings some more while Ng and Mario read on the chairs opposite. Half my brain was trying to think of what the sleeves should be like, and the other half was imagining getting the money and going to a travel agent and throwing a big wad of cash down on the desk and saying, 'Your finest return ticket from Perth, please.' I was having a great time imagining the bit with the money-throwing, but after ten minutes I could feel Mario's leg jumping around under the table.

'You right there?'

'I can't read for *all* of recess,' he said. 'I have to go kick something. My legs need it. Come on.'

Ng shrugged. 'I could kick,' he said.

'I'll stay here,' I said. 'I've gotta keep drawing.'

'Come on,' Mario said, pulling my arm. 'It's more fun with you there.'

'I can't. I've got to work on this.'

'You can come back at lunch for a bit.'

'No, I can't. I've got a meeting with Zara at lunch.'

Mario rolled his eyes. 'Tell her no. Come kick with us.'

'NO,' I said, yanking my arm away. 'I've got to *win*, okay? You know I need that money.'

They both stared at me. I looked around the library, and saw that everyone was watching us.

'Please keep your voice down,' Mr Hamilton said.

I hadn't realised I'd been so loud. I crossed my arms.

'Forget it,' Ng said to Mario. 'We'll see him later.'

'When?' Mario asked as they walked away. 'He's always busy. Can't play now. Has a "meeting" at lunch. At school! Doesn't even hang out on the weekend.'

I must've caught that same eye-rolling disease because when I heard that I rolled my eyes. I mean, I'd hung out with Ng after Mum's game and everything. They were being super dramatic about it. I'd told them why I wanted the money, and they knew how much I missed my dad. I mean, they'd had to spend all of last year listening to me give them advice about how their parents could be better people so they wouldn't want to break up with each other. And their dads both still lived at home, so it must have worked.

They might be all about footy and nothing else, but I wasn't. In here, they were just distracting me anyway. I picked my pen back up.

It was time to work.

When I got to the stumps at lunch, Zara, Avery, Murphy and Thi were there already, looking absolutely super serious. I'd been smiling because I was kind of excited, but I'd seen enough business meetings on TV to know the only smiling person was always about to get fired, so I stopped.

'Hey, guys,' I said. And even though the last time I said

thank you to the stump crew they'd started lecturing me on all the times I'd sucked, I said, 'Thanks for doing all this.'

'No problem,' Zara said. 'We're all getting cheap shirts and we'll be famous by association when you're successful. Anyway, I've come up with a business plan.'

'Already?'

Zara clicked her fingers and Thi rushed up with her clipboard. I really had to ask Zara how she did that to Thi (who would surely kick me square in the teeth if I tried it on her) so I could turn Mario or Ng into minions too.

'Here,' Thi said, handing over a sheet of paper.

NAME OF BUSINESS: 'Sew What Enterprises Pty Ltd'

TEAM

- President, Founder & CEO: Homer Falzon Schneider
- Vice President: To Be Announced
- Sales Officer: TBA
- Human Resources Officer: TBA

COSTS

- Needles
- Thread
- New Material
- Bandaids

REVENUE

- $15 per item, minimum
- Past pricing has been lower BUT we will say that these were 'GRAND OPENING' prices

- Now the prices are SET and CANNOT BE CHANGED

MARKETING STRATEGY

- Posters
- Business Cards
- Newspaper ads
- Billboards?
- Morning Television???

GOALS

- Tailor every sports outfit in Grade 5–6
- Tailor all normal uniforms in Grade 6
- Tailor all normal uniforms in Grades 3–5
- Tailor all normal uniforms Prep–Grade 3
- Grow business to incorporate more tailors, a warehouse, and overseas opportunities

COMPETITORS

- Homer's Pa
- ???

RISK ANALYSIS

- Pricked by needles
- Hien shuts it down
- Accidentally ruin clothes (budget needed for mistakes)

FUTURE PROJECTIONS

- One month, four shirts a week: $240
- One year, when business has expanded: ~~$2880~~ ~~$20,000~~ $2,000,000

ROUND 18 STATS

Business Plans: 1
Confusion: High

I blinked. Then I blinked a few more times.

'It's great, isn't it?' Thi said proudly.

'I mean, it's ...' I blinked some more because it was something I remembered how to do. 'What's ... what's revenue?'

'Like, the money you'll make,' Zara said.

'Riiiight.' I looked over the page again. 'And my Pa is ... my competitor?'

'Yes,' Avery said. 'I guess we'll have to have a meeting about how to take his business down?'

'Hmm,' I said. 'I like this bit, though. Where I'm the president, founder and CEO. Except I don't know what a CEO is. Is it ... a Captain ... Over ... Everyone?'

'Not even close,' Murphy said. 'And that would be COE, not CEO. It means Chief Executive Officer.'

'Cool. I've always thought I'd be the chief of something some day.'

'Like, of a football club?' Thi asked excitedly.

Somewhere in my mind there was the sound of an umpire's whistle and the satisfying thump when your boot hits the ball just right for a kick, and then there was the thought of being in charge of making people have that feeling every day. I shook it off. 'Well, for now I'm the chief of this. Of you, specifically.'

'Don't get any ideas,' she growled, pointing a pen at me.

'What other costs do you think you'll have?' Zara asked.

'I don't know. These sound about right. More material would be helpful in case I need to make someone's shirt wider or longer.'

'Right. So then we have to take a portion of the money you make and set it aside for things like that.'

That I definitely didn't agree with. 'What? Take my money?'

'Yes. For expenses.'

'Expenses?'

'To buy the new material. And pay for advertising. Remember how we asked Willow to draw up those posters? She'll have them ready by tonight, she says.'

'But didn't you say Thi was going to give her some pens or something?'

'Yes. But we have to get the posters printed.'

'Oh.'

'And who's paying for that?'

I blinked.

'I'm paying for that because I live right next to a printing place,' Zara explained. 'And then you are paying me back.'

'Okay?'

'Great!'

I looked at the plan again. They were all words that I theoretically understood, but it was like they didn't make sense together. 'Goals?'

'Yes,' Zara said.

We stared at each other until Murphy leaned in and said, 'Like, how you'll succeed in the future.'

'Overseas ...'

'Look,' Zara said, sighing, 'a business plan details a *plan*. This is not all going to happen this week. We're making projections for the future. Like those sales for a year.'

'Wait, does that say two MILLION dollars?'

'Yes. But that's not *this* year. We have to build up to it. It is a *projection*. We're hoping for *next* year.'

Two million dollars.

There was the sensible part of me, the part that almost never got to go out in the world, that was saying that two million dollars in my pocket was not going to happen. Even if I was amazing at this, which I could get to be, and even if I was fast, which I definitely wasn't yet.

But, let's face it, for years there'd been a bigger part of me that had always ignored anything sensible because that was boring, and boring was for other people. And that part of me saw the word million and just *knew* it was possible. My dad was working hard to save the money to eventually move back to Melbourne – to me. The least I could do was work even harder, and make so much money he could do it in months instead of years. It would make it so easy for him to come back.

'So do you have any other ideas?' Zara asked.

'I don't know. I can't think of any. I'm just the shirt-fixing guy.' Then I remembered this morning, handing Ng and Mario their shirts. 'Wait! Another thing I have to spend money on is brown wrapping paper and string, for when I hand over the shirts.'

'You wrap them? That is *amazing*,' Zara said. 'So professional! And you call yourself "just the shirt-fixing guy".'

I was, secretly, pretty pumped when she said that.

'Report from the rest of the team?' Zara asked the others.

'I've paid Willow her new pens,' Thi said.

'Did you have to spend actual money?' Zara asked.

'No, kind of? Mum got a huge discount on them, so it'll be about the same discount I'll get off the shirt from Homer.'

Zara narrowed her eyes. 'But you need to be compensated for your *time*, too.'

'It's fine,' she said, looking at me and giving me a small kind of smile. 'I mean, it's not like I'm compensated for my time holding clipboards for your other stuff.'

'That's different!' Zara yelled. 'For reasons I will think of later! Moving on.' She cleared her throat. 'Avery, Murphy?'

'We've come up with the music for the jingle,' Avery said, holding up his little tape recorder. 'I can play it for you.'

We crowded around to listen as Avery pressed play. A jangly, cheerful piano tune burst out of it, sounding all busy, then there was a longer, stretched-out part with the piano playing the same melody but much fainter, alongside a kind of quiet chaotic rattling and the sound of a sewing machine stitching through material – it sounded like something thick, maybe denim. Then it became loud and busy again, and finally, when it ended, there was the sound of scissors cutting fabric in two short, sharp bursts.

Even when it was over, I could still hear it playing in my head. 'Whoa,' I said. 'That is really catchy.'

'We're pretty happy,' Murphy said. 'It might change when we come up with the lyrics. You guys have any ideas?'

'Pfft,' I said. 'I can't write an assignment for school, so there's definitely no way I could write a song. The only thing I can do is, you know, cap your sleeves, hem your shirts, fix your shoulders and make your clothes feel right.'

Avery and Murphy exchanged a look.

We spent the rest of lunch talking about stuff like risk management ('Do *not* drop your needles on the floor and forget and have your mum walk on one or she will *sue* us,' Zara said), and who was going to be Vice President ('Probably me,' Zara said, 'since I already tell you off a lot'), and drawing up the form that my clients (clients!!) would sign at the shop when it opened.

When the bell rang, Zara said, 'All right, so, we'll open the shop tomorrow. You and I can be there on the first day. It'll be what in the industry they call a *soft opening*. We'll start small tomorrow, increase our reach with posters and the recess radio spot … it'll be great. Okay?'

'Okay,' I agreed.

But it was better than okay.

Because if this worked out, it wouldn't matter if all of Dad's teeth fell out. I'd be able to pay to get him here, no matter what.

I loved watching Mum train.

Sure, I kind of wanted to work on my tailoring, but Pa and Nanna were out and I couldn't see how I'd get any of that done at Mario or Ng's houses if I went over there. So here I was, at a football training session, like one of us was every single day of the week. Obviously, the general vibe at Mum's practice ground was way more buzzy than it was when I trained at my local oval, where there were generally only cheers from the people watching if someone brought a new dog. Here the grounds were huge, some of the stands were undercover, there was a merch shop, and people came to watch even if they weren't related to the players. Everything here was faster and bigger and just felt ... *more*. I sat in the stands with a can of lemonade, a sandwich and a muffin, and I watched my mum roll.

She was powerful. She ran fast and far and charged through everybody. She was also encouraging, applauding everyone's good work and yelling out nice things, which made it all the more terrifying when they played a scratch game and she just completely mowed down all those people she'd just been nice to. It was scary to watch, and also really, really impressive.

Mum's coach, Douglas, who I secretly called Less Doug (mostly because then I wasn't so intimidated about being around him), came and found me after training while Mum was drinking her twentieth cup of Gatorade outside the team rooms. 'Your Mum told me you've got an injury,' he said.

'Nah, it's okay now.'

'You better take it seriously,' he said. 'The club's counting on you to build your skills and join us later.'

'I'm eleven,' I reminded him. 'It's not like I'm going to be drafted in yet.'

'They're always watching,' he said mysteriously, looking around. 'You're too young now, but soon you won't be. You don't want to be injured out of a career before it even starts.'

'No, I know. I'll look after it. It's really fine.'

'Oh! You know that for sure, do you? You a doctor? That

what you're studying in grade four these days?'

I really knew too many sarcastic people. 'I'm in grade six! But no.'

'Well, then. Guess you better listen to your mother, the one person you know who's actually studied a bit of that stuff, huh?'

In the car on the way home, I said to Mum, 'I don't need to go to a doctor.'

'So you've said.'

'It's fine, I promise! You even said it yourself when you saw me the other day.'

'It's just hard, you know? You keep saying that, but then I see you limping at training and I don't know what to do. Now that I'm the only parent in town, I don't have anyone to bounce my ideas off. You dad can't actually see how you're doing, so when I tell him you say you're fine, then he's like, "Well, he's probably fine then." What am I supposed to do?'

'Listen to Dad,' I said.

'Hmm,' she said. 'That sounds terrible. Isn't that why we split up? So I didn't have to?'

'Mum,' I said, hurt.

'Oh, I'm just kidding. I just told you I asked him! But I'm going to keep a keen eye on you, okay?'

'Okay.'

'Did Doug tell you the other thing?'

'What other thing?'

'I made the team for this week.'

'You what?! That means ...?'

'Yeah,' she said, beaming. 'I'm definitely going to Queensland. I mean, I hoped I was going to, that's why I made plans for Nanna and Pa to look after you, but ... yeah. I did it.

I'm playing an interstate game,' she said, and she was smiling so big that all I could do was high five her so hard that my hand hurt all the way home.

ROUND 19 STATS

Days Until Shop Opens: 0
Shirt Money Earned So Far: $20

'I tried my shirt on last night,' Mario said when I got to The Bad Corner in the morning. 'I cannot tell you how good it felt. I figured out the meaning of life while I was wearing it.'

'Oh yeah?'

'It's the shirt. The shirt is the meaning of life.'

'Well, make sure you have this exact conversation with everyone else you know too, because we're opening the shirt-fixing shop today at lunch.'

'You what?'

I could feel myself puffing up like one of those birds that likes to show off in nature documentaries. 'I'm opening a shop. I am a shop owner. I'm a ...' I tried to remember what it said in the business plan. 'I'm a CEO.'

Ng ran up, panting. 'A Cheese and Egg Omelette?'

'Nah, it's a Common Emu Owner,' Mario said.

'You're both complete prongs. It's a—' I coughed while my

brain tried to catch up with my mouth. 'Chief Executed Officer.'

'Hmm, pretty sure that means you're dead?' Mario said.

'You might mean Executive,' Ng said.

'You both didn't even know what it meant two seconds ago!'

'Didn't we?' Mario said, stroking the beard he didn't have.

'Whatever,' I said. 'I'm gonna fix everyone's shirts and make a million dollars and Dad can move back home and it'll be great.'

'What do you need us to do?' Ng asked.

'Yeah, do you need us to, like, run the register, or be your security detail or something? Or take notes? Do we need to apply for a job?'

'I have my pen licence,' Ng said. 'And I bet Mrs Loo would give me a good reference.'

'Um, it's okay,' I said, shrugging. 'I've actually got it under control, I think. Zara's helping me out today.'

It went really quiet for a moment. I could hear the cars rumbling around us and all the kids hollering across the road in the playground. I didn't like it when things were quiet. 'Thanks, though,' I said. 'You can, like, definitely tell everybody! When you're kicking around or whatever.'

'Yeah,' Ng said. 'Or whatever.'

The music started through the loudspeakers and we picked up our bags from the ground and headed over. Something felt weird in the air, like I'd said something wrong. Really, all I'd done was given them the chance to, like, not do work at school on their break. I didn't know what the big deal was. Maybe I'd try and talk to them about it later when I'd sorted out what was happening, because Sulking Instead Of Talking About Things was pretty much why my parents split up and I was not interested in divorcing my two best friends.

Before I could do too much more thinking about it, I was distracted by everyone looking down at the ground as they walked through the school gates. There on the footpath, in chalk, was an arrow next to the word 'RECESS'.

Even though class was about to start, I followed the arrows along with all the other kids who were checking them out. The last arrow was in the junior playground, pointing to the slide. Underneath it there was a wooden room with a window frame cut out of it, otherwise known as the most premium piece of playground equipment for the under-six audience. Back when I was younger, we'd pretend it was an ice cream truck, or a tractor, or a shop that sold butts; today, all the wood around it was coloured in bright chalk and there was a sign hanging from it.

'What is it?' Ng said from beside me.

'It says "CLOSED UNTIL 11AM",' some kid said.

I opened and closed my mouth while Mario said from my other side, 'Is this you?'

'Um,' I said, 'maybe?'

We raced back to class, with everyone else who'd been distracted by the signs, and I made a beeline for Zara. 'That chalk,' I said, 'was that you?'

'It's great, isn't it?' she said, grinning. 'It was an overnight idea. I get all my best ones when I'm supposed to be doing something else, like washing the dishes or cleaning my room. Luckily, Thi had chalk in her house, because she's Thi, and we got here early. I watched you follow those arrows, along with most of the school. If I'd written "order new shirts here", literally nobody would turn up. Instead, people are whispering about it.'

'They are?'

Tom came up to me and said, 'Did you see that chalk stuff? I heard there's going to be a gig at the playground. I heard Murphy got some band to turn up. I heard it might even be Clover Park.'

'Um, I'm right here,' Murphy said from next to him.

'Murphy! How did you get Clover Park?' Tom said.

'I didn't?'

'Well, who did?'

'Nobody?' Murphy said.

'They're just turning up on their own?'

'This is painful,' Avery whispered.

'It's not a gig,' Taylor said. 'It's a casting call for a movie, I heard.'

'Did you actually hear that or are you just desperately hoping for that?' asked Rissa, who was Taylor's sometime friend and an actual movie actress, which meant she knew they didn't hold surprise auditions in school playgrounds.

'I think it's definitely a murderer and this would make a great horror movie,' Hayley said happily.

'I don't think murderers let you know their plans,' Ava said. 'Besides, it's a shop. Just ask Homer.'

Everybody turned to me and I said, 'Uh.'

'Well, this has all been very interesting speculation,' Mr Skia said loudly, 'but I don't believe any of you, so maybe can we do some work?'

When we were all sitting down at our tables, Thi leaned over and whispered to me, 'How did Ava know?'

K. pushed their chair in and said, 'Ava knows everything. Remember when she knew Ms Fletcher was leaving the school before anyone else *and* she knew it was because she was pregnant and even that it was twins?'

'She also said Mr Oates was secretly a lizard in a human suit,' Thi said. 'Also, this whisper wasn't for you, no offence.'

K. saluted and moved slowly backwards, making quiet beeps like a reversing truck.

'I don't know how she knew before I did,' I whispered to Thi. 'I think it's a good idea if we just assume she knows everything all the time.'

I felt a little weird all morning. Kind of like before a game, when I'd spend the mornings full of energy I needed to save for the match, but I couldn't figure out where to put it so I'd just talk a lot and try and eat everything in the house and remember all my best moments in matches. I tried that now, remembering when we'd played the Northern Corellas and I'd leapt into the air on some kid's back and caught the ball in an incredible mark and everybody cheered; or the time the weather was perfect and my shoes were new and we annihilated the other team and I was amazing; or the game when I scored three goals and Mum and Dad took me out for pizza afterwards and Mum told me that even though it was cloudy she'd had to put her sunglasses on so nobody would see her crying from excitement.

Revisiting those memories did *not* help.

After I'd smashed down an apple at recess, I headed out to the junior playground. On my way, I kicked a rock along the ground and thought about whether anybody would even care about fixing their shirts, or if they would want to pay for it if they did.

Then I realised: I was nervous. Like Mum, I didn't really do nervous, because that means you've got more time for thinking than doing, and I was always a doing type of person. But I'd thought and I'd thought, and I really wanted to be able to fix people's clothes and I really wanted to make money and I really wanted to see my dad and it was somehow entirely different from all those times I'd really wanted to win a game or play a match. Maybe it was because I'd had years of training and practice for playing football, and I'd had zero training for how to run a shop in a playground.

There were so many people in my way at the junior playground that it was getting hard to concentrate on being nervous. It was only after I'd elbowed my way around all the kids there that I realised they weren't there to stand around getting in people's way.

They were there for the shop.

ROUND 20 STATS

Minutes Until Shop Opens: 0
Crowd: 15,000 (approx.)

Zara leaned through the shopfront window and spun the sign around to say OPEN. The crowd got louder, and she hollered, in the same booming voice she used in class debates, 'HELLO EVERYONE!'

There was silence, and everybody looked at her, and then she turned to me and waited. Zara being her most Zara self was like being in a thunderstorm: awesome to be near, but you might get electrocuted. She had her electrocution face on now, and I said, helpfully, 'Uh.'

'What Homer is trying to say,' Zara announced smoothly, 'is that you are all here for the grand opening of Sew What, a tailoring business that for the low, low fee of fifteen dollars – just fifteen dollars! – will fix your PE shirts to make them stop strangling you.'

Someone yelled, 'Does he do some kind of spell to stop them trying to kill you?'

Zara yelled back, 'Marcie, they're not trying to kill you, they're just badly made.'

'I tried to tape rocks to my collar to keep it from doing that strangling thing,' some kid called out. 'But then I got bruises from the rocks when I ran.'

'That's pretty proactive,' whispered Thi, coming up next to me.

'Well,' Zara said, 'Homer's here to offer you a real solution.'

The buzz of the crowd was working on me just like it did in a game, and I stepped up. 'I fixed my PE shirt,' I said, 'and you wouldn't believe how much freedom I have. I beat all my friends in PE last week because I didn't have to spend all my time yanking my shirt down.'

'But don't just ask him,' Zara said. 'Ask his friend Tom, who is wearing his new shirt right now.'

I blinked, but it definitely was Tom she'd hauled out from inside the shopfront. He was wearing his PE shirt and, dammit, he looked like some kind of ridiculous god. Everyone even went *oooooo*, which I knew I would never ever hear the end of.

'How does it feel, Tom?' Zara asked.

'Like I'm not wearing anything at all,' he said, while Thi made a throwing-up sound beside me.

'Very good, Tom, please never say that again. To anybody interested, we've got slips here that you can fill out with your name and grade, and you can bring your forms back with your fifteen-dollar payment and FRESHLY WASHED SHIRT in a bag. If you bring a stinky shirt in, we will throw it back at you, all right? The Sew What shop will be staffed by one of the company's employees at recess on Tuesdays and Thursdays, and UNDERSTAND,' she said, glaring, 'that we will only be able to do a few at a time, so you may have to wait. But, my friends, it will be worth it.' She put a stack of paper and a bowl of pencils out. 'Now, you may take your forms, and we await your interest – and your future comfort.'

It was like an attack. Kids ran everywhere, grabbing forms and sitting with their friends to talk about it. Only grade fives and sixes even *had* the sports shirts, but kids from other year levels were grabbing the forms too. I heard one super tall younger kid say, 'I wonder if he can fix it so my shirt isn't so short that everyone keeps poking me in the bellybutton?'

There were kids with pencils hanging out of their mouths like walrus tusks and kids turning paper slips into airplanes and some prep kid who was figuring out how much of the form she could fit up her nose. But I also heard all these kids whispering stuff like, 'Do you think he does sequins too?' and 'I have this band patch I wanted to put on something, you reckon he could put it on my shoulder?' and 'Could he make the sleeves be longer than my hands?'

I hadn't even thought about other things. About doing *more*.

Because I could probably do sequins. I could definitely stitch a flag to a shoulder. And I could learn how to make a sleeve longer.

Zara was answering questions when I went up to the window. 'No, it's not free,' she was telling one kid, and then she turned to the next and said, 'Fifteen dollars. It says it right there on the form. I know it's expensive. Do you think your mum works for free?'

'Zara!' I said to her. 'This is incredible.'

'Yeah, I'm the best,' she said, turning to me and grinning.

'How did you get Tom to get up and do something nice?'

'He owed me a favour,' she said mysteriously.

'You used up a *Tom* favour on Homer?' Thi asked.

'He still owes me a few more. Anyway, this is also something good for me to work on, for my future. I'm learning a lot. Like, don't give out forms with lots of words to kids who can't read yet, or they will just bury them in the sandpit.'

'I'm so impressed,' I said.

'I'm glad to hear it,' she said. 'Also, you're on duty here on Thursday for when everybody comes back. Thi says she might do some days, but still I'm not sure she's invested enough to give up her entire recess for this.'

'Eh,' Thi said. 'I'm not sure she is either.'

'Hey!' I said, and she grinned.

'Excellent, so you'll do Thursday together. All right,' she said, turning to a kid who'd rocked up crying about getting their pencil stolen. 'You can have another one. If Jemima tries to take this one off you too, stomp on her foot and run away.'

'Um, I guess you don't have to stay on Thursday if you don't want,' I said to Thi, feeling embarrassed. 'I can do it on my own. I mean, you've already done heaps.'

'I know I have,' she said. 'I even got all those pencils those kids have up their noses right now. It was an order at Mum's work for some mini-golf place and they never picked them up. Anyway, I was mostly not interested in working the shop because I thought it was just going to be me and I'd get bored. But if I have company, it probably won't be so bad.'

I could feel a really goofy smile trying to take over my face, so I turned away and pretended to look around so Thi couldn't see it. And honestly, I couldn't believe the huge crowd of interested kids bothering Zara with questions. All these kids wanted to get their clothes fixed. They wanted to look on the outside how they felt on the inside. And I was going to be the one who helped them.

And spending a recess sitting in a prep-sized shop with Thi for company wouldn't be so bad for me either.

We met up again at lunch.

'Okay,' Zara said, getting a notebook from under her chair, 'so I guess we need to make sure any slips I make in future say things like "WE ARE NOT DOING ADDITIONAL REQUESTS" because I heard about twenty kids say they were going to ask for, like, glitter or tassels on their shirts. And not even their sports shirts! Just their normal ones.'

Thi tapped her pen on her teeth. 'Maybe we need to make a space for reasonable requests, like if they need a button replaced, or something?'

'Or,' I said, 'I could just … do them?'

Zara turned to look at me. 'What do you mean?'

'Well,' I said, and my hands felt all itchy, like I wanted to be stitching something with them, 'what if I did all these things that people asked for?'

'You can't put sequins on a school shirt!' Zara said.

'Why not?'

'Because … hmm.' She drummed her fingers on the armrest of her chair. 'I guess because nobody has?'

'Because nobody has offered?' I said.

'You could get more money for this,' Avery said.

Exactly, I thought.

‘But do you have time?’ Zara asked.

‘I mean, it would depend on the thing. I can’t put sequins over a whole shirt, it would take me weeks. But I could do some. Or, what did you say? Tassels? I don’t think that’s too hard.’

‘Or,’ Murphy said, ‘like, could you sew a kazoo into my collar that I could blow on when Mr Oates’ back is turned in class?’

‘I reckon I could for two dollars,’ I said.

‘Nice.’

‘Okay, so how do we write that on the slips?’ Zara said. ‘It needs to sound super professional.’

Thi put up her hand. ‘Price on request for other changes?’.

‘Perfect!’ Zara wrote it down. ‘Okay, this is great. Once we’ve got these out, and the posters, and the song for recess radio, I reckon we’ll be all good. Then it’s all up to you, Homer.’

‘I can do it,’ I said, bouncing on my feet. ‘I can be good, and fast, I promise.’

The others kept talking, but my hands still felt all weird, like they needed to do something. I couldn’t just sit and talk like the others were. I wished I had a shirt here so I could just fix it right now and be done with it.

‘Homer,’ Thi said, ‘you look like somebody who needs to move. Maybe go run around the oval or something?’

‘Are you kicking me out of my own project?’ I said, pretending to be incredibly offended while doing exactly what she said and bolting away through the gap between classrooms to get to where there was space.

I ran in on the lunchtime footy game and Henry whacked me on the back. ‘I thought you’d forgotten how to get here from the classroom,’ he said. ‘We might win again with you here.’

Except we didn't. Not because we didn't try – I was full of built-up energy – but because Mario and Ng didn't kick or handball the footy to me once, even when I was clear and in front of the goals. I ran up to Ng at one point and said, 'Mate, I was wide open! What gives?'

'Don't know,' he said. 'Must've just missed you.'

Funny, since I could've sworn he'd looked right at me. Or, maybe, not funny.

Despite the weird game, I was hyped up all the way home, then felt great working on my jersey sketches in the lounge while Mum made dinner. 'Muuuuum,' I said, 'I'm out of yellow and black pencils. Can you buy me some?'

'Just yellow and black? Really?'

'Yeah. I mean, pencils are cheap, right?'

'Well, they are when I buy a cheap packet of all of them from the two-dollar shop, but I feel somehow that buying only yellow or black will cost way more? Maybe we'll go find some on the weekend.'

'Aren't you going to be interstate on the weekend?'

'Oh, yeah! I mean, it's just one game, right? They won't mind if I miss it to get some pencils.'

I tapped my pen on the notebook. 'How does it feel, being out there?'

'Like during a proper game?'

'Yeah. Is it different from when you played before?'

'I guess it is. You know how it's different playing in front of a crowd instead of just playing at training, right? It's like that, but … more. You feel like you owe it to the people around you to be good. You're already trying to be your best, but they give you this extra boost to help. And people call your name, and people boo you, and everyone's yelling about umpires, and it just … it doesn't even feel real, sometimes. It feels absolutely amazing, like the whole world is yours.' She stirred the pasta sauce she was making. 'I don't even know if that made sense. I just can't wait for you to have that same feeling one day in ten years, or whatever. When you're out there too. Feeling the rush of having a whole crowd behind you. Knowing that you're good enough to be there.' She'd stopped stirring. 'Why do you ask?'

'I don't know,' I said. 'I just like hearing you talk about it.'

'Why aren't you practising?' she said. 'Don't you have some pre-training training to do?'

'I'm sketching.'

'Ah, working on your wrist muscles,' she said. 'I get it.'

After dinner, I was halfway through a really good sketch when Mum started yelling about Why Wasn't I Already In The Car, We Are LATE, so I put my smallest sketchbook in my shorts pocket and went running out to the car. I finished the sketch, all hunched over in the passenger seat, just as Mum parked.

Training was awesome. I still had heaps of energy left over from how well the shop went, and I could feel it in every leap I made, in every kick I did, in every pass I caught. Mario and Ng were back to kicking to me again, and when I made an amazing goal from the boundary line right through the posts, Mario raced over and tackled me to the ground while screaming.

When it was over, even Crabtree, who only gives out one compliment a day, said, 'You did good, Homer.' By the time I got to Mum afterwards, I felt like I was on fire, but in a good way.

'Mate!' she said. 'I can't believe you. You were great out there. I'm glad I don't have to play against you or you'd smash me. You weren't even limping! *And* some of the other parents came up to tell me how good you were today, which is great, since feeling superior to the other parents is the only reason I enrolled you in football in the first place.' She bopped me on the head with my notebook. 'You dropped this on the ground in your excitement to get there, you goof. What's with all the bird heads?'

'It's for the jersey competition,' I said. 'Yellow, black, white cockatoo. It's why I need the new pencils. I've got all these amazing ideas and I reckon I'm in with a chance, you know? If I win the money then Dad can for sure get down for my first football game in case he's spent all of his plane money on his teeth and—' Mum had gone a strange colour, and I stopped. 'What's wrong?'

'I thought you knew,' she said, covering her mouth with her hand. 'You didn't say anything about the competition when you got home last week.'

Something was creeping its way through my body: a bad feeling, like someone was pulling a thread slowly through my veins.

I asked, slowly, 'Thought I knew what?'

'You can't enter the competition,' she said. 'Because my club's sponsoring it. It'd be unfair if you won. I'm so sorry … I thought Mr Crabtree told you.'

The thread pulled tight.

'I can't …?' My voice felt like it wasn't even mine. 'I can't enter?'

'Oh, Homer. I'm so sorry. I—' she reached out for me but I shook my head. The thoughts in my head were knocking around in there: moneydadplanetwohundreddollarsallthattimeIspentdra wingmoneyplanes*DAD*—

'Homer?'

'It's fine,' I croaked, and opened the car door, threw the notepad inside, and kicked it underneath the seat. I sat the whole drive home with my head in my hands, my thoughts thrashing loudly around my skull like yellow-and-black cockatoos trapped in a cage.

ROUND 21 STATS

~~Jersey Ideas: 25~~
~~Good Jersey Ideas: 3~~
~~Jersey Competition Prize: $200~~
Shirt Money Earned: $20
(Perth Ticket Fund: $20)

Nobody else was at The Bad Corner when I got there.

I'd been so angry on my way in that I rode there in half the time it usually took, and when Mario wasn't there to get angry at I just got even madder, gripping my bike's handlebars and imagining tearing them off my bike Hulk-style except then I'd have to pay to get them fixed and I'd have even less money than I already did. I'd laid out my savings last night, hoping it had somehow gone up since the last time I'd counted it, and added up to twenty-eight dollars. Not only was it not more, it was actually *less*, because it turned out Mum had put an IOU note in there when she'd borrowed some coins to catch a bus. And then I yelled at her for stealing, and then she told me to stop being unreasonable, so if anybody needs any tips on how to get into a massive fight with your mum, I'm the guy for the job.

Mario and Ng still hadn't arrived when the music started, so I stomped over to school and put my bike in the shed and saw the two of them walking along a footpath next to some hedges. I thought for a moment about the best timing, then told myself I was in a grand final and ran up to the two of them and tackled them into a bush.

'What the hell?' Ng yelled, pulling leaves out of his mouth. 'What is your deal?'

'You weren't at the corner,' I whined.

'So you decided to beat us up?' Mario growled. 'Real normal reaction there, Homer.'

'But I needed to talk to you,' I said.

'We don't talk to people who push us into trees,' Mario said.

'But you talked to Tom just yesterday,' Ng reminded him.

'And I made sure to push you into the soft tree!' I said. 'I even waited so you got past the spiky one *and* the one that's full of bees. I am way better than Tom.'

'Forget it,' Mario said, as the bell rang. 'We can talk at recess. Unless you're doing your jersey thing that's so important.'

'I'm not,' I said, feeling my face going red and following them while they walked away. 'I can't.'

'Did you get banned from the library again?' Ng asked sympathetically.

'No! And that was years ago and how was I supposed to know you weren't supposed to use the books as frisbees? That wasn't even written up in the rules.'

'I mean, it is now,' Mario said.

'I thought you weren't talking to me?'

'It's okay if I'm making fun of you.'

'Why are you sad, anyway? You were great at training. That's why we weren't at the corner,' Ng said. 'We got in early to practise so we can beat you.'

‘And it sucks because you haven’t even been playing for like a week and you were still smashing everyone else there last night,’ Mario said, and when I looked at his expression I almost realised something for a moment, until I remembered that we were talking about *my* sadness right now.

‘I can’t enter the jersey competition,’ I said. ‘Because Mum’s team is sponsoring it and it’d be unfair.’

Mario stopped. ‘Mate,’ he said. ‘That sucks.’

‘After all that time you’d been working on it?’ Ng said.

I nodded. I couldn’t talk for a moment, and we kept walking.

‘That *really* sucks,’ Mario said. ‘Can we … can we do something?’

‘Maybe you could still come up with your shirt design, and we’d just enter it under our names?’ Ng suggested.

‘That seems like it could end pretty badly if I was busted,’ I said, ‘but thanks?’

‘Zara could start a petition,’ Mario said as we got to the classroom.

‘Excuse me?’ Zara said from in front of us. ‘How dare you assume I’ll help you with a petition.’ She crossed her arms. ‘So you better tell me what I’m fighting now so I can spend the day getting mad about it.’

‘Forget it,’ I said, shaking my head. ‘I already thought of all this stuff. But Mum’s right. And I don’t want to get her in trouble with her club or anything. It … it just blows.’

Ng put his arm around me. ‘It really does.’

‘One good thing is that you’ll be able to come kick around with us again at recess,’ Mario said, drop-kicking his bag through the classroom door. ‘We can annihilate you using the power of our extra training.’

'Maybe at lunch,' I said. 'At recess I've got to go sort some stuff out with the school shirts. You guys go play footy or whatever.'

Ng and Mario looked at each other. 'Yeah,' Ng said. 'Or whatever.'

'Sorry,' I said, 'but it's important.'

'No problem,' Mario said, but somehow, his voice made it seem like maybe there *was* a problem. Anyway, I had even an even bigger problem, and that was that I needed more people I could complain to.

While we were supposed to be figuring out the area of an irregular shape, I poked Thi across the table with my pen and whispered, 'Thi! I can't enter the jersey competition.'

She was staring intently at the line she was trying to rule. 'What are you talking about? And also, shut up. I'm trying to get this done before everyone else.' She ignored me, finished it, then looked up. In a moment, her face went from intense to sad. 'Oh, no. It's because of your Mum being part of the team sponsoring it, isn't it?'

I leaned back in my chair. 'Well, if it was so easy for you to figure out, why didn't you tell me?'

She gave me a withering look and I said, 'Okay, okay, I'm just pretty bummed out about it.'

'All that work you put in,' she said, reaching over and patting me on the arm. 'That's not fair.'

'Yeah, well, at least you'll probably win now.'

'Aw, come on. You know I'm better at things when I'm competing against somebody I know.'

She looked so genuinely sad for me, or maybe herself, that I felt like I'd given away some of my feelings for somebody else to deal with for a while. Everybody always said it was good to share, after all.

At recess, Zara did not have time for me to sulk. 'Homer! I'm glad you're here. There's been so much talk about the shirts in the yard. Avery even made a compilation.'

'A what?'

'I collected the voices of people talking about it,' Avery said, holding out the tape recorder he always carried everywhere so he could make music out of literally everything he heard. 'Listen.'

We all leaned in. It was fuzzy, but I could hear all these different voices coming out of the speaker: '—can get your shirt fixed so it's not strangling you—', '—get extra better at sports and even writing—', '—fifteen dollars which is cheaper than a new shirt—', '—that kid whose mum did that mad goal at the end of round three is making shirts better—', '—he'll do whatever, even put a jet pack in—'.

'Is that Ng's voice?' I said. 'Is he telling people I'll put a jet pack in their shirts? I thought they hadn't been invented?'

'Good ear.' Avery grinned. 'Just consider it free advertising.'

'I bet we'll have a bunch of people in tomorrow,' Zara said. 'Think about all these new additions. You're going to make heaps of money. I can't wait. I'm thinking of writing up a contract that says after you make your first thousand dollars you have to give us a little bit of it for our help. That seems fair, right?'

I was just standing there, my mouth opening and closing, because I couldn't talk. She honestly believed I'd make a thousand dollars.

A million dollars had sounded great. But a thousand?

That sounded real.

ROUND 22 STATS

Jersey Competition Prize Money: None
Shirt Money: $1000 (Soon)
Successful Fittings: 0

Thi turned up at my front door at half past four, wearing basketball shorts and a loose white t-shirt with her backpack over her shoulder.

'Mum says I can't come over to a new friend's house without bringing something,' she said, getting out a bag of peanuts. 'I hope you're not allergic.'

'I'm all good,' I said. 'And I love peanuts.'

Pa appeared at my shoulder. 'Ah! You must be Thi. Homer is very determined to get your shirt looking extra perfect.'

'Really?' Thi smiled. 'Well, that's good.' She held up the peanuts again. 'I brought these.'

'Grazzi,' he said, beaming. 'Would you believe just yesterday I made a whole bunch of peanut biscuits and ran out of peanuts? It's a shame we ate all the biscuits already, but these are exactly right.'

I knew he was lying – there was no way they'd make

biscuits and not bring them to share with me, their favourite and also only grandson – but it wasn't the first time I'd heard Pa lie to a customer to make them feel special. Mum always told me to be honest, but Thi was absolutely beaming at him, so it seemed like lies that didn't hurt anyone were okay. I'd have to remember this moment the next time Mum told me off for lying about not having homework. I mean, nobody really gets hurt if I don't do my homework either.

'Okay,' I said, 'you brought your shirt, right? You can go change into it now, if you want. The bathroom's on the left, just past the kitchen.'

She took it and vanished. Pa said, 'Peanuts! What a nice girl.'

The doorbell rang again. K. was outside, wearing denim shorts and a long-sleeved t-shirt with pandas on it, saying, 'Sorry I'm late. Also, sorry I had to bring my sister, but it was the only way I could convince my mum to let me come. Somebody needed to take River for a walk.'

K. had so many brothers and sisters that I actually didn't know how many there were. This one looked about five years old. I didn't really know what people were supposed to do with small kids unless they were holding a football. 'Uh, is she allergic to peanuts?'

'Nope.'

'Excellent!' Pa said. 'Sweetie, can you do drawings?'

'Only of dinosaurs,' she said.

'If you draw me a dinosaur, I can give you some peanuts!'

River thought about it. '*Five* peanuts.'

'You drive a hard bargain,' Pa said. 'I accept.'

Thi came out and K. went into the bathroom to change.

I looked at Thi wearing her sports shirt and then remembered again that to do a fitting you usually had to put your arms around someone for measurements and I suddenly did not know how to talk.

Nanna, who'd been sitting calmly on the couch pretending she wasn't listening to football podcasts on her wireless headphones, saw my face, got up, came over to Thi and said, 'Oof, I can see how these shirts would strangle someone. Do you mind if I take some measurements around your waist?'

'Go for it.'

I breathed out. 'Thi's on the Cockatoos' first girls' football team next year,' I told Nanna.

'Thi is great at footy,' River said behind me. 'K. said so.'

'I reckon she'll be captain,' I said.

'K. says Thi is good at pens,' River said.

'It's true,' I said. 'She does always have pens.'

'K. says Homer likes Thi,' River said.

There was a thump in the bathroom like somebody had just banged their head on a door.

'K. says lots of things, huh,' Pa said smoothly. 'I hope you listen to him when he tells you to brush your teeth too.'

'You say "them", not "him",' River said. 'That's what makes K. feel like the most right.'

'Oh! I'm sorry,' Pa said. 'I hope you listen to them when they tell you to brush your teeth too.'

'No,' River said.

'So glad I brought you,' K. said, appearing from the bathroom. 'I don't regret this at all.'

Thi hadn't said anything. I was half-frozen, half-not. I mean, it wasn't like I *did* like Thi. Probably. And even if I did, which I didn't, I definitely hadn't told K. about it. So there was probably no reason to be embarrassed.

'Maybe you can take K.'s measurements?' Pa said gently, holding out a tape measure.

I took it and walked up to K. 'Is this weird?'

'It wasn't until you asked.'

As I put the tape measure around K.'s waist, I imagined how their shirt could sit on them to make them look their absolute best. Where the seam on the arms would sit to not pull too tight or sit too loose. Trying to make it so that K. would smile when they put it on.

That's all I wanted, really – to give people that feeling. The one where you felt good about who you were, partly because of what you were wearing. You just felt *right*, like nothing on your body was holding you back or felt too small or too big or uncomfortable. It didn't matter what kind of size you were, or what anybody thought of you, because you were wearing something you loved and you knew you were the best-dressed person in the world.

You could feel the same way in footy, really, like those days where you'd trained hard and were completely prepared and having a total blinder. I didn't know how clothes and football could be so different and so alike at the same time, but I guess if I knew how feelings worked then I would be helping my therapist instead of the other way around.

I wrote down all the measurements Nanna and I took and then stood back, looking at my friends. The room was quiet.

'K.,' I said, 'do you want me to add a button to your collar? Since you like your normal shirt buttoned all the way up?'

'Can you do that?'

'Sure.'

'That'd be great.'

'And we'll adjust the shoulders to make it stop doing that annoying thing, obviously.'

'That'd be *super* great.'

'And you wanted cap sleeves, right?'

'It'll make my arms look longer. I think they're too short,' K. said, holding their arms out sadly.

'K. has good arms for hugging,' River said. 'Also, I finished my dinosaur picture. It's a pteranodon.'

'That's amazing,' Pa said. 'You absolutely deserve your five peanuts. But you can only get five more if you draw the dinosaur a friend.'

River thought about it. 'Okay.'

'You can get changed back if you want,' I told K.

I went and stood in front of Thi and stared at her.

'What do you think?' she asked, in a small voice.

'I'll … I'll fix your shoulders,' I said.

'Cool! And what else?'

I studied her a bit longer, then threw my hands up.

'I don't know! You already look good.'

River started giggling. 'K. was right!'

'Shut up,' I said, crossing my arms. 'She just does. Oh! I know. What about if I stitch a little navy-blue-and-white striped flag on your hem with ribbons? The Geelong flag? Like your notebook?'

Thi clapped. 'That would be *perfect*.'

'Is there anything *you* want changed?' Nanna asked her.

'Not really. I mean, it's just my PE shirt, and it's not like I wear it outside of school. The shoulders are the worst part.'

She went off and got changed when K. came out. Once she shut the door, K. whispered, 'I'm sorry, I shouldn't have said anything to River. I was trying to make us late so you and Thi could have more time together, but she wouldn't listen until I explained what I was doing, and when she heard that there was romance drama she was even less interested in waiting.'

'Hang on, why were you trying to be late?'

K. said, 'I mean, you like her.'

'What are you talking about?'

K. and River and Pa and Nanna all exchanged a look.

'You've all eaten too many peanuts,' I said, rolling my eyes.

'If you say so,' K. said.

River held up her dinosaur drawing. 'The brachiosaurus is Thi,' she said. 'She's wearing her shirt with stripes on it. And the pteranodon is Homer. You can tell because of the way the eyes are love hearts.'

'So lovely!' Nanna said. 'I'll get you your extra peanuts now.'

'We should probably go,' K. said, dragging River away.

Thi came out, pulling her normal shirt down and handing me her sports one. 'Is everyone leaving? Okay. Well, nice to meet you, Homer's grandparents,' she said, waving and following K. out.

Once I'd waved them off at the door, I said, without turning around, 'Do not tell Mum about this.'

'Sorry,' Nanna said, holding up her phone. 'I was texting her live updates. I thought it would be a nice surprise for when she's finished training.'

'Can I get some new babysitters? I'll pay out of my own pocket money.'

'Oh, hush,' Pa said. 'So you're in love. Aren't we all? It's time to get to work.'

Dad called while I was setting the table for dinner. 'Perfect timing,' I said. 'Nanna and Pa are making me do all the work while they lie around doing nothing.'

Nanna glared at me from the oven, where she was pulling out the Maltese roast she'd spent hours making. I winked at her and turned away.

'Sounds legit,' Dad said. 'How's tricks?'

'Good. Mum's at training. I'm fixing up some shirts.'

There was a long pause. I checked my phone, but Dad hadn't been cut off.

'You still there?'

'Yeah, yeah. Just wasn't sure if you were going to say anything else about the shirts. Has Mum been beating any personal bests at training?'

'Dunno. She just gets tougher to beat each time.'

'Love to hear it. I can't wait to see you smash all the other teams this season. I'm thinking I'll pay some broke teenager to film your games for me when I can't be there to see them.'

'But you'll be there for my first game, right?'

'Definitely. Like I said, I already arranged for it off, no backsies. I used my Deprived Papa eyes when I brought it up. It broke them, Homer.'

'All your teeth are okay?'

'What? Of course they are! It was just one filling. Besides, this week's drama is that I drove over a nail and had to get my car tyre replaced. What do you think next week's thing will be? Will the whole apartment explode?' He laughed, and I made some kind of sound that was definitely a laugh and not a scream.

Mum came into my room that night at ten o'clock and watched me working on Thi's shirt. It turned out that Nanna hadn't been texting her, which was more proof that my grandparents were liars, which would be good to remember the next time Nanna asked if I was lying about being the one who ate all their peanuts. At least it meant I hadn't had to suffer through Mum asking questions I did not have the time or mood to answer.

'It's time to go to sleep, sweetie,' she said, coming over and putting her hand on my head.

'Nah, I'm nearly finished.'

She sat down next to me. 'I know I'm usually pretty chill, and I've tried hard to cultivate this whole persona of being the relaxed parent who lets you joke around and stay up late, but I'm not asking, I'm telling. Put it down and go to sleep.'

'You don't understand,' I said.

'Okay, then tell me what I don't get.'

'I *need* to finish these.'

'I know. But you don't need to finish them *tonight*.'

'I've got more coming, though! Tomorrow is the day I get my first order for the new shirts and I heard from Mario when he started talking to me again that Henry wants one and apparently Hayley's desperate for one and then someone else said Marcie will say yes after I agree to a list of requests and—'

'Great! That's great. Wait, what do you mean Mario wasn't talking to you?'

'Nothing.'

She looked at me and said, 'All right then. And if you really mean it's nothing, then none of that changes the fact that you need to go to sleep right now.'

'But Mum—'

I expected her to interrupt and stopped. Instead, she just watched me.

'But what?' she said eventually.

I imagined the conversation. I'd say, *I need the money*, and she'd say *what for*, and I'd say *to go see dad*, and then she'd say he was coming soon, and I'd have to say *but he had to spend all the money for the plane on tyres and teeth*, and then she'd turn it all into some big talk about him doing his best and us dealing with it. Or maybe she'd feel bad about not being able to pay for the ticket herself. I just wanted to get this stuff done, get heaps of money, and then be able to tell her that she didn't have to worry about making Nanna and Pa look after me on her interstate weekends because I'd buy my own plane ticket and go hang out with Dad instead.

But telling her this would be a whole thing, and I did not like whole things.

'See? I knew you were tired. You completely zoned out there.'

'I'm awake! Let me do this.'

'You've given me no good reason. I'm the boss, and you have to go to bed.'

'Please.'

'Hearing you say that for the first time in your life is very exciting, but it's not enough. You have to rest. You're a growing boy.'

'This morning you told me to stop growing because it made my pants too short.'

'Yes, but it's not like you've ever listened to me before. You want to keep growing, and you need rest to do it.'

I held so hard onto the needle in my hand I thought I might snap it in half.

'Don't make me be the mum who takes this stuff away from you,' she said. 'Neither of us want that, but I'll do it if you don't go to bed, okay?'

I put the needle down. She kissed me on the head and watched me get into bed.

'You brush your teeth?'

'Sure,' I said, remembering that it was sometimes okay to lie.

'Okay. Sleep well. You've always got tomorrow.'

'I've got training tomorrow.'

'You've got the weekend,' she said. 'And you don't even have to go to my game. A whole weekend, just you and my parents and all the clothes-making you want. Okay?'

'Okay,' I grumbled.

It wasn't okay, though. The weekend was too far away, and I still had to figure out how to make K.'s sleeves work.

Luckily, she hadn't said anything about me not being able to sketch ideas.

I reached over for my torch and got to work.

ROUND 23 STATS

Successful Fittings: 2
Shirts Made Better: 4
New Shirts to Fix: 3
Days Until First Game of the Season: 30
(Days Until I See Dad: 29)

A few months ago, my favourite clothes shop, LaFontaine, had a huge sale on t-shirts. Since their t-shirts were the only thing I could afford, and by 'afford' I mean 'the only things there that were under $100 so maybe I could get one for my birthday one year', I went along with Dad and the thirty dollars I'd earned cleaning out Mr Huber's gutters. There was a queue halfway down the road and we waited for forty-five minutes before Dad, who has probably never stood still for forty-five minutes on a weekend his whole life, refused to wait any longer and made me leave. (Tom turned up the next weekend in a premium teal-and-black LaFontaine t-shirt that looked so great I told Mum later I understood why she was breaking up with Dad, but that didn't go down as well as I'd thought it would.)

'You okay?' Thi asked now.

I stared at the crowd in front of the playground's shopfront. A crowd of kids queueing for *me*.

'Sure,' I squeaked.

'I'm convinced,' she said, then headed on in.

As soon as they saw Thi with her clipboard the kids went wild. Tiny wild voices screamed in my ear about lace and jet packs as I pushed past them to the shop. There were two poor prep kids holed up in there, terrified at the crowd outside, and Thi, who really was always prepared, gave them three cat erasers and then helped them escape through the mass of people. Then she put the clipboard on the shelf, pulled up her socks, looked down at me sitting frozen on the tanbark, and winked.

'Who was first?' she yelled.

'ME!' some kid hollered. 'I snuck out of class early to be here! I hate my shirt!' She threw her form down. 'And I want bells on it!'

Thi looked down at the paper. 'Wynter, huh? And you want … bells.'

The girl leaned in and whispered, 'Then I'll sound like Christmas. Every. Single. Day.'

Thi looked over at me. 'Bells?'

I thought about it. 'Sure. Should only cost me, what, two dollars?'

'Five dollars,' Thi told Wynter.

Wynter handed the money to Thi, and Thi handed it to me, and I could feel myself start to glow like stadium lights at night.

The next person was Marcie.

'I heard you put curses in your clothes,' she said.

I poked my head up over the ledge. 'What? How did you know?'

'Ava told me.'

'How did *she* find out?'

'Why would I ask?'

It was a good point. 'Well, yeah, I can do curses. As long as they're short.'

'Curse*s*, you said. So I can have more than one? Can I have six?'

'You have to pay for each separately,' Thi said.

'Do you sew them in while sitting in a ring of candles and salt to really make sure they're going to come true?'

'Maybe if you paid for the candles too?' I said.

'And the salt,' Thi said.

Since Marcie only had six extra dollars, we bargained down to two curses and I promised to ask Mum if I could light her green apple scented candle in my bedroom while I made them.

Olivia J was next, and she slammed down the money and said, 'Mine has to have a fringe along the hem.'

'Fifteen dollars extra,' Thi said without blinking.

'Thi,' I whispered, 'it'll probably only cost …'

'Twenty,' she said loudly. 'You're right.'

'Ugh. Are you kidding? Forget it,' Olivia said, then picked up her shirt and stormed away exactly two steps before spinning back around, dropping the shirt back on the ledge and saying, 'But I really do need that collar fixed.' She dropped two more dollars on top of the shirt, stared me down and growled, 'I'll think of something else you can do instead and I'll tell you in class.'

Hayley pushed in beside her and said, 'Can mine have, like, eight pockets in it? For … things.'

'What kind of things do you need for PE?' I asked.

'Important things,' she said mysteriously.

For the next ten minutes, kids handed their shirts over with way more ideas than I'd ever imagined. Only a few were terrible ideas like Ng's jet pack one, but some of them, like Olivia R's request for a drinking pouch with a straw that went into her collar, made me wonder if I should maybe have a base design for a mega-perfect school shirt that did all the best things. Drinking pouches. Extra pockets. Adjustable sleeves with buttons. My fingers itched to sketch out some ideas.

We took ten shirts before Thi declared the shop closed for the day. The kids who hadn't had an opportunity to yell at me about sewing a Nike logo or whatever onto their shirt groaned, and one kid even cried. I guessed this is what the designer at LaFontaine felt like when they ran out of t-shirts the day of their sale. Like you could never make everyone happy.

But *I* was happy. I had a whole bag of shirts – Thi, who always thought of everything, had safety-pinned each form to the right shirt – and I had a plan and, ridiculously, one hundred and eighty-two dollars. In one lunchtime, I had earned almost enough money for a Perth to Melbourne flight. If I worked fast enough, it'd only take a couple of weeks to get enough money for a return ticket, for sure. I still had a whole shopping list of stuff like bells and straws and sequins and embroidery thread for curses and ribbons so somebody could lace up their collar instead of using buttons. And I thought maybe I'd use a little bit of it to buy Thi a KitKat or something to say thanks. Or flowers? No, that was too much like saying I liked her. Which I did, maybe. But I didn't want to make it *seem* like I did. Though getting flowers was just nice anyway, like the time Mario had brought me a huge bunch from his garden when I had the flu and they smelled good and made my room feel nicer and less full of boogers.

But you can't eat flowers. And you could definitely eat a KitKat. I'd think about it some more.

I still felt incredible that afternoon when Nanna and Pa met me at home to take me to training, since Mum was busy going to some AFLW dinner event thing after work. Pa had altered her favourite fancy dress for the event because she'd become super buff since the last time she'd worn it, and she'd paraded around in it last night making sure she wouldn't bust straight through the material if she accidentally flexed her biceps.

I had all ten shirts laid out to show Nanna and Pa when they arrived. Pa picked his way around the piles of shirts with their lists, leaned in to read one of them and said, 'I'm sorry, you need a triangle pocket for this shirt so Giang can store slices of pizza in it?'

'Surely you'd need some insulation for that so it doesn't go cold,' Nanna said.

'I charged an extra dollar on top of the pocket fee,' I said smugly. 'I figured Mum wouldn't mind if I cut up one of her insulated shopping bags.'

'I figure she will mind,' Pa said. 'We'll come up with something.' He surveyed all the shirts. 'This is a hell of a lot of work, you know.'

'It'll be fine!' I said. 'Also we'll need to go to Maker Acre to get all this extra stuff people need,' I added.

'Oh we need to, do we?'

'Paaaaaaa,' I whined, 'this is my small business you're talking about here! Don't you want me to make something of myself? Don't you want to brag to all of your friends at your community garden about how your grandson is a successful businessperson and he's not even out of primary school?'

He crossed his arms and looked offended while Nanna snorted beside him.

'I've got the money,' I said.

'Tomorrow night,' Pa said. 'We'll see.'

ROUND 24 STATS

New Shirts to Fix: 13
Shirt Money Earned: $202
Round ticket Perth → Melbourne → Perth: $400

'Surely,' I said to Mum, 'if I have to be awake because you have to fly for work, I should get paid too?'

It was eight o'clock in the morning and Mum was about to drop me off at Ng's on the way to catch her flight to Queensland for her game, once she'd checked for the sixteenth time that she had all her gear. She put a fifth hair tie on her wrist, checked her meds, her jersey, her shorts and her shoes. 'Pretty sure I packed my phone charger,' she said. 'Text me whenever you need, okay? Maybe don't call in case we're training. You've got Doug's number in your phone, right?'

I nodded.

'All right! I'm nervous. Why am I nervous? Polly says Queensland games are her favourite. Maybe I'm going to have the best game of my career so far! I can't always be nervous the week after we lose. No team wins every game. But Homer,' she said, grabbing at my shirt, 'what if we *were* supposed to be the first team to win every game and we didn't because I didn't try hard enough?'

I stared at her.

'I know, I know, don't look at me like that. We're a team, it's not just down to me. But I want to do my best by them – they've treated me so well and they drafted me even though I'm over thirty. Oh my god! Homer! I'm about to travel interstate to a football match that *I* am playing in! Can you believe it? Whoa.' She shivered from her shoulders to her feet. 'I can't believe that I'm me sometimes. I'm so lucky. And I get to come home to you and my parents here, keeping my house safe and super clean and definitely leaving me good leftovers, right? Okay. I'm pumped. It'll be fine. Right. I think it's time to go.'

Now that it was real and she was really leaving, I was suddenly not that okay with it. As she walked out to the car, my feet stuck to the ground. I knew it was all in my brain, but I still grabbed myself by the thigh and tried to yank my leg off the ground like I was pulling myself out of quicksand. Mum came back in and saw me and said, 'Oh no, is it your ankle again?'

'No,' I said, and talking seemed to break the spell cast on my legs. I walked over and said, 'See? Just mucking around.'

'You? Never.' She looked down at my ankle. 'You sure?'

'Yes,' I snapped.

She held up her hands. 'Okay, jeez. Get your bag, bud. It's time we rolled.'

Next to the car, before she got in, I said, 'Um, Mum, can I have a goodbye hug?'

She flew into me and wrapped her arms around me so hard that I immediately felt better and also suddenly terrified for anyone she encountered on the field. She really was tough.

'I'm sorry you can't come,' she said into my hair. 'Maybe another time.'

I didn't like the idea of both of my parents being in different states. I mean, about three years ago they went on a holiday to Tasmania and I was cool with that, but somehow, them being separately away from me felt worse. Mum was all that way up north, and Dad was all that distance west, and then there was me, south and east and basically an orphan. I clung hard to her shirt, and she gave me one last alarming squeeze and let me go.

'We have to go,' she said gently. 'I love you, okay?'

I nodded.

As we drove, I called Dad, just to say hi. When he picked up the phone, he said in a muffled voice, 'Homer! Are you okay?'

'Yeah, I'm okay! I just wanted to say hi.'

'Hi? Homer, it's not even five o'clock in the morning.'

'No it's … oh.'

'I love you, but I'm really tired, okay? Yesterday I worked late and my microwave stopped working and I ate cold beans for dinner like I was camping and I just kind of need this sleep, okay? I'll call you later this morning. Wait. I mean tonight.' He yawned. 'Later.'

'Okay,' I said. 'Bye.'

'Oh, Homer, I didn't realise you were calling your dad,' Mum said as she drove. 'It's, what, four in the morning there?'

'Yeah.'

She patted my knee. 'You're okay. It's his fault for moving to a different time zone.'

'I thought you said the moving thing was nobody's fault?'

'Moving on,' she said. 'Was he okay otherwise?'

'How much is a microwave?' I asked.

'That is definitely moving on the conversation,' she said. 'I don't remember. Three hundred dollars?'

I looked down at the floor. My socks, I realised, were two slightly different shades of white. I rubbed my ankles together angrily, as if that would help.

At Ng's house, his dad seemed to know what was up before I even arrived. 'My mother used to travel a lot when I was your age,' he said. 'I would miss her, and so would my older brother, but we both pretended we didn't. He'd use up all the oil in the house and make me jau zaa gwai every time she went away, even though on normal days for breakfast he'd just punch me in the arm.' He held up a perfectly fried doughnut stick. 'I thought you might like the same. Without the punch.'

'Can you come over and be sad more often?' Lily asked from the kitchen bench.

'I'm with her,' Ng said, eating his third doughnut. 'If there's some way I can make you sad every week, let me know.'

At school, I kept trying to sneak extra bits of jau zaa gwai out of the serviette in my pocket without being noticed, but K. said, 'You right there?'

'Yep,' I mumbled around the crumbs.

'Was your mum at that dinner event thing yesterday?' Thi hissed. 'I saw it on the AFLW website. Did she get to meet anyone famous?'

'I didn't get time to ask this morning,' I whispered. 'We were too busy getting ready for her to fly out.'

'Can you call her and ask?'

'Yeah, sure, I'll just ask Skia.' I put my hand up but she launched herself over the table and grabbed my arm. 'Homer! Oh my god. Later!'

I spent most of class feeling really confused about whether I should be happy about hanging out with Pa and Nanna and making stacks of money, or sad because Dad kept breaking all his stuff, or excited because Mum was about to play her first interstate game. Without even really noticing what I was doing, I headed straight to the stumps for recess.

'Perfect,' Zara said when she saw me. 'Avery and Murphy have finished their song.'

'Whoa.' I looked at the two of them, who were grinning. 'Already? That's so cool! Can you play it?'

Avery pulled out his tape recorder and we crowded around it. This time, the music started more quietly and there were all these voices over it – the ones he'd recorded the other day, but cut a little shorter: '—get your shirt fixed—', '—get extra better at sports—', '—cheaper than a new shirt—', '—making shirts better—', '—he'll do whatever—'. Then the song started in full and a chorus started singing, 'Cap your sleeves, hem your shirt, fix your shoulders till it no longer hurts.' Then, just before the end, they sang, 'Sew What will fix it for you! Tuesdays and Thursdays at recess!' Then, dramatic scissor-cut sounds, and a drum solo that took the song to the end. Avery pressed stop on his recorder, and I just stood there for a moment while the last of the song bounced off the walls around us.

'Well?' Zara demanded.

'It's …' I couldn't even speak. 'It's real.'

'Almost definitely,' Avery said.

'I mean it! It's actually real. It's like an actual ad on the actual TV. It sounds … so good.'

'You seem shocked,' Murphy said, raising an eyebrow.

'Obviously you're good at music,' I said. 'That's not news.

But the whole ad! How did you get so many people to sing it?'

'Remember in music the other day when Ms Hingee sent you out to Hien's office to give her all those incursion forms? We did it then. Good acoustics in the music room, obviously.'

'You kept it a secret?' I said. 'Why?'

'More of a surprise than a secret,' Zara said. 'Though I can't believe nobody told you. Especially Tom, who loves to show off when he knows something another person doesn't. And Mario and Ng, who are just terrible at keeping secrets, let alone from you.'

'Yeah,' I said, frowning. I couldn't believe that Mario and Ng hadn't told me either. I'd spent the morning with Ng, and nothing. I hadn't really spoken to either of them at training yesterday, but they could have *tried* to talk to me.

They played the song a bunch more times and it got completely stuck in my head. Afterwards, in class, I kept humming 'cap your sleeves' under my breath until K. shuffled so far away from the table that they fell off their chair.

At lunch, I headed to the oval, thinking I could probably do with some practise after last night's training. I'd been distracted, and a bit all over the place, wishing I could be home making shirts for money for Dad instead of being made to do push-ups over and over because Crabtree was in a bad mood. Pa had said something about me limping and I'd said it was fine and I just hadn't been playing enough at school so my ankle was getting weak. If I actually kicked around today, maybe it'd be fine and I wouldn't have to listen to Pa talk about it again or give me that Pa kind of look like he didn't believe me.

On the way to the oval, Wynter stopped me in the middle of the footpath. 'You!' she yelled. 'Did you do my shirt yet?'

'I'm buying the bells tonight,' I said.

'I am dying of excitement,' she said. 'See?' She collapsed onto the ground and lay there completely still while I edged around her nervously, hoping she hadn't actually died.

Three steps later, Marcie and Jhyll were standing in front of me, Jhyll with her hands on her hips. 'You didn't even do all your class's shirts first,' she said. 'You absolute jerkjack.'

'Hey! That's going a bit far. You didn't turn up at the shop yesterday!'

'Why would I? I'm literally your *friend*.'

'Are you?' I asked, genuinely confused, since for the past six years she'd either just ignored me or asked Marcie to cast spells that turned me into a slug.

'And you're doing Marcie's. What's she ever done for you?'

'Turned up at the shop and waited in line?' I said.

'She's just jealous,' Marcie said, rolling her eyes. 'It's blocking her aura. She won't be able to rollerskate properly until she's yelled at you and got this out of her system.'

'It's not that!' Jhyll yelled. 'I couldn't skate this morning because I was *tired*!'

I edged away from them as well but when I turned to escape, Tom was there, leaning against the grade three classroom wall.

'Tom,' I said.

'Homer,' he said.

We didn't say anything for a minute and then he said, 'So if I'd waited to get my shirt done I could've, like, picked all these other cool things that the rest of the kids are doing?'

'You could've asked me when I did yours,' I said, shrugging. 'You just didn't.'

'You didn't *tell* me.'

'Well, next time the shop's open you can line up and I can do something to yours if you want. What do you want done?'

'I don't *know* what I want,' he said, crossing his arms. 'Isn't that the point of you being there? Telling us what would suit us? And why would I have to line up? I'm your friend, remember?'

'Everyone has to line up,' I said.

'Zara didn't,' he said. 'And I heard Thi came to your house for a *fitting*.'

I didn't like how he said that. 'Yeah, but Zara also planned the whole shop and wrote me up a business plan? And you didn't even pay, remember?'

'Oh, so you're asking me to pay now you're famous?'

'What? No!'

Tom gave a big, long sigh. 'Good. So I can just drop my shirt off this weekend and you can do something to it?'

'Literally no. I have a huge pile of stuff to already do.'

'Great, I'll drop it off on Monday,' he said, and walked off.

While I tried to groan loudly enough for Tom to hear, I noticed some tiny grade two kid staring at me. 'That's the shirt guy!' they whispered to their friend.

I stayed to listen in.

'I heard his shirts can make you fly,' the friend said.

'Duh, people can't fly. The shirts make you break world records, though. Mum said that I can use some of my birthday money to get fairy lights sewn to my shirt. Will you line up with me next time the shop's open?'

'Only if you give me one of your cherry tomatoes right now.'

I hadn't even thought about fairy lights. How would that even work? Where could you keep the batteries? Unless it was solar-powered and you could leave it out in the sun when you weren't wearing it. I wondered how you'd wash it.

I was almost at the oval. I could hear the punt of the ball and the thumping of everyone on the grass. When I got to the hill, I could see Thi running after Mario, who was bouncing the ball as he bolted off laughing. Mario was right – all this playing at lunchtime did mean he was getting better. Watching Mario like this reminded me of his dad, who always rocked up to every training session and watched intently, not even looking at his phone. Back when my dad was there too, they'd sit together and talk about tactics and games from twenty years ago and try to come up with nicknames for all the kids that absolutely did not stick. I wondered for the first time if Mario's dad missed my dad too, and whether he'd be happy as well when Dad rocked up for my first game.

If he could still afford to come now that he had to buy a new microwave. And pay for whatever disaster was going to happen next to try and burn up all his money before he could even use it to get to me.

I had to get these shirts done. I had to make that money. So I might as well figure out how the fairy lights worked now, before that kid even asked, and draw up what they'd look like on a shirt. I turned around and headed to the library, thinking about how I'd feel like I was all full of lit-up fairy lights when I finally saw Dad again, and trying very hard not to think about everybody racing for the ball behind me.

ROUND 25 STATS

Shirts Made Better: 5
New Shirts to Fix: 12
Shirt Money Earned: $202
Cost of a Microwave: $300
Round Ticket Perth → Melbourne → Perth: $400
Days Until Shop Reopens: 3

Saturday mornings are either for games or for sleeping in, and anything else is a crime. So when Nanna started shaking me awake on Saturday morning, I dug in under my doona and mumbled, 'I'll call the FBI if you keep trying to do this.'

'We don't have the FBI in Australia,' she told me. 'I think you have to call the Australian Federal Police. Also, it's ten o'clock, and you have to get ready.'

'Ready for what?'

'The doctor.'

I sat up. 'The what?'

'It's obvious there's still something wrong with your ankle. Our neighbour's brother's daughter is a doctor and we've always gone to her and she's very nice, and she's working today, and we got you an appointment!'

I shook my head. 'It's fine! It's not a problem. I *told* Pa it was because I wasn't practising enough at school and I promise

I'll start doing it again next week, okay?' I was desperate and went for the guilt angle. 'And I bet Mum would think it's weird to take her only child to the doctor without her knowing about it.'

'Pa texted her. She's fine with it. More than fine, actually.'

Traitor.

'Anyway, your appointment's at eleven-thirty, so you need to get up and get ready, get some breakfast into you, and get in the car. It's on the other side of town.'

Thi's shirt was finished now, but the bag with the rest of them loomed sadly from the corner.

'But Nanna,' I said, with big eyes, 'I have all those shirts to fix.'

She laughed. 'Oh, my beloved grandson, do you honestly think *that* excuse is going to work? "You're right, we should put off seeing a health professional about your injury because you have some shirts to sew"? Yes, I'd definitely get a Grandmother of the Year award for that one. Now, get up. I promise I'll make Pa buy you some jellybeans from the chemist afterwards.'

All Nanna and Pa's needle-sharp shower made me think about was how I wanted to be using actual needles to fix those shirts in my room, and the water couldn't wash away how stressed I was that I wouldn't get them done on time. Breakfast didn't help either, even when Pa let me have as many pieces of toast with jam as I wanted, and neither of them cared when I walked pointedly around the house showing off my lack of limp.

In the car, after forty-five minutes of listening to angry people on talkback radio while I just got madder about everything, we finally pulled up outside the clinic. It was already way too close to lunchtime on my first day of tailoring and I calculated that with a fifteen-minute appointment and another forty-five minute drive home, I was still an hour away from starting. *And* I had to fit lunch in with all that.

I took a deep breath. If I went straight in and the appointment was quick – which it would be, because I was fine – then maybe I could get started on the shirts properly by half past twelve.

Turned out, I could *not* go straight in.

They didn't call out my name until nearly twelve o'clock. I'd been sitting with my head in my hands, reading old magazines that were about gardening and didn't even have any fashion shoots in them, while Nanna and Pa kept looking at me and then at each other. When someone finally called my name, Pa stood up too.

'I can go in on my own,' I said.

'Nope,' he said cheerfully.

I went in. Dr Brudy was wearing a high-necked grey woolly jumper, cropped black pants and a nice smile. 'How can I help you today, Homer?'

'It's my ankle,' I said. 'I fell over in PE and hurt it a week ago but now I'm fine.'

Pa waved his phone around. 'It's been two weeks. He keeps saying he's fine, but he's just getting worse. We watched him at training yesterday and he was stumbling a lot, and favouring the other leg, and limping when he walked. I can show you the footage.'

'But you say you're fine and it doesn't hurt?' Dr Brudy asked.

'Yeah.'

'But you still limp and favour the other leg?'

'I didn't notice,' I mumbled.

'Hmm,' she said. 'Can you take off your shoes and socks and hop up on the bed here, please?'

As she examined my foot, Pa said, 'I think it hurts more than he's saying.'

'Oh?' She looked at me. 'Are you being brave, rather than admitting it hurts?'

'It's not like that. It's …' I didn't know what to tell her.

Pa said, 'We think he's pretending it's not happening so he doesn't get dropped from his football team on medical grounds.'

I stared at him. He wouldn't look at me.

'That's not true,' I said.

'His mother's an elite footballer – she's interstate right now playing – which means everyone's got eyes on him,' Pa said. 'His father's also living in Perth for the moment and is next coming down for Homer's first game, so the pressure might have something to do with it too. I feel like he might have to sit out for a few weeks to heal, but he keeps insisting he's fine and playing, and I don't want to – I don't want to see him really hurting himself trying to prove something.' Pa was a generally mellow type of guy, but he sounded angry here, his voice speeding up and getting harder.

'Hmm,' Dr Brudy said. 'I've been manipulating your foot while he was talking,' she said to me, 'and you haven't flinched. Is it not sore when I do this?' She bent it back.

'No.'

'And this?' She pushed my foot from side to side.

'No.'

'Right. So when does it bother you?'

'It doesn't.'

'Hmm,' she said again. 'Can you walk around the room for me?'

I hopped up and walked around the room. She watched me closely.

'There is a minor favouring of the other leg, you're right,' she told Pa. 'But without a report of any pain, it might just be a kind of leftover reaction to the injury he had a few weeks ago.'

'That sounds right,' I said.

'It doesn't,' Pa said. 'He's underplaying it.'

'I'm fine,' I said, jumping up and down. 'See?'

'I'm going to show you some exercises to strengthen the muscles in your leg,' she said. 'I think that's the way to go at the moment. You'll need to do them every morning and every evening, all right? Here, I'll show you.'

Once she'd taken me through the exercises and told me to come back in two weeks if it didn't improve, she walked us outside. Pa looked at Nanna and shook his head, while I pointedly looked at my watch. It was already a quarter past twelve, and we hadn't started any shirts at all. Then, in the car, Nanna said, 'Why don't we go somewhere nice for lunch?' and I almost launched myself out of the window.

'Depends on what Homer thinks,' Pa said. 'Out, or sandwiches at home?'

'Sandwiches!'

'Maybe *I* wanted to go somewhere nice for lunch?' Nanna pouted.

'Tomorrow, love,' Pa said, and put his hand on her knee.

At home, I helped to make the sandwiches because I am a Very Good Grandson and not because I was desperately trying to get everyone moving. Nanna was cutting very precise avocado slices and Pa was drying tomato slices on a piece of paper towel while I dragged Vegemite all over my bread, slammed slices of cheese on top and wolfed it down over the sink so I didn't have to waste my time putting a plate in the dishwasher, then told my grandparents their sandwiches looked very lovely and ran up to my room, got inside and shut the door.

I looked at my watch again. Nearly half past one, and I hadn't done anything yet.

I opened the first bag, and Wynter's shirt was on top. We'd gone to Maker Acre last night after school and picked up all the extra stuff – which cost way more than I thought because it turns out you can't just buy six bells, you have to buy a hundred – and now it was in a pile next to my desk. I reached in for a handful of bells, then got to work.

Once I finally started, I was there, in the magic. Today, it felt like being out on the field, when the ball was in your hands and you could see somebody waiting for you to kick it to them and nobody was in your way. You kicked it, they caught it, and everybody would cheer.

The shirt was in my hands. I had a clear path to the goal, and all I had to do was line it up straight and make sure it landed in the right place.

I didn't notice how long I'd been working until there was a knock on my door.

'Yeah?' I croaked.

'It's me, Homer,' Pa said through the door. 'I've got

something for you.'

I tried to stand up, but my body did not want to cooperate. I had been hunched over the desk for what felt like a thousand years, and I stood up awkwardly and hobbled to the door, opening it.

'Yikes, kid. Are you okay?'

'I hurt,' I said, holding my back. 'Is this what it's like being old?'

'Somebody tells you they've got you something and you make fun of their age?'

'I can be meaner if you'd prefer?'

He knocked me gently on the head. 'Honestly.' He held out a hot chocolate. 'Thought you needed a break.'

'Yes, please,' I said, holding out my cramping hands for the mug.

'Homer,' Pa said, holding the cup away from me, 'can you tell me something?'

'Sure?'

'I can see how enthusiastic you are for this, and I love it. You know I do. My own kids were never interested in going to a craft store or wanting to make clothes. Your Mum just wanted to kick a ball around, and your Aunt Lia would've worn pyjamas all day long for all the care she had about clothes. You're a passionate kid, and it's why I'm worried about you.' He leaned down. 'I need you to promise me something. You're not in pain, are you? And pretending not to be because you're afraid of not seeing your dad, or not making the team?'

'I'm already on the team,' I said.

'You know what I mean. You know I moved to America from Malta when I was a teenager, right, to live with my aunt and uncle? Well, over there they are the kings of not taking things like this seriously and then injuring themselves out of sport before they are even adults. I was on the track team in high school, and my buddy Mike, he was something else. You've never seen a kid like him. He flew.' Pa got a faraway look in his eyes. 'It was his knee. He injured it a month before a big track meet and didn't take care of it. We were in our senior year and we'd all heard rumours about college scouts and all of that coming along, so he just ran through the pain.'

'And he was okay?' I asked, even though he clearly wasn't going to be.

'No. His bad knee buckled on a staircase. I'd seen him struggling on steps for weeks, but he told me it was nothing. I don't think I'll ever forget watching him fall down those stairs.'

'Why? What happened?'

He shuddered. 'He lived, but his leg – I can't. Anyway, he didn't run after that.'

'Ever?'

'Well, I haven't seen him for a few years, but I'm still going with "no".'

I narrowed my eyes at him. 'Is this real, Pa? Or are you just telling me the plot of some American movie I've never seen to teach me a lesson?'

'It's true! Ask Nanna. I told her all about it, and she met him when we went to America years ago. I'm not making it up for a lesson. But is there a lesson you need to learn?'

'Nope,' I said. 'I promise you that's not what's happening. I'm not – wait, what's a senior? Is it like how I'm in the senior year of primary school?'

'It is not like that.'

'Oh. Anyway, I'm not like Mike. I'm not running through pain.'

'Are you sure? Because it seems like it to me.'

'I promise,' I said, holding out my hand. 'Pinky swear.'

'Promise you're not lying to me?'

'I promise I'm not doing a Mike.'

'Okay.' He sighed and looked around at the mess I'd made all over the room. 'Well, do you need a hand here?'

'Maybe?'

'Then let's get started.'

When Mum arrived home on Sunday night, she was glowing.

'Mum!' I yelled through the window.

She tore into the house with her bags. 'Homer!' she said. 'How good was I?'

'You were amazing!'

'That goal!' Nanna said. 'You were so far out! I said you couldn't make it.'

'She did,' Pa said. 'I agreed there was no way.'

'I said you could!' I yelled. 'As soon as you spun it in your hands when you were lining it up I knew you were gonna make it.'

'And I did! Oh my god, I felt so good. I'm so wired I could power our whole house. We won! Polly's mark – did you see? Almost kicked the hair off Annabel's head. I thought I was going to throw up at half-time when we were losing, but we did it – we did it!'

'I'm so proud of you,' Pa said, holding her tight. 'My own daughter!'

'I need a shower,' Mum said. 'Then you can fuss over me more.'

It was already late when Pa and Nanna left, waving off Mum who was cradling a plate of sausages and salad on the couch, wrapped in a dressing gown. I sat next to her and put my head on her shoulder. She was soft, like the stuffing inside a jacket.

'You were great, Mum.'

'I was so nervous at home, and when I first got on their grounds – it felt like another world. But then I got that ball in my hands and I just remembered, Homer, how it was what I was built to do.'

'You're a natural.'

'Yeah,' she said. 'You get many of your shirts done?'

I didn't really want to talk about that part. When I'd told Pa on Friday night that I wanted to finish all ten shirts by Tuesday, he'd laughed so loud that the Maker Acre assistant told him to keep it down. He said I'd be lucky to do four shirts by then, and I told him he was wrong. Turns out, a professional tailor knows what he's talking about.

It was making me feel pretty stressed, really. I wasn't sure how I was supposed to fit in all this shirt-making around all the footy training for me and the footy training for Mum and all the school and all the everything else. Maybe I should ask Hien if I could go to school part-time.

'Three shirts,' I said. 'Maybe I can finish another one by Tuesday.'

'That's great!' she said. 'Well done.'

I was still cranky about it, but Mum's game this afternoon had reset me a bit. Watching a camera – on TELEVISION – zoom into my mum's beaming face after her epic goal while all her teammates jumped on her back had been something else. I'd forgotten about the shirts for a couple of hours, and I even almost remembered how I wanted that to be me one day.

'I heard about the doctor,' Mum said. 'So she reckons you're just recovering?'

'Yeah,' I said. 'That's what she thinks.'

'We'll keep an eye on you, though.'

'I thought you said to always keep your eye on the ball?'

'I've got enough eyes for both.'

I grinned.

'Want to watch the replay?' I asked.

'Watch myself on television? Are you kidding?' She put her plate down. 'I can't believe you waited this long to ask.'

ROUND 26 STATS

Shirts Made Better: 8
Shirts Still to Fix: 9
Shirt Money Earned: $202
Maker Acre Expenses: $27.50
Days Until Shop Reopens: 1

Sometimes I don't like being an only child. It's lonely, especially when your dad moves away and there's even less people around to hang out with you. There's nobody extra to steal dessert from at home. Nobody to play two-player video games with when your parents get sick of it. All that kind of stuff.

But sometimes, it was okay.

'KID! Get out of my way!'

I was trying to sew a curse on a tiny white piece of fabric. It involved a lot of staring closely to make the words work. What it didn't involve was having Mario's cousin come flying at me with a soccer ball in his hands.

Mario sat up from where he'd been lying on the grass next to me, trying to spin a football on his finger. 'Johnny! Why are you even out here? Mum said *I* could be out here!'

'There's enough room for your little ball-kicking as well as real football like I'm doing,' Johnny said. 'At least when there isn't somebody in the middle of the grass like you and this random kid.'

'That's Homer! You've met him, like, a hundred times.'

Johnny stared down at me. He was wearing jeans that seemed way too tight for him to be playing any kind of sport and a black t-shirt with a logo so tiny I couldn't even read it. He was only fifteen, which I knew because I had actually met him a hundred times like Mario said, but he looked like he was about forty.

'Homer,' Johnny said to me, 'you're in my way.'

'This is where the best light is,' I said, holding up my needle while Johnny squinted.

'Yes,' Johnny said, crouching down close to me and saying in my ear, '*My* light.'

Mario's dad came over and pushed Johnny over from his crouch. 'Johnny, just because your big brother kicked you out of the house doesn't mean you can come out here and kick around the smaller kids. Do something useful and help Mario in the garden. We need some potatoes for dinner.'

'No chance,' Johnny said, dropping his soccer ball on the ground and kicking it around me in a circle.

'Potatoes!' Mario yelled. 'Homer, come help me pull some up.'

'But I'm doing *this*,' I said, holding up my needle again. 'I need to finish Marcie's shirt tonight so I can give it to her tomorrow.'

Mario looked at his dad, who shrugged and went back inside. I pulled at the thread and got to work. All of my 'r's looked different from each other. Words were hard.

After a while, Mario came over with a pile of potatoes.

'You know, it didn't take that long. You could've helped.'

'But you just said it didn't take that long,' I said, concentrating. 'So it's all good.'

'Sure it is,' Mario said. 'So glad you came over to not actually talk to me at all.'

'I've got to do this,' I said. 'Nanna and Pa took me to the stupid doctor on the weekend so I couldn't get enough shirts done and then the recess radio ad went out today so people might've heard it even though they probably didn't listen, but just in case I really need to finish the ones I've already started so I can start fixing more and make some money and,' I took a breath, 'you know.'

'Yeah, I do know, but doing this with me would've taken you, like, three minutes and not actually stopped you making money to see your dad. You can take three whole minutes off, right?'

'But it'd throw me off my letters, and it only took you six minutes, and it's not like you've got another job to do like me, do you?'

'Nope,' Mario said, and picked up his potatoes and went inside.

Once I'd finished Marcie's first curse/spell/whatever – it said 'VAMPIRES BEGONE', even though I'd pointed out to her that it wasn't like she'd see many vampires during the day when we had PE anyway, since they couldn't go out in the sun – I realised Mario hadn't come back outside again after delivering his potatoes, and also that it was getting pretty dark. I went into the house and found him with his brothers and cousins watching cartoons.

'Hey, Mario, I—'

'Shh,' he said.

'But—'

'I'm watching cartoons,' he said.

I went to sit next to him, but he didn't move over. I sat on the floor and wished I'd brought extra fabric to work on Marcie's other curse, but at least one was done.

Mario's mum and dad made gnocchi for dinner out of the potatoes, and we were banished to the kids' table outside to eat because there wasn't enough room inside. Mario stabbed at his gnocchi and stared at the back door. Usually I talked because Mario talked, but when he didn't talk I didn't know what to say, and so I didn't say anything for the whole of dinner.

We were still watching cartoons when Mum came to get me, but by then we were in our pyjamas and there weren't as many cousins around. Mario's mum answered the door and I heard them talking in low voices while I got all my stuff ready.

'What's up?' I asked as we drove home.

'What's up with me? I was going to ask what's up with you! Nicole says you barely said anything and spent most of the time on your own doing sewing stuff. I thought it'd be nice for you to hang out with Mario for once while I was at training! That's why I organised it.'

'You should've asked! I had stuff to work on. It would've been easier with Pa.'

'They can't look after you every day of their lives, Homer. They already do a lot.'

'Don't they want to see me?' I stared at her.

'Homer, don't be ridiculous. They love you, but they already see you heaps, and sometimes they just might want to do their own thing. They've been constantly parenting one kid or another for thirty-two years. Give them a day here and there.'

I looked out the window, watching the houses rush by.

'Are you and Mario fighting?' she asked softly.

'No! I don't think.'

'Are you sure? Nicole thought you might be.'

I shrugged.

'Can't imagine why you'd be fighting with that kind of perfect communication,' Mum said dryly. 'Let's get home, huh?'

I finished Marcie's last request – 'CAN SEE GHOSTS' – and sewed it in by torchlight with an unlit candle on the desk next to me after Mum yelled at me to stop setting fires and get to bed. I had four shirts to give back at the shop tomorrow. It wasn't ten, but it was something.

I headed straight into school in the morning, peeling down the road right past The Bad Corner and chucking my bike into the back of the shed where it probably wouldn't hit anybody else's. I had all the shirts packaged in brown paper with string, and I'd put everyone's names on labels with tiny letter stamps.

I'd planned to go find Thi and show off – I thought she'd be super impressed with the stamps – but as soon as I got away from the bike shed some kid accosted me next to the library and said, 'You're the guy from the poster!'

'The what?'

He pointed. There was a poster right next to my head that I'd completely missed. It said 'SEW WHAT' in big red letters over a comic book-style drawing of me holding a needle like a sword and fighting a school shirt. It was completely rad. I'd have to give Willow a brutal fist bump when I saw her next.

Thi came out of the library holding a notepad and said, 'Uh, this a friend of yours?'

'This is the guy from the ad on recess radio!' the kid told her excitedly.

'No way! Did you know I saw him eat somebody else's boogers for a dare?'

'Hey! That was *one time*.' I crossed my arms while my fan club shrieked and ran away. 'I was looking for you,' I added once they'd all gone.

'What's up?'

'I have your shirt! And four others,' I said. 'I did all your names with stamps,' I pointed out, because it had taken forever and I wanted her to be as impressed with me as I was.

'They look great,' she said, looking over her label before shoving the package in the backpack. 'So this means we can get, what, four more orders at the shop today?'

'Five!'

'Four,' she said, shaking her head.

'I could do more! And maybe next weekend I can do more again. I was super distracted this weekend. There was this whole thing with the doctor about my ankle and it was such a waste of time.'

'Yeah, I bet,' Thi said in a strange voice.

I pointed at the notepad. 'Still working on that jersey design?'

'Yeah. Deadline's soon.' She held it close. 'I'm sorry. You must still be pretty sad about it.'

'Kind of? But this is good! You'll win the contest, we'll

make more money at the shop, I'll still have some cash, it'll be great. No problem.'

'Yeah,' she said, grinning. 'No problem.'

'I guess this is a problem,' Thi said.

Turns out, everybody really does listen to recess radio, even the ads. At the shop, there were even more kids lining up than last week and they were all asking questions, and there were more preps crying that they couldn't use the shopfront for games even though Thi had extra pencils to bribe them with, and then there was a pile of grade fours singing Avery and Murphy's jingle on top of the monkey bars, and it was just, you know, a lot more chaotic than you want things to be when you can only take four new orders.

Thi managed the queue, a terrified-looking Murphy backed slowly away from everything while wiping away her happy tears from everyone singing her song, and I ran into the chaos to find the other kids whose shirts I'd finished. Wynter excitedly jingled her parcel all over the place while Roman tore his open and slapped my back hard like I was choking. Marcie said she would remember me when the vampires didn't get her, and Olivia J said, 'Whatever.' Still, as soon as she was out of the crowd, I saw her unwrap it slowly and carefully next to the flying fox.

The first four kids in line put their orders in – one kid just wanted the shoulders done, another wanted the ribbon football flag they'd heard rumours about ('Sorry,' Thi whispered), another wanted her nickname, BLASTER, sewn onto the back, and the fourth one wanted a pocket for a single Skittle.

'Just one?' I asked.

'Just one,' they said.

'All right, that's it!' Thi shouted, and everybody groaned. 'Come back again on Thursday for another try, but there will probably only be one—'

'Two,' I hissed.

'—two spaces available. Thanks for your time and have a great day.'

'Very professional,' Murphy said.

'Your ad was too good,' Thi told her.

Training was pretty normal that afternoon – I still hadn't really talked to Mario, but I felt powerful and was all over the ball anyway and everything was excellent until close to the end, as we were lining up to tackle Crabtree. Everyone was talking about what they were going to do on the Easter holidays, and I didn't really mind that I didn't have plans until Bucky said, 'I'm going to Perth with my dad. Last time we went he took me whale watching and we caught boats everywhere we needed to go and one night I stayed up until three in the morning.'

'No, you didn't,' Aaron said.

'Did too! The sky turns red after midnight.'

'Does not,' Jerome said.

They kept fighting over it, but I was distracted about the idea of Bucky and his dad on their big stupid Perth adventure. Boats, whales, staying up late. Dad said Kings Park in Perth was one of the nicest places he'd ever been, and in Fremantle you could take a ferry to Rottnest Island and look at the quokkas, and I'd done a whole project on quokkas in grade three and could totally be a tour guide about it. Bucky even said his dad would take him back there to watch an AFL game later in the year. I wondered if Dad would do something like that to make up for the other twenty games he'd have missed with me by then.

I rubbed my face in anger. I'd made another fifty-three dollars today. It was sitting in an envelope in my schoolbag, waiting for me to take it out and put it into my money box. I was so close already. Bucky never had to worry that his dad wouldn't be here, because he was always up in the stands smoking when he thought nobody was looking and shouting 'CARN BUCKS' and 'YEAH LAY INTO HIM' and stuff, and you couldn't miss him even if you wanted to.

When it was finally my turn to tackle Crabtree, I pretended he was Bucky and slammed right into him. 'Mate!' he wheezed. 'That was a rough one. The aim of a tackle is to get the ball, not actually injure your opponent, yeah?'

When we were driving home from training, Mum said, 'I'm really not sure about your ankle. I see what Nanna and Pa were worried about. You were okay at the start, but by the end you were trying to stay off it again.'

'I'm doing the exercises!' I lied indignantly. 'I'm fine! The doctor said it was fine and just residual or whatever!'

'I'm only pointing it out,' Mum said. 'Maybe a break for a week would be good?'

A break. I'd have more time to work on my shirts if I wasn't at training on Thursday. It'd make life a little easier.

My phone beeped. It was a message from Dad. 'Hang on,' I said, 'I gotta message Dad back.'

'I could hardly interrupt this,' she said.

Heya sport. Destroy everybody at training today?

Too much. Crabtree had to tell me off about it.

Haha! Great work. Don't tell your mum I said that. Actually, she'll probably laugh. Can't wait to see you in action.

I can show you the shirts I've been working on, too, I typed, and sent him a picture I'd taken earlier of the chaos of thread and measuring tape and fabric on my desk.

Your mum lets you go to training with a room this messy?

I looked over at Mum. We'd already pulled into our driveway, and she was sitting patiently in her seat, rolling her hoodie string into a spiral.

You ever want to talk about something other than football? I typed.

Sure. I can talk about working out too.

He started sending a mountain of fitness emojis, one after the other. He was trying to be funny, probably.

Can't wait to see you at the game, I wrote, finally.

And he replied: *It's all I've been waiting for.*

I put my phone back in my backpack. 'I'm fine,' I told Mum. 'I'm going to training on Thursday. And to every other session too. Always.'

ROUND 27 STATS

Shirts Made Better: 10
Shirts to Fix: 11
Shirt Money Earned: $255
Days Until First Game of the Season: 24
(Days Until I See Dad: 23)

On Wednesday morning, I handed over K.'s shirt in its brown paper. K. squeaked and said, 'Hell yes! Why isn't it tomorrow already?'

'I hope it feels okay,' I said.

'It will,' they said, and grinned.

Later, when we were all on the floor watching a video about tectonic plates on the whiteboard, Henry shuffled over to me across the carpet and said, 'Mate, I'm so impressed with your whole shirt business thing. It's really awesome.'

Zara leaned over to him and whispered, 'He's not going to let you skip the queue, so stop trying.'

I had, in fact, been about to ask Henry if he wanted me to do his shirt, but I shut up. He shook his head and said, 'Nah, I was just going to ask if he was coming to play again on the oval any time soon, since we're getting destroyed without him. It's only fun when we're winning all the time.'

'That's a terrible message!' Zara said.

'Zara, you threw your cricket bat onto the PE shed roof when I caught you out last year, you absolute sore loser,' he said.

'You saw nothing,' Zara hissed, and when she looked back at the screen he whispered to me, 'I kind of did want to skip the queue.'

Once he'd shuffled away, I shuffled over to Willow. 'Those posters,' I said. 'They're next level.'

She beamed. 'Thanks! It took me ages to get your face right. Turns out your nose is really hard to draw.'

Murphy was the last person to shuffle over. 'I don't think I said this, but I'm really impressed with your whole tailoring thing,' she whispered. 'Like, everybody always knew I was into music, so when it got out that I was writing it too, nobody was really surprised. But you – you're trying to do something that nobody's really used to you being into, and that's probably super hard. So, you know, good for you.'

It was the most I'd ever heard her say in her life. 'Hey, thanks,' I said.

'And when you get around to doing my shirt, I want you to put, like, a drum in the chest so the next time Tom kicks a footy into me in PE it makes a cool sound.'

'Deal,' I said.

When I was heading out the door for recess, after staring at the reflection of my nose in the window for a bit and wondering why it was so hard to draw, I realised there was some kind of hold-up at the entry. I looked up and saw Thi making her way back through the crowd, but she wasn't smiling.

'It's Hien,' she said. 'She's asking to see you.'

'Hien? Why does she want to see me?'

Thi put her hand on my arm and didn't say anything. Then she reached into the crowd, pulled Avery out of it, and told him: 'Go get Zara.'

He nodded and melted back into the crowd.

I still didn't really understand. When everyone had shoved through the door and I saw Hien standing there, she smiled at me in a not-entirely-smiley way and said, 'Hi, Homer. I wondered if you had a moment to come to my office?'

'I've actually got to talk to Zara about—'

'Oh, you know what? I shouldn't word it like that, it sounds like I'm asking. What I'm really saying is: Homer, come to my office.'

That was when I noticed she was holding one of my brown packages in her hand, but it had been taped back together again not as nicely as when I'd done it.

And I realised, finally, what this was about.

Somehow, Zara was already waiting by the door when we got there.

'Ah, Miss Gruschow, we meet yet again,' Hien said. 'This is your doing, is it?'

'Entirely,' Zara said. 'So you might as well let Homer and Thi go.'

I started to speak but Hien held up her hand. 'This isn't court. Nobody's going to jail here. We're just talking.'

She led us all into her office. Thi looked nervous, probably because she'd never been in here before, unlike Zara and me who were experts at being told off.

'Okay,' Hien said as she sat down behind her desk. 'Let me get this straight. I have had a phone call from a parent saying their kid asked for money to fix their PE shirt. They were wondering why they had to pay to fix a problem with shirts they'd already paid a lot of money for, and then they were even more surprised when the shirt turned up in their house with a bottle opener in the hem.'

'Olivia said she drank a lot of kombucha after school,' I explained.

Hien held her hand up again. 'This question they asked was a very good one, since I didn't know anything about either the shirts being damaged in the first place or somebody in the school asking for payment to fix them. Imagine how ridiculous I sounded when I said I didn't know what they were talking about and asked them to bring the shirt in question.' She tapped the package on her desk, and I started to feel like this wasn't just a small chat. Like maybe something was about to go horribly wrong.

'So,' she said. 'Who was responsible for this?'

'I am,' Zara said immediately. 'Like I said before. It was entirely me. You can forget these two.'

'I did some stuff too,' Thi said, and her voice was way smaller than usual, like somebody had put it in the wash and it had shrunk. 'I helped.'

'She's lying,' Zara said, glaring at her. 'It was entirely me.'

'I will accept what Thi said, thanks.' Hien leaned forward on her chair. 'The packaging was done beautifully. Was that you too, Thi?'

She didn't look up, but she shook her head.

'It was me,' I said finally.

'Well! It's very good.'

I remembered how teachers loved it when you learned things from your elders, and I said, 'My grandfather says presentation is important.'

'He's not wrong,' she said. 'What you're saying, Zara, is that this was your idea and you made Homer do the work?'

'Yes,' said Zara.

'No!' I said, louder now. 'I did it.'

'No, I did,' Zara said.

'She's just trying to get into trouble because she thinks it makes her look more like a rebel,' I insisted.

'Am not!' Zara said.

'I did it and asked her to help.'

'He didn't! He never asks anyone for help, Hien, you know that.'

'CHILDREN,' Hien said, and we both shut up. 'I saw the shop yesterday, before I even received the bottle-opener shirt, and I'd heard rumours in the staffroom about it before that, and all three of you were mentioned. I was going to talk to you yesterday, but you closed down your store while I was on my way there, and then somebody fell over in the playground and I needed to fill out paperwork for the rest of recess. I *saw* you, which means that I know you're all involved in some way. Let's stop fighting over that, and take this down a notch. Have any of you read the uniform guide in your handbook recently?'

I said, 'We have a handbook?'

Hien sighed. 'Yes. You get a fresh one every year with your take-home pack. It's very clear on uniform policies. Mostly, that there are certain parts of the uniform that are required. You know: t-shirts must have logos; dresses must be the same checked pattern; pants, shirts, skirts and skorts must all be blue.'

Zara sat up in her wheelchair and said, 'I don't think you've really considered students that have financial difficulties—'

'IF,' Hien interrupted, 'you had read the handbook – which I'm a little surprised about from you at least, Zara, knowing your usual knack for studying the rules so you can find loopholes – you'd see that there is a very clear line in it that explains we are absolutely able to help anyone in financial trouble acquire their uniforms.'

Zara sat back.

'Sadly for you,' Hien said, 'there's also a line about making *amendments* to school uniforms. Do you know what that word means?'

'Changes,' Thi whispered.

'Exactly.' Hien sighed. 'It is very important to us that all the children have the same clothes so that nobody has to feel different from each other. I know that everybody gets very dramatic about wearing uniforms, but it removes stress about fashion from the school experience and supports the equity we want to foster here. Doing this really crosses the line from uniform – which is a word in itself, meaning the *same*, remember – into free dress. You've also got to think about safety issues on the school grounds. Homer, you like to tackle people. What if someone tackled you while wearing a bottle opener and scratched up your face or your eye? These accessories could tear of clothes, or cause bruises – all kinds of things. They're distracting. And they're against the rules.'

Zara said, 'Hien, I've been meaning to talk to you about

how putting us all in uniforms violates our freedom to express ourselves and—'

Hien put her hand up. 'Zara, I am absolutely sure you'll have a list of compelling arguments against the school uniform. I will probably even agree with some of them. This is not the time for that discussion. We are discussing a rule that already exists, which, by the way, you all signed that you had read and understood.'

'I don't remember doing *that*,' Zara blustered.

'I don't either, but luckily, this is exactly the kind of thing we keep on file for these discussions.' She pushed three slips across the desk, signed by each of us, saying we read and understand the rules of the handbook.

'My signature was faked?' Zara tried.

'You've been spending too much time with Tom,' Hien said, then sighed. 'Kids, look. I'm impressed by your initiative, and I understand you were trying to something positive. But this is a flagrant disregard of our rules, the safety of the school and the equity we strive for. Therefore,' she said, 'I am shutting your shop down.'

ROUND 28 STATS

~~Days Until Shop Reopens: 1~~
Round Ticket Perth → Melbourne → Perth: $400
Shirt Money Earned: $255
Extra $ Needed to Get to $400 = $145

There was some kind of fire travelling up my body from my toes to my fingers. I could feel it burning all through me, like bursts of flame coming off my skin, each one exploding with a word like: *no. dad. closed. money. closed. no. plane. dad. NO.*

I hadn't made anywhere near enough money yet. All those daydreams I had where we'd meet up at the airport, and I'd get to see him for the first time in months – it was like they caught fire too. I had, maybe, two-thirds of the money to get him one way, after all this time, all this work I'd done drawing jersey designs and making shirts to get the money and training for footy so he'd still want to come and see me and—

'And,' Hien went on, 'you have to give the kids back their money.'

'WHAT?' I exploded.

'But Homer already did the work,' Thi said desperately.

'It doesn't matter,' Hien said. 'You can't exchange money

for goods at school. Because,' she added, 'we're a *school*. Not a store. It's in the handbook.' She tapped it. 'This isn't a place for business. It's a place for learning.'

'But not for learning to start a business?' Zara snapped.

'Obviously we hope the skills you learn here are transferable to whatever you want to do as an adult. If that's open up a business – great. I hope the maths and English basics we've taught you will assist you in doing that. But it doesn't mean you can open one up here. The school can get in trouble if you sell things on our grounds.'

I remembered something and nearly fell out of my chair to yell it out. 'What about the school fete last year? We were allowed to sell things then!'

'Yes. Because we had permission to do so, and, more importantly, because it was a fundraiser for the school. It wasn't about profits, it was about being able to afford new equipment and buildings and upgrades for the school.'

'Jhyll sold hair ties and made a profit,' Thi said.

'I'm saying the *point* wasn't profit, not that anybody was banned from making some.'

'What if I donate part of my money to the school?' I asked, standing up. 'I can do that!'

Zara nodded furiously in agreement.

'You kids are doing a great job at defending your choices and making a case,' Hien said, not smiling, 'but you're missing the point. There isn't a case to be made here. You cannot amend the school uniform, and you cannot have a shop in the school to sell your alterations. You can make clothes and sell them at the next school fete, if you really want.'

I didn't even know when the next fete was, which meant it

was too far away. 'But Hien,' I said, 'I need the money.'

She leaned forward. 'Homer, are you okay? What do you need the money for?' She looked around at Thi and Zara. 'Maybe you two should head back outside for now—'

I was boiling up, like the carpet tiles underneath my feet were a stovetop and my breath was angry steam. 'It's mine!' I shouted. 'I earned it! I spent hours on those clothes! You can't just take it away from me and—'

'*Homer!*' Hien said, standing up as well. 'I have not been angry with the three of you because I don't think you were deliberately causing trouble, and I am giving you the information you need to move forward. But I will *not* be spoken to like this.'

The fire inside roared out. 'You can't just take people's money away from them! That's stealing! It's *mine*!'

'No, it's not. It belongs to those children. I will do you a favour by intercepting any angry phone calls I get from parents about what went down here, but that is the last thing I will do for you. It is now time for you to leave my office. Tomorrow morning before class you will come and give me the money you've already been paid.'

'But I *need* it,' I said, fighting with Hien and also with the tears behind my eyes, which were putting out the fire even though I didn't want them to.

Hien came around the desk and stood close to me. 'That wasn't a question, and this is your last moment to get out of my office without seeing further consequences. I expect an apology for your words once you've calmed down.'

My dad came with me to this office once. I'd been in trouble for bringing our old cat Norman to school, in my backpack. He was very lazy and didn't even get out of my bag, but Olivia R saw him and told on me, and Dad had to come pick Norman up. Dad had told Hien it was a misunderstanding, that I'd asked to take Norman to school one day and Dad had said yes thinking he'd bring him to drop-off sometime to say hi, and it was his fault he wasn't clear about when and how Norman could come to school. I still had to wash bird poop off the office railing for Hien while spending time Thinking About What Could Have Happened, and obviously Dad told me off at home later for not Thinking Through My Actions, but still. He'd come, and he'd stuck up for me.

He wasn't here now, though. He wasn't anywhere nearby. He wasn't even in the state, and my one chance at getting back to him again was gone. I'd been so close – I'd had $182 plus $53 in my hands and it was almost enough to go see him *tomorrow*, or even *right now* – but now I had to give all that back, every dollar. Worse still, I was supposed to return more money than I even had, since I'd spent heaps at Maker Acre on bells and letter stamps and all this stuff I'd never even use now.

Thi leaned forward and broke through the illusion of Dad sitting there. 'Homer?' she said.

I walked out.

Zara followed, with Thi close behind, shouting over her shoulder to Hien that she was sorry. I got out of sight of Hien's office and then whirled around on both of them so hard that Zara's tyres squealed when she braked.

The inside of my body felt broken, like my heart and lungs were made out of glass and Hien had smashed them all with a hammer. When I tried to speak, my voice sounded broken too.

'You know what?' I hissed. 'It was all fine. I was just quietly doing all these shirts for my friends, fixing the messed-up shoulders, and if that's all we'd done then Hien wouldn't have even noticed it. Everybody would've gone around in their fixed-up shirts and I would've been paid and it would have all been fine.'

Thi had been so quiet in Hien's office that I was surprised when she came right up to me and shook her finger in my face. 'Excuse me? You *wouldn't* have been paid. That was my idea. You were doing it for free before that and *I* was the one who told everyone to pay you.'

I threw up my arms. 'I was going to ask for money eventually! You and Zara and your friends just butted in and made everything so much bigger and put up posters and made ads and it just made everything *worse*!'

'*Worse*?' she snapped. 'You're trying to handball blame here by saying me and Zara and "our friends" butted in like you've never even met us before, but you were *extremely* happy to have us all work on plans to make it all successful for you, which *by the way*, we did for *free*, because we are *your* friends, even though I am feeling *very* unfriendly towards you right now.'

There was a sucking sound next to us. We both whipped around to face Zara, who was slurping up the dregs of a juice box.

'Don't let me interrupt you,' she said. 'This is very entertaining.'

I turned back to Thi, clenching my hands open and closed like I could feel the money in them and was trying to grab onto it. 'I wish you'd just left me alone,' I growled. 'You've ruined *everything*. Why didn't you just concentrate on playing footy, since that's all you ever think about?'

Zara stopped slurping.

Thi stood up very straight and took a deep breath. I thought it was to calm down, but when she spoke again, she was infinitely louder and angrier.

'LISTEN UP,' she roared. 'You were my *friend*, you jerkjack! If I only cared about football then why was I helping you, huh? You wanted to be known as a tailor, and we made people see that about you. You wanted customers, we gave you customers. You think any of *us* are happy about this? You think *we* wanted it shut down? After all the effort we put in?'

'YOU put in?' I yelled. 'I was the one making everything! And if I don't have the money I can't ever see my dad again because he can't afford to come to see me and I can't afford to go see him and you don't even have to care because both of you have dads that just live with you in your houses and you don't have any idea at all what I'm going through! Thi can just play her football like she always does and Zara can take over the world and I'm left with nothing.' I stopped and took a deep breath. 'I won't *ever* see him again. And if you hadn't had to be all freaking *Zara* about everything, none of this would've happened!'

'Homer,' Thi said, 'shut up.'

It's not like I hadn't heard worse. I mean, I go to a school, I've been to footy games, I've watched television, I've met teenagers. But hearing Thi – *Thi* – say that made me actually shut up.

'Homer,' Thi went on, in a voice I hadn't heard before, one like Skia's voice when he's Not Angry But Disappointed. 'You think Hien wouldn't have figured out what was going on eventually? You'd already offered to do different things to people's shirts. She would've noticed the next time she turned up to a PE lesson on one of her surprise visits. It was a mistake for you to fix these, but it was a bigger mistake that I even bothered helping you when all you're doing is yelling at us and blaming us. You suck,' she added, and she looked me right in the eye. 'I was trying to help you be happy because you were sad. I was trying to help you make clothes when everyone only saw you as a football player. But now everybody will know that you're not a football player, or a tailor.' She shrugged. 'You're actually just the worst.'

Zara sucked in her teeth.

'Let's go,' Thi said to Zara.

And they did.

ROUND 29 STATS

Wins This Season: 0

Nanna and Pa were waiting at home for me after school that day.

Nanna was rolling out some dough. Pa was putting a button on something. It was like some kind of chirpy family movie, except these weren't my happy parents, because my parents weren't happy together.

Pa said, 'Okay, champ, I reckon if we work hard today we can get thro—'

'I'm not making any more clothes,' I said. My voice felt hard, like my throat had turned to stone. 'Hien shut it down. And I have homework. I'll see you later.'

I went up to my room and sat at my desk. There were notes all over it about measurements for the shoulders on the school shirt, pages of jersey ideas, scribbles with plans for a jumper I wanted to make for winter. I scrunched up every page and shoved them all into the bin, pushing down to get them all in. I thought for a moment about setting it on fire, but last time I did that to get rid of some homework I didn't want to look at, it ended up with the smoke alarm screaming at me and a big circle of plastic that melted onto the carpet, so instead I went downstairs, got a can of lemonade out of the fridge, then took it upstairs and poured the whole thing into the bin and poked it with my ruler while it got all mushy.

There was a knock on the door. I didn't say anything.

'Homer?' Nanna called.

'I'm busy,' I said, staring at the bin.

'Okay. Your dad's on the phone, wants to say hi.'

'I'm busy,' I said.

There was whispering outside. 'Are you sure?' Nanna asked. 'Just a quick hello?'

'I'm busy,' I said, getting up and crawling under the covers of my bed. 'Tell him I said hi.'

After a moment, faintly, from under the covers, I heard her say, 'Homer says to say he loves you.'

I put the pillow over my head and blocked my ears.

When Mum shook me awake, it was dark.

'Hey, honey,' she said. 'Is everything okay?'

'It's fine.'

'Is that why you went to bed at four o'clock with your shoes still on? Pa says you didn't even wake up for dinner. Nanna made pastizzis and for the first time in recorded history there were still some left when I got home.'

I buried my face in the pillow.

'I mean, there aren't any left now, I ate them all. Does that make me a bad mother?'

I didn't say anything.

'Is there something wrong?'

'No.'

'Nanna said something about you not being able to do your shirt-fixing anymore.'

I lay still.

'It's a good thing though, right? Now you can relax and design your own clothes. I mean, surely it was boring fixing the same thing over and over instead of making new things to wear?'

When I still didn't say anything, she said, 'Are you sick? Do you feel okay?'

I nodded into my blankets.

'I'll be downstairs,' she said, rubbing my back. 'If you need anything, or just want to talk, you let me know, okay?'

After she left, Pa came upstairs and opened the door without knocking. 'I found a pattern in the shop,' he said softly, from the doorway. 'It was for a bomber jacket design I had to make once for a whole bowling team, and I remembered how you'd liked your cousin Luca's jacket at Christmas. I thought perhaps we could go out and get some good canvas material for it next weekend. And I can help you out.' He paused. 'I'm sorry you can't fix the t-shirts anymore, but I guess it does make sense that kids can't do that kind of thing at school.'

I sat up and glared at him. 'Oh, so you're on their side too?'

He looked surprised. 'Obviously I'm on your side, Homer. I'm just saying, it's probably against their rules, and—'

'What, so everybody realised it was against the rules? It's not a surprise to you, huh? Maybe you could have told me about it earlier, like maybe before I got my hopes up?'

Pa didn't really ever raise his voice, even though Mum laughed whenever I said that and told me he'd probably lost his voice after all the yelling he'd done at her and her sister when they were kids. Anyway, turns out he'd just been saving it up for now, because he was pretty loud when he boomed: 'HOMER!'

Still, I wasn't done. 'I worked hard on those!' I shouted. 'And I didn't even get to keep the money! What's the point? Why should I do anything for anyone? Why should I try and fix things when apparently the rules say that they have to stay broken? Everyone wants to walk around in uncomfortable clothes? Fine! Let them! I don't want to make a bomber jacket. I don't want to fix anything for anyone anymore. I don't—' and I leaned forward so he could hear me, even though I was already yelling, '—*care* about their clothes. Or mine. Or anyone's. I'm done.'

There was a little gasp from the door. Clearly, Nanna and Mum had come to listen. I said, again, very loudly, in case anybody else had missed it: 'I. DON'T. CARE. ABOUT. ANYTHING.'

Pa crossed his arms and took a deep breath. I sat up straight so his booming voice didn't knock me over, but when he spoke, he was back to normal. 'Well, that's that then,' Pa said. 'I guess it was nice to work with you on clothes while it lasted. I'll just go back to doing it on my own.' He turned to Nanna, and she put her hand on his arm.

And they were gone.

When Mum came back in after saying goodbye downstairs, she wasn't soft anymore. 'Now you listen to *me*, Homer. I know this hurts, I know you've got stuff going on, but if you think you can talk to my parents like that, you are *wrong*. I'm not going to talk to you anymore tonight because you're just lashing out, but I expect you to find a way to apologise to them in the morning.'

She sounded just like Hien. I'm the one who had everything taken away from me, and in return, I'm the one who has to say that he's sorry.

I lay back down in the bed and turned away from her.

'No,' I said.

'Yes,' she said, 'but I'm not asking you again until the morning.'

I woke up early on Thursday. It was so early that Mum wasn't even up, and the sky looked like no one had turned the colour on properly yet. I got dressed, brushed my teeth and took a banana out of the fruit bowl, wrote a note for Mum saying I was going to school early – I was mad, but still calm enough somewhere deep inside to know I didn't want the police called because she thought I was missing – and snuck out of the front door.

I didn't actually want to go to school, but I also didn't really know where else to go, so I ended up heading there anyway, just like my note had said. Everybody at Before School Care was inside, so I went to the oval and walked over to the tree stump where Murphy had hung out for most of her school life before she'd started talking to other people. I'd always seen her on top of it, hunched over a notepad being mopey, and I climbed up now and looked out over everything.

For the first time, I realised why she'd liked it here so much. You could watch all over the school while being far enough away that nobody bothered you, but close enough that you knew what was happening. Maybe she hadn't really always been mopey. Maybe she'd just liked it here sometimes.

It was all so empty. Nobody was around yet for cross-country practice or extra athletics training because it was still pretty early, and there wasn't anything to watch. The longer I spent on the stump alone with my thoughts and nothing else, the more my brain tried to remind me how everybody had helped me with the shop. I didn't like thinking about that, because really, I'd just been tricked by Thi and everyone into making everything complicated and loud and ruined.

'Hi,' a voice said, and I fell off the stump.

Once I could open my eyes again, I saw Ava there, standing above me.

'Ava?' I said, sitting up. 'I didn't see you! Where did you come from?'

'Tunnels,' she said mysteriously.

'That's weird.'

'People say that a lot about me. But actually it's everyone else that's weird.'

'Makes sense,' I said, dusting myself off.

'You can't make my shirt better,' she said.

'I know,' I said. 'I don't want to talk about it.' I really didn't, but also I said, 'You didn't even ask me to.'

'I was waiting for the time when you'd know what I wanted.'

'Ava, there's no way in a million years I could guess what you wanted on your shirt.'

She looked at me patiently and I sighed.

'Well, I mean. I'd have changed the collar so it opened in both directions, which means you could have worn it backwards if you want, because that seems like something a weird person would do. And I would've sewn a compass into it so you don't get lost in your tunnels.'

'There you go,' she said. 'You knew exactly what I wanted.' She held a ball out to me. 'I found this while I was in the tunnels. I thought maybe you'd like it.'

She walked away, and I looked down at the ball she'd given me. It was dirty, oval-shaped, small and soft, with a Thomas the Tank Engine logo on it. I felt this rush of rage at it and went to throw it over the back fence, but as I tossed it in my hand first to wind up, a memory hit me like a kick to the head.

Me with a small ball like this, running around an oval. Maybe even this oval – maybe even this ball. Nobody else is around. It's just me and Dad. He's kicking it to me from close by and I'm laughing because I can't pick it up. I'm really small, I realise. Not even coordinated enough to pick up a ball properly. I think I'm laughing at Dad's serious face. He's not mad or anything, just patiently trying to show me what to do, over and over again, even though I'm not listening because it's much funnier to not catch the ball. It's that choking laugh that little kids have, and I can feel it in my throat, wheezing from it.

The memory turned off, slowly, like a fan slowing down. And I just stood there, in the middle of that oval, holding the ball, alone.

ROUND 30 STATS

Shirts Fixed: 10
Shirts To Fix: 0
Shirt Money Earned: $-27.50
Days Until First Game of the Season: 23
(Days Until I See Dad: ?)

The rain began just after eight-thirty, but I didn't leave the stump until the first bell rang to go to class. Inside, I didn't talk to anybody at my table, and Thi wouldn't even look at me. K. passed me a note that said: *you okay?* and I shook my head and put the note in my folder.

I believe you, the next note said, *since you usually eat the notes I send you.*

I couldn't even smile. The third note said, *I'm here if you need to talk*, and I just wrote NO on the back of it so K. could see and then put that one in my folder too.

I paid attention. I did my maths sheets. I showed everyone how to handball in PE. Turns out, it was heaps quieter for your brain this way. You didn't have to talk to anybody or smile, or anything.

You could do the class work, sit on the stump during breaks, and just wait out the whole damn day.

When I got home, Mum said, 'Call your grandparents and apologise, or you're not going to training.'

'Okay,' I said, and went upstairs to lie back on my bed.

Ten minutes before training started, Mum threw open the door and said, 'I can't believe you called my bluff on this. You can't miss training. It's about being part of a team, and you can't let your team down. Get your gear on and be in the car in two minutes or I will put your shoes through the shredder.'

Even through my bad mood, I still wanted my shoes, since they looked a bit like LaFontaines if you didn't look up close and they didn't give me blisters at school like my last pair had. I got up, changed, splashed my face and went out into the car. Mum didn't speak to me the whole way to training and stayed in the car when I got out.

The evening air was clean, and the ground was soft but not wet. It was a perfect day to play, and I decided to work just like I'd done at school. No mucking around. I stretched and ran and handballed and kicked and watched the ball.

Crabtree blew the whistle for our scratch match and I tore into the centre. There were elbows and knees and I couldn't see the ball anywhere. I ducked around, but my body wasn't responding to all those years of training even though I'd thought it could. Everything was wrong and wonky and the ball was far over there and I ran straight for it but everyone was in my way, Aaron blocking me here, Jerome there right underneath me, Bucky in from the side and a push and—

I saw red, then white. I was on the ground, and people were shouting. My head was hot. Someone was yelling right next to my ear, 'Is he okay!?'

'Yes!' I said, but when it came out of my mouth it wasn't a word but a scream.

'It's his ankle,' Crabtree was saying, and his voice wasn't like it usually was. It was something less scratchy and mad. 'He's been favouring it, then he twisted and—'

Bucky was right nearby saying, 'I'm sorry, I'm sorry, I didn't think I was going to—'

Mario was there beside me saying, 'Ng's gone to get your mum, okay? You're okay, Homer, you'll be okay.'

Somebody was holding my hand.

I wanted to get up, but when I tried, Crabtree was in front of me, pushing me down, telling me to wait.

And then Mum was finally there, and she didn't look mad anymore.

'Come on,' she said, touching my face. 'I think it's time we took this seriously.'

The last time I was in hospital was for Mum, when she hurt her shoulder in training. Nanna and Pa had driven me there to see her, and she was so little on that bed, her arm in a sling, her face really pale and her voice super shaky. It had been hard, watching her be in pain, but it had also been good watching how everyone cared for her. Polly had turned up with Mum's favourite disgusting green juice, and I was allowed to sit up on Mum's bed on her good side, and to keep her happy we all told jokes and Pa did a live-action re-enactment of the time Mum broke her arm falling off her bike when she was eight. The man in the bed next to her even asked us to keep it down because if he laughed any harder he'd have another heart attack.

It wasn't like that now. Nanna and Pa were out with some friends and hadn't answered Mum's text. Dad wasn't here, and Mum said he was busy and we couldn't call him right now, though he'd sent a text saying he was thinking of me. It was just us, with Mum looking as pale and shaky as she had when she'd been the one here. We'd already waited in the emergency room for three hours for somebody to come and give me crutches and ice and move us to the next waiting room, and we'd been here for an hour too. I was sitting on the hard plastic chairs, looking at my bare foot.

'It's red,' Mum said, 'but it's not swelling up or anything. How does it feel?'

'Weird,' I said.

She went back to patting my hair, like she had been for the last hour. I'd already had to tell the nurse what happened, but mostly I couldn't really explain it. Mum told the story, which she'd got from Crabtree and Mario and Ng and Aaron and Jerome and Bucky and Jay and everyone who'd talked at her after it happened, while they got some ice and tried to figure out what to do and I was there on the ground curled up in a ball and not able to talk.

'Mostly,' Mum had said to the emergency nurse, 'it's that he's already been to a doctor and they don't think anything's wrong, but he's just getting worse, and he won't talk to me about it properly, and I'm so worried that it's something …' she trailed off, and looked at me. '… else,' she finished.

But there were all these other people with way worse problems than me. Someone came in holding her face, with blood all over her hands and a friend trying to hold her up because she couldn't walk properly. Someone else came in and even though they were quiet and I couldn't see any injuries or anything, they still just looked entirely wrong, and they went straight in. A little girl came in who'd broken her arm. When I saw a man who had a bandage around his eye go in I pushed Mum's hand off my hair and said, 'Mum, I think we should go. Everyone here has got it worse than me.'

'No.'

'What?'

'I don't care about anyone else here,' she said. 'I care about you, and making you better. You've had something wrong for weeks and we need to fix it. I don't know how, but the people here will.'

I sat back in my chair and bounced my foot up and down. Mum was sending messages on her phone. I'd run my phone battery flat playing games and messaging Ng and Mario, and I'd looked at all the fashion magazines until I was bored, which wasn't long since they were like ninety per cent ads for watches, and then I flicked through car magazines and learned so much about the history of Holden that I thought I might as well write it down for one of those 'whatever you want' assignments that Skia liked to make us do, which was a good indication of how bored I was.

'Mum, do you have any paper in your bag?'

'Hmm? No. Oh wait, I do! I have this.' She opened her bag and passed over the notebook I'd been using for the jersey competition ideas. 'I found it in the car today, because I decided to use my sulking time to clean up so I'd least I'd have something to show for it all.'

I stared at the notepad like I'd never seen it before. All these ideas that I'd had seemed like they'd been drawn by someone else one million years ago.

Pa had given me the soft brown leather notebook back when I'd first said I wanted to learn how to make clothes. Those early drawings were super crappy, but I got better. I wasn't anywhere near as good as Willow, who could draw a shirt like it was really hanging off someone's shoulders, but the sketches of t-shirts I'd been doing by the end were better than the boxy T-shaped ones from the start. As I flicked through the pages, I found where I'd first drawn my uncomfortable PE shirt, with little dotted lines over it where I'd thought about how to fix it.

Then I found a sketch I'd done of Thi in her PE shirt, and I closed the book. I couldn't think of her now. All day today she hadn't even looked at me. And even though I was mad at her for ruining everything with her idea to help me, I still felt kind of sick inside. I leaned down and rubbed my ankle.

'Are you okay?' Mum said. 'What's wrong?'

'Sore,' I said.

'I wish they'd at least give you some painkillers, but they can't in case you need something or go into surgery or—'

'Surgery?' I sat up. 'What?'

'Well, I don't know! I'm just a physio. I never thought I'd say that, but this is beyond me. And I don't know if you'll need more than exercise. I just … I don't know. What I do know is that I can't see you like that again.'

'Like what?'

'When you screamed,' she said, looking at the ground. 'I thought my heart was going to come out of my mouth. I was on the phone to your dad when you screamed and he …'

A voice behind us said, 'He what?'

We both turned around. Mum gasped.

It was Dad.

ROUND 31 STATS

[*error retrieving statistics*]

'Homer,' Dad said, and I couldn't speak, but I could jump up and wrap my arms around him and hug him like he'd been away for years, like I hadn't seen him at Christmas, like I'd never hugged him before, like if I held on for long enough maybe this time he wouldn't leave.

'How are you here?' I asked, when I could finally let go.

'Funny story,' he said, sitting down in the seat next to me. 'Well, not that funny. So, like your Mum said, she was on the phone to me when you fell, and I heard her say … well, I probably can't repeat it,' he said, looking at the other people in the room. 'Anyway. She said that Ng was running towards her and she'd get back to me, but she sounded scared, and then I was scared, and while I was waiting for her to call back, I checked flight times, and I just kind of thought, "well, it's not like I'm very far from the airport", since my office is not too far away as long as there's not a crash on the highway, and then I thought, "what if I drove there, in case?", and I was already in line at the ticket counter when your mum texted to say she was taking you to the hospital, and I thought of you in a hospital without me and, well … here I am.'

'But how did you get here so fast?'

'Well, it's been nearly five hours since then.'

'God, really?' Mum said, sighing. 'I don't think we're high on their waiting list.'

'How are you, Homer?' Dad got down on the floor. 'You stood up okay when I got here.'

'Yeah, he keeps using the foot,' Mum said. 'It's a whole problem, like I was saying. But when he fell today, I thought I'd get over there and it would have snapped off or something. I'm worried they're missing a fracture.'

'When we get in they'll do an X-ray,' Dad said. 'Angela, you want to go get yourself a coffee or something at the café?'

'Sure.' She kissed me on the cheek. 'Text the second the doctor calls you in, okay?' She patted Dad on the head like he was a puppy and walked away.

'That was a nice greeting,' Dad said. 'You must really be hurting. Mum says you've been in denial about your ankle.'

'Yeah, I guess.'

Dad sniffed. I looked over at him, and he wiped his eyes.

'What is it?' I asked, alarmed.

'Is it because of me?'

'What?'

'You training too hard when you shouldn't have been. It was one of the things your mum and I couldn't agree on. I said you needed to be pushed, and she said you were a kid, and I said you didn't see kids getting anywhere without encouragement, and she said what I was doing wasn't encouragement, and … I'm sorry. I don't want to get into it with you. It's just … I thought she was wrong about that. But I wasn't there to tell you when to back off if you had to. And if she wasn't—'

'She told me,' I said. 'She said I should back off and stop training while it hurt.'

'Why didn't you?'

'I don't know.' I rolled my ankle and looked at it. 'It didn't hurt.'

'But apparently you were limping all the time?'

'Yeah … I don't know.'

'Homer,' Dad said, and put his arm around me. 'I'm sorry about all of this.'

We were quiet for a bit. A doctor came to the swinging doors and called out the name of the person who had been waiting just before me, who'd looked like they'd maybe sprained something. I thought I was probably next. I thought about Mum saying something about surgery. I looked at another kid, who'd come in after me, all pale and shaking like we were waiting outside in Antarctica.

'Why does it take so long to go in there?' I asked, pointing at the door.

'Well, they put the people who have more urgent problems in first. It can make you feel like you're being ignored, but you're not.'

'That girl there,' I whispered. 'She looks worse than me. Can I ask them to take her in next instead of me?'

'Why would you do that?'

'I'm okay,' I said. 'I can wait.'

'I don't think it works that way,' Dad said. 'The nurses and doctors know what's up with everyone here. And something's wrong with you, and you need help. They'll have a proper look at you. X-rays, MRIs, ultrasounds, I don't know – we'll just keep asking until there's an answer.'

'What if there's not an answer?'

'We'll figure it out,' Dad said. 'And I'll be here until they do.'

'What about your work?'

'I guess I was hoping that by the time I got here you'd already be patched up, and we could hang out tonight and I'd catch a flight back in the morning and make it to work before lunch. We'll see, though.'

'You couldn't come to Mum's game,' I said.

'I know.'

'But you came now,' I said, and I could feel the spark of anger coming back, the spark that had gone out when I'd seen him.

'Before now you hadn't just had a huge injury,' Dad said. 'When I missed my flight it was frustrating, and I was sad, but *you* were fine. Now, you're not fine.'

'You said you couldn't come a lot.'

'And I can't. But if you need me, like really need me, I'll come in emergencies, you know that, right? When I called my boss to tell her you were in hospital she said, "Of course, if you have to go, go".'

I kicked the back of my left heel with my right toe. 'You can still come to my first game as well though, yeah?'

'I don't know, bud. Super last-minute flights are pretty expensive. Two, if you count the one tomorrow. Or the day after, if this takes a while, and then my sick leave … actually, I might not have been there long enough for sick leave yet.' He blinked.

'I'm sorry, it doesn't matter, this bit's not important to you. We'll work something out.'

'I thought you didn't have the money because of your dentist and stuff,' I said.

'I had this much money,' he said. 'Before I left, your mum and I made sure I had enough to get back if you needed me. But not much more.'

'So coming now means maybe you can't come to my first game and stay that weekend?'

'Maybe.'

I moaned again and leaned over to look at my ankle.

'Are you okay? Can I help? Have you got anything to take? You probably can't—'

'I know. Mum already told me. I can't have any painkillers.'

'Surely they can do something?'

As I leaned over, I saw the journal on the floor, from when I'd knocked it off my lap standing up to hug my dad. I picked it up and looked at the back, where I'd stuck football stickers all over it. On the front, I'd glued clothes I'd cut out from Grandpa's magazines.

I took a deep breath.

'Dad?'

'Yeah, mate?'

'I think I want to quit the team.'

He blinked at me. 'What?'

'And there's something else.'

He was rubbing his face. 'God, do I want to know?'

I didn't know how to say it. My lips felt stitched shut. I rubbed my mouth and whispered, 'Can we leave here without seeing anyone?'

'Why would we sneak out? Is this about your mum?'

'Not sneak out! We can get Mum first. I mean, tell them we don't need to see a doctor.'

'I mean, probably, but that's not generally what happens, you know, because you need help. Remember? Because of the injury?'

'Dad?'

'Yeah?'

I took a deep breath, like I was lining up for a goal I knew I would miss. 'My ankle doesn't hurt.'

'So you keep telling everyone.'

'No, I mean, it doesn't hurt. That first time I fell, it hurt the tiniest bit, but it was fine, like, ten minutes later. It didn't hurt at training. Or today. I just fell.'

'What do you mean?' He sat up straight and leaned in. 'What hurt so much that you screamed?'

I wasn't the type of person who knew what words to say when things were hard. When things were hard, I usually made them not-hard, with somersaults, or jokes even if they weren't funny. But there wasn't enough room for a somersault, and I didn't have any jokes now, not even unfunny ones. I could only think of cheesy things that I felt too embarrassed to say. I went through them in my head anyway while Dad stared at me, waiting.

Finally, I said, 'Life.'

The doctor came out of the door and said, 'Homer Falzon Schneider?'

Dad stood up and handed over the ice pack and crutches, and said, 'Thanks, but I think we've been waiting for the wrong kind of doctor.' I got up and stood next to him, and he said, 'Let's go find your mother. I guess we need to talk.'

ROUND 32 STATS

Days Until I See Dad: 0
Season Average Injuries: 0

In tailoring, there's this thing called darning. When you've got a hole in something, you use thread to crisscross over the damage, fixing it so you can still wear it. If you're good at it, you can barely tell there was a hole in the first place. If you're not, it only takes a while before everything falls apart again.

It took me a while to figure out why I was thinking about darning when we drove home from the hospital in silence. We'd picked up some drive-through Hungry Jack's, since everybody was hungry and nobody had eaten, and it was only when I'd licked the last of the mayonnaise off my fingers at the kitchen bench that I realised I'd been paying more attention in Skia's metaphor lessons than I thought.

'So,' I said, putting my hands on the bench, 'I didn't really mean for it to be a thing.'

I explained about how when I'd first fallen on my ankle, everybody had fussed over me. How Dad had told me to look after it. How it'd been … nice. How the next day it was fine, and I didn't really think about it, and I hadn't meant to fake it so that people would be worried. How people would tell me I'd been limping but some of those times I hadn't really noticed I'd been doing it. Like it was my body doing it without me realising, even though that whole time I knew I hadn't hurt it. But I couldn't say anything when everyone would get concerned, and I'd just tell myself I'd stop doing it, but then I'd be at training and somebody would point it out again anyway. It was like I couldn't control it.

'But,' Mum said, 'why?'

'I don't know.'

Dad said, in a voice much smaller than he usually used, 'Is it because of me?'

I couldn't really say anything. Then Mum said, covering her mouth with her hands, 'Oh. I think … I think maybe you did limp more after you'd been talking to or thinking about your father.'

Dad put his head in his hands.

'No!' I said, feeling awful. 'It's not … it's not that.'

'Then what is it?' Mum asked.

'It is that,' Dad said.

'It's everything,' I said.

'But when you fell today,' Mum said, leaning in, 'you looked like you were in so much pain! Your poor friends didn't know what to do. I had to text everyone's parents to tell them you weren't dying once we got to Emergency. You really didn't fall?'

'I mean, Bucky did knock me over,' I said. 'And I'm pretty sure I've got a bruise on my butt from it. But it didn't … it didn't hurt my ankle.'

'Then why did you scream? Homer, you frightened me so much.'

‘I could feel it all the way from Perth,’ Dad said, and his voice was all weird. ‘How Angela reacted, how she sounded – I’m surprised I even needed to get on a plane. I almost just flew here myself from stress.’

‘I’m sorry,’ I said.

For a moment, the house was so quiet it was like nobody had ever lived here. I picked up the wrapper for my burger and scrunched it into a ball and threw it from hand to hand.

‘I guess,’ I said, ‘I screamed because I was losing all these things that were important to me, like the jersey competition, and the shop—’

‘What competition?’ Dad said.

‘What shop?’ Mum asked.

‘Okay,’ I said, putting the wrapper down. ‘Let me explain.’

When I woke up the next morning, it was already eight o’clock. Usually by eight, Mum had yelled me awake and was making me do star jumps while she picked all the almonds out of my cereal, but all I could hear were quiet voices downstairs. I padded down to the kitchen and both of my parents were there, standing across the bench from each other with the faces of two people who’d definitely just been talking about me before I came downstairs.

‘Hey, kid,’ Dad said. ‘How are you feeling?’

‘Tired,’ I said.

‘Thought you might,’ Mum said. ‘Anyway, I better go finish getting ready for work.’

Dad said, ‘So, turns out, I’m actually staying a little longer. I have to go into the Melbourne office to fix up a few things, and

I'll have to fly out on Saturday to be back in Perth on Sunday so I can head in and make sure everything's sorted for the week, but I figured you could come to the office with me today.'

'Um,' I said, 'I know you've been away a while, but I still have school on Fridays?'

'Well, about that. Your mum and I thought maybe you could do with a day off to collect your thoughts.'

Until now I hadn't really thought about what I'd say when I went back to school. Like, when my friends asked about my ankle and I didn't have a cast, or a bandage, or anything. I mean, I generally didn't really think about what other people thought of me, but I still didn't want them to think of me as a liar, when I wasn't, not really. I was just a less-than-truth-er.

After Mum left, Dad made me the toast he used to when I was little, shaped like a football, with red jam and tiny slices of onion for the stitches. I never ate the onion, because ew, but I did today, as punishment for everything, and I even heroically kept the sputtering to a low choke. He ate an apple and watched me.

'What?'

'I just haven't seen your face in a while. I think you got older.'

'I saw you, like, three months ago.'

'That's a long time in kid years.'

'It felt like a long time,' I agreed. 'Are you going to get in trouble at work?'

'No,' he said. 'They're people too. They get that things come up, but I have to make it work out. That's why I'm going in today and returning for Sunday.'

'I'm sorry,' I said.

'You didn't ask for me to come,' he said. 'I decided to come.'

'But now you can't come when it's important. Like for my first game.'

'Maybe not,' Dad said, 'but I think maybe coming yesterday was important too. Also, if you're quitting, there won't be a first game for me to come to. Isn't that right?'

I licked the rest of the jam off my fingers. 'Oh. Yeah.'

'Mum says she's calling your therapist today to get you some new appointments.'

'Oh.'

'I guess we thought you were okay, but that was before the move and ... well, you can keep not being okay, and that's okay. What I mean by that is that it's normal. I had counselling when you were a baby.'

'Really?'

'Yeah. I was getting really short-tempered and cranky and taking it out on you and your mum, and it wasn't your fault, it was mine. I was tired, and you were little, and I wasn't very good at being a dad yet. Now, of course, I'm the best at being a dad.'

He meant it like a joke but then he looked at my face and said, 'I guess not, since I moved away.'

'You're still the best dad,' I said to him. 'It's not like I want another one.'

'Hmm. Is that a compliment? It's hard to tell.'

I was finding it hard to talk. Like there was something stuck in my chest and words couldn't get past it. If this is what Murphy felt like when she didn't talk, I should probably apologise to her for being a jerkjack about it for, like, six years.

'I love you,' I said.

He looked at me again, but differently. 'I love you too. So much that I had to move away. So much that I'll do anything to come back. And if you need me, I'll be there. Me living away from you is not fair, and not what any of us thought life would be. But if you think about everything in a different way, life is really good at the moment. I've got a job that means I'm finally going in the right direction to make me happy and us comfortable. Your mum's got a job she likes and now a second, lifelong-dream job in the sport our entire family is obsessed with.' He looked at me sadly. 'But I guess not you, if you're quitting. Anyway. She's happy, I'm on a good path, you've found your clothes thing, Mum says that girl in your class keeps looking at you for longer than other girls do—'

'Dad! What?'

'She says that you also look at her slightly too long too. She also told me not to say anything, but I can't keep quiet about this. It's nice!'

I stared at the floor and felt my whole body turn red.

'Yesterday, everything sucked for all of us. Today, things are better already. You're getting a day off school, I get to stay and watch Angela's game tonight, and your mum – well, she knows you're safe and not physically hurt, and we're aiming to help you feel better up here too.' He tapped his head. 'It's a good day.'

He wasn't wrong. While I got ready upstairs, I could see outside that it was warm but cloudy: good playing weather for Mum tonight. I thought about how distracted she might be because of what had happened yesterday, so I sent her a text: *I feel better today. Love you.*

I just had to hope that was enough.

ROUND 33 STATS

Kicks to the Heart: 2
Big Discussions Tackled: 4
Emotional Goals: 3

'You're going to love it at the office,' Dad said on the train into the city. 'One of the downstairs desks is free. You can do your schoolwork, read a book and play unlimited games of Solitaire.'

'Of what?'

'IN MY DAY,' Dad boomed, 'spending a whole day playing Solitaire on a computer would have been the absolute dream. You'd have been the envy of everyone you knew.'

'Is it like Call of Duty?'

'Yes. But if instead of war, there were cards. And instead of soldiers, there were cards. And instead of enemies—'

'I get it, I get it, the olden days were a time of horrible suffering. I'd argue that my childhood is worse, though. I mean, I have to listen to you say all this.'

'*Excuse* me?'

'Though I guess you have to listen to yourself as well?'

He raised his eyebrows. 'I could make you sit in the skip in the alley outside instead if you'd like?'

'I'll be good.'

Once we hit the city itself, I said, 'Why don't you leave me at Pa's shop?'

'No,' he said, straightening his tie in the reflection of the train door. 'I want to keep an eye on you. Make sure you, you know. Are okay.'

'I'm fine,' I said.

'Yes, obviously. I'm here because you're fine.'

We didn't talk much more until we got to Dad's office and he deposited me in an empty, boring room with a view of a brick wall and told me to do the schoolwork my teacher had sent and not to call him unless I was on fire or dead.

By about ten o'clock, once I'd dragged myself through the questions about fractions Skia had set, I considered setting myself on fire, which seemed like a slightly easier option than dying. By eleven, when I'd finished writing up how to make my favourite breakfast in exactly eight steps, which probably would have been easier if I'd picked something harder to explain than Coco Pops, I was actually finding the blank wall opposite interesting.

At midday Dad took me down to the café at the bottom of the building and bought me a salad roll that I ate looking out the window at everyone walking by. I hadn't been to the city since me and Mum had gone in December to look at the Christmas window decorations, and I'd been cranky because that was the first year we'd done it without Dad and she couldn't remember where the restaurant was where we'd usually go afterwards to get spearmint hot chocolates, and she'd thought that getting a different type of hot chocolate was acceptable when it obviously wasn't. I'd kind of hoped, without asking, that Dad would take me to the spearmint hot chocolate place for lunch, but he didn't even get anything to eat himself, and as soon as I'd smashed through the roll he took me back upstairs to my computer, nodded with a serious face over my fractions, scuffed my hair and then said he'd be back at five.

I wondered, after a while, whether I was supposed to be spending this time doing some Thinking About My Actions, and if that was why I'd been sent here and not to Pa's shop, where I could do something useful instead of sitting around. Or maybe Pa didn't want me there after I'd yelled at him. Even if it was his fault. A bit. Then I was mad because somehow I *had* started Thinking About My Actions. Instead, I decided to do something way more productive with my time and cut out some paper-people, and then made some clothes to put on them, but they kept tearing when I coloured them in so I got mad and then scrunched them all up in a ball and kicked it around the carpet for a while using two bins as goalposts. Then I got mad about playing footy and spent the last two hours becoming really good at Solitaire on the computer, which was, annoyingly, super fun after all.

It was half past five before Dad made it back to me. We went past a supermarket and stocked up on bread rolls and potato salad to eat at Mum's game, then headed to the train station fast to get out of the rain that had started to spatter all over us. We'd both been pretty quiet the whole time, but on the train we were surrounded by all these people in footy gear making friends with each other and slowly I could feel myself starting to get just a little, tiny bit happy.

At the game we set up just the two of us, right next to the fence, eating our rolls and sharing a litre bottle of orange juice. The rain started to get pretty full-on and Dad put up the giant umbrella he'd taken from his office's merch stash. 'The office should pay for our tickets for all the free advertising,' he said. 'This thing is enormous.'

'Didn't we get the tickets for free, though?'

'You're going to make a terrible businessperson someday with that attitude.'

When the siren blew and Dad started up his excited screaming/cheering, I started to feel all strange. I'd been to games before – like, hundreds of them – and I'd heard Dad yell before, and I'd usually join in like we were both wolves. But I couldn't speak or yell or howl or whatever it was we did. It was like the world was maths and the equation was wrong and the fractions didn't add up and I couldn't work out the answer. Like Mum Playing + Dad Here should = Great Game, but instead it felt like somebody was trying to convince my brain that 2 + 2 = Celery. I looked down at my ankle and thought maybe I'd been lying about it *not* hurting, because something was hurting right now but I couldn't figure out what it was or where it was or—

'ANGE! YES! YESSSSSS!'

Mum was running onto the field with her team. Dad was absolutely flipping out beside me, screaming her name and yelling everyone else's names and telling the other team that Mum, specifically, was going to take them down. Everyone else around us was yelling too, cheering their favourite players and ragging on the other team and laughing and filling up with excitement.

'Dad,' I said, looking at him closely, 'are you crying?'

'Am I *crying*?' he shouted, crying harder. 'Of course I am! That's my Angela, up there, where everyone can see how good she is! Do you know what this is like, Homer? When we were kids, girls couldn't even play football at all! Just, nothing!

There were no women's football games to watch on TV or see in person, and girls had to quit to play something else when they were teenagers! They deprived girls of this, and they deprived all of us of extra football for a hundred years! But now, look how great it is!' He wiped his eyes. 'Look how great *she* is.'

'I mean,' I said, watching Mum side-step on the grass, 'she's just warming up.'

'But she is the *best* at warming up,' Dad said, then sighed. 'Mate, I'm so glad I get to see this. She's worked so hard for it. We all have, even you.'

'Me? I'm not even playing anymore.'

'I know. But you're just a kid and now your mum's always at training and your dad's interstate and you've done such a great job being a good kid.'

'But my ankle?'

He put his arm around me. 'It's not like getting your feelings mixed up stops you from being good. It's one of the rules of being a kid. You have to get things wrong, otherwise how do you learn? Like me. I messed up at work last week – accidentally sent the wrong file to somebody in charge.'

'Are you going to get fired?'

'Fired? No way! Well, I did think I was for a few hours. But it just meant I had to apologise, and send the right file. My colleague told me to rename files when they weren't in use anymore so I didn't do it again, and then he told me about the time he deleted the file he'd been working on for a week and was due the next day.'

'Was *he* fired?'

'Nope. *His* colleague showed him how to back up all his work, then told him about the time he left the front door of the building unlocked and somebody broke in and stole all their fake plants.'

'Sounds like you work with a lot of people who aren't very good at their jobs?'

'You are learning the wrong lesson here, squirt.'

The rain was pummelling down now. 'My jeans are getting wet!' I whined.

'Du bist doch nicht aus Zucker,' he said, shuffling up closer with the umbrella. Telling me I wasn't made of sugar was one of his favourite things to do and I hated it, but right now, hearing it for the first time in months, I wished he was here to annoy me way, way more often.

The siren blew again, and suddenly it was on.

Mum lived for rainy weather. Watching her in it today was like watching some kind of overexcited puppy. She was all over the ground, darting around like she was ready to take anyone on. She got covered in mud and whenever she grabbed the ball the water that had soaked into it flew up and slapped her square in the face. Nobody could keep a hold of the ball – it was too slippery to catch properly – but she leaped around and attempted to take marks and got lost in squelchy piles of players and when she came out she'd be laughing.

Dad whispered, 'She's amazing. Seeing this in person is something else.'

In the second quarter, everyone's slippery fingers cost Mum's team two goals and she stopped laughing. They were down by ten points and she had her serious face on now, sliding desperately after the ball to touch it before it went over the boundary after a kick, and when she lined up for a goal she slammed the ball right into the post for a point instead. Dad was yelling, 'ANGE! YOU GOT THIS! DESTROY THEM!' and slapping the fence every time she came within 75 metres of us.

When she flew up for a mark off the shoulders of Big Haitch – the most jacked person on ground, probably including the entire audience – everyone went wild. Some complete strangers beside me started screaming 'AN-GE-LA! AN-GE-LA!' and Dad joined in until his voice went croaky. There were all these people yelling for Mum and she kicked the ball from halfway down the field all the way to the goal square and then Polly bolted after it and managed to get a boot to it and steer it through for a goal and they'd done it, they'd nearly caught up.

Dad had to lean over and put his hands on his knees to catch his breath back. 'How do you do this excitement every week?'

I shrugged and looked away.

'Homer, I'll be here as much as I can. And this isn't your mum's only season, so maybe I can be there for one of them.'

'Yeah.'

'And in the meantime we still get to call and talk, right? This isn't the olden days where we had to write letters and wait for weeks to hear anything.'

'But you're so far away and in the wrong time zone,' I said.

'I know.' He sighed. 'I don't really have all the answers for this. We're trying to make a bad thing work as well as it can. I just don't want you to think you have to be one hundred per cent in charge of your own happiness. You're still a kid. Your Mum and I have work to do too. I'll be better at calling and … you know. At listening, too, maybe.'

'Maybe?'

'Well, it's hard! And I've been to your parent-teacher meetings, so I know this is something you struggle with too. I see it in you like I see it in myself. Like, you talk about your fashion stuff and I'm happy for you, but I don't know what to say, so I guess I change the subject to what I can talk about. And I don't want to talk too much about my new life and all the things I'm liking about Perth because I don't want you to think I prefer my life there to the one I have with you. So I guess I just talk about what's safe, and that's football, really.'

'I don't want you to be sad in Perth, though,' I said. 'You can tell me some other things about your life. I'll pretend to be happy for you.'

He laughed. 'And I'll pretend to understand when you talk about thread density and sleeve types.'

I went back to watching the game. Something felt like it was opening up in my brain. Dad wanted to talk about other things but couldn't. I wanted to talk about other things, but he hadn't heard. He wasn't a good listener, but I *was* a good listener. Just not in class, when Skia was trying to teach me something I didn't care about.

But it was probably just a class thing.

Probably.

Stephanie, the half-back, was doing one of her famous fast sprints while bouncing, and Mum was near the goals, yelling for the ball. Steph booted the ball towards her, so hard and far that water spun off it like a firework. Mum took a second to judge, then ran at Big Haitch's back again and leapt up for it, then grabbed. The football slipped out of her outstretched hands and into her face, and then she fell backwards off Haitch, and was for a moment falling through the air like a raindrop before smacking hard into the ground.

She'd landed on her bad arm, the one that had kept her out

of the first few games. My heart flew into my throat while she lay there, and all I could think was that if she'd hurt it again she'd be sidelined for the rest of the season and then what if nobody drafted her next year and—

'Mum!' I screamed, grabbing at Dad and pulling him away. 'We gotta go over there and—'

'And what? She's all right. She's already up.'

I turned back around, and he was right. It was just a normal fall. She was standing now, helped up by Big Haitch, no less, rolling her shoulder, wincing a little. She knew how to fall – had trained for years for things like this – and she was fine. But for just a second, I'd felt a rush of panic, and I properly realised what I'd been doing to everyone in my family for the last few weeks.

'Dad?' I asked. 'Can we go find Nanna and Pa?'

'Is it just because you want the snacks they have?'

'Like twenty per cent for snacks,' I said. 'And eighty per cent because I have to tell them I'm sorry.'

'For not listening?'

'For being a pain in the butt.'

ROUND 34 STATS

Apologies to Make: 5
Chances That Jumping the Fence and Running Across the Field Will Distract Everyone Enough to Forget I Need to Apologise Instead: 20%

We went around the edge of the grounds, showing our lanyards to the security guards and explaining who we were. Eventually we found Nanna and Pa with their feet up on the cooler in front of them.

Nanna got up and gave Dad a hug. 'Timo! Good to see you again. Enjoying the game?'

'I can't believe you get to do this almost every week,' Dad said. 'How do your voices survive all the cheering?'

'I bring hot water with lemon and honey,' Nanna said, holding up her thermos.

'Um,' I said to Nanna and Pa, 'when Mum fell just now – was that what it was like when you saw me with my not-actually-sore sore foot?'

'Yes,' Pa said. 'It was exactly like that.'

He was standing up, patting Dad on the back, smiling at me with his big wrinkled face that always was there and I said to him,

'I'm sorry I yelled at you. It wasn't your fault that I got in trouble for messing up all the shirts. It was mine.'

'Look,' he said, 'you were right about one thing. We probably should've thought about it not being okay with your school. I didn't even think about it for a moment, because I was excited about doing all this tailoring with you.'

'He really was,' Nanna put in. 'He was coming up with all these ideas for you to add to your school shirts, but I told him he had to let you do it.'

'What kind of ideas?' I said.

'Making a pocket from mesh,' he said. 'So you could fill it with tea and dip it straight into a cup of boiling water.'

'How much boiling water do you think they have around primary school-aged kids, Pa?'

'That's what *I* said,' Nanna said. 'Then I thought maybe we needed to speak to your teacher about having a kettle in the classroom for tea emergencies.'

'I'm sure Zara would help me campaign for it,' I said, then remembered all my friends were probably super mad at me right now for lying about my ankle. Or maybe even slightly madder at me for yelling at them. Possibly.

The siren rang out for half-time. 'Are you fellas heading back to your wet side of the oval now?' Nanna asked.

Pa nodded over my shoulder. 'It looks like you have more incentive to stay here.'

I turned around and saw Mario and Ng weaving their way through the seats. 'You guys!' I yelled, while Dad made a little noise of excitement and ran over to slap Mario's dad on the back. 'Why are you here? I thought you were mad at me.'

They looked at each other. 'Since when do we come to

the footy for you, ya goof?' Mario said. 'We come because it's football.'

'And to support your Mum,' Ng said.

'And because my Dad lets me buy hot chips,' Mario added.

'And because it's the only time my parents let me stay up after ten,' Ng finished.

'Is your Mum's shoulder okay?' Mario asked.

'I don't know. I think so.'

'Why are you here, anyway?' Mario asked. 'Tom said you were having today off to get your leg amputated.'

'What? No! That is not happening. And Tom hasn't even messaged me or anything so how would he know what was going on?'

'Have you *met* Tom?' Mario asked.

'Henry said he'd heard from Pilar who heard from her mum who heard from your mum that you were okay, though,' Ng said. 'I tried to listen to what he said instead of Tom.'

'Yeah, you don't even have a cast or anything!' Mario said. 'You must have had a really great surgeon.'

'No surgeon,' I said. 'Not even any doctors.' I looked down. 'I'm sorry if I scared you yesterday. I wasn't … I wasn't really hurt.'

They both stared at me.

'Like, I wasn't hurt yesterday, or before that either. I just …' I wiped some rain off my face. 'It was just … there was some stuff going on and it seemed easy to just … fall over, I guess. Hien banned the shop.'

'I heard,' Mario said. 'That sucks.'

'I heard you quit footy,' Ng said.

'Yeah.'

'Why? You love footy!' Mario said.

'And you're good at it.' Ng said.

'And you have heaps of footy cards,' Mario said.

'And everyone on the team likes you,' Ng said.

'And you were the one who always wanted to play it at lunch since, like, prep,' Mario finished.

I kicked hard at the ground, not even caring about how much mud I got on my shoes. 'I know. I just can't at the moment.'

'Is it because of your dad?' Ng said. 'Like, because you and your dad always practised together and now he's never here and you're mad about it?'

I looked up, staring at him. 'What?'

'You know. Like when your mum worked weekends for ages and so it was only your dad taking you to footy games. So when you think of footy, you think of him, and now he's not here, so you're like, "wahh, footy is all empty and stupid," or something, I don't know.'

Mario was staring at him too. 'Whoa. Are you a counsellor or something? That was really deep.'

'It was,' I said. My brain was ticking, hard. 'I don't know. I mean, maybe you're right?'

'You know it,' Ng said. 'I'm literally the best.'

I remembered sitting in Mario's backyard and not helping him pull up potatoes even though he loved gardening and he'd just let me sit there doing my own thing for, like, an hour beforehand. I had barely even seen Ng and usually I was over at his house annoying him all the time while he tried to play video games, or making him come over and annoy me while he talked about video games. And the other day, he'd asked to play video games and I'd picked a fight about it until neither of us got to do the thing we wanted.

And I remembered how I said that they only cared about footy and nothing else, when actually they cared about growing food and video games.

And. Also.

They cared about me too.

You can't just say things like 'thanks for caring about me' out loud though because it makes it sound like you're in one of those romance mangas that K. always reads in class, so I said, 'I'm sorry. I think that I kind of got bad at … being me.'

'Look,' Ng said, 'I didn't want to say. But if I was Skia, and I was marking you on how much of a Homer you were, I'd have given you, like, twenty per cent.'

'Fair enough,' I said. 'I reckon you're right about the Dad thing, Ng. And I think it messed me up in other ways. Like, I was trying to make money so I could go see Dad, but because of that I spent all my time just freaking out about that and not any time, like … enjoying the things? Like hanging out with you guys and doing stuff that wasn't drawing terrible ducks and terrible shirts. I wasn't even happy most of the time either. I like to make clothes, but when I had to frantically fix them all just so I could see Dad it stopped being as much fun. I wasn't *making* anything, just fixing things.' This was a lot of talking and not a lot of doing, so I jumped up and down a few times. 'I'll be a better friend. Like, award-winning. Best on Ground at being a pal. An Oscar for Paying Attention to Your Buddies. King of—'

'Yeah, jeez, okay, we get it,' Mario said. 'Like, you sucked, but also I knew you were all tied up in your brain and all this other stuff was going on.'

'It was like you became a grown-up suddenly,' Ng said.

'You were all, "No, kids, I can't hang out with you, I have to go to work to make money!" It was a real bummer.'

'What are you going to do now, though?' Mario said. 'About seeing your dad more?'

'I don't know,' I told him. 'I guess I just have to save my pocket money and stop spending it on Dope Ropes all the time and just eat some of yours instead.'

'That sucks,' Ng said. 'Especially because neither of us are going to share.'

'Sorry,' Mario said to me, 'but he's right.'

I kicked them in the shins, but gently, mostly because I was pretty sure they'd give me, like, a centimetre of Rope if I asked. And if I stopped being a jerkjack for a bit.

The siren was going off again for the end of half-time, and I went back to stand with Nanna, Pa and Dad. They were all staring at me seriously.

'What? Is it Mum?'

'Not Mum,' Pa said. 'I have a business proposition for you.'

'Huh?'

'We've been shutting the shop early to come help you out after school, but really, I can bring my work home as much as I want. I thought perhaps you could help me out some afternoons when your Mum's at training? There's a lot of little work that needs to be done, and I could do with someone to help me.'

'Me? Help out? Like making clothes for you?' I could hear my voice going all high with excitement.

'All right there, you might want to lower those expectations a little. I mean tasks like re-threading bobbins, sorting threads, preparing supplies, double-measuring for me, those kinds of things. And you can practise hemming on spare bolts of material, so maybe we can see how you go at some point. Of course, I would pay you.'

'You'd pay me?'

He nodded. 'Not a lot, mind. We're talking a couple of hours here and there. Ten dollars a week, maybe. Possibly twenty.'

It was a lot and not much. A month ago, I'd only been earning four dollars a week in pocket money, and spending four of those dollars on Dope Ropes. A week ago, I'd had hundreds of dollars coming my way. Two minutes ago, I'd had nothing. And now, maybe, I'd have twenty-four dollars a week that nobody could take away from me.

Halfway through next term, I'd have enough for a plane ticket. Or for my LaFontaines. I'd definitely have enough for some Dope Ropes to share with Mario and Ng.

The siren blew again. Everyone came running out of the change rooms. And at the front of the pack was Mum, her shoulder taped up, completely fine.

Just like I'd be. Hopefully.

'Okay,' I said. 'Yes please.'

ROUND 35 STATS

Goals: 6
Life Goals: 1
Current Apology Success Rate: 100%

They lost by three points.

It was a good game, though, and Mum went back on in the last quarter and smothered two goal kicks, so really it could've been way worse. The rain didn't let up the whole time and my shoes were like tiny bathtubs strapped to my feet.

On the way to Nanna and Pa's car, Pa nudged me and said, 'Isn't that your friend over there?'

I looked around and saw Thi and her family walking through the carpark in matching yellow raincoats and gumboots. Everything had gone really well with saying sorry to Nanna and Pa and Mario and Ng, and Thi was way nicer than all of them, so I straightened my raincoat and said, 'I'll be back in a second.'

I sloshed through the car park and hollered, 'Thi! Thi!'

She turned around and saw me, then sighed, said something to her parents and hung back. 'What?' she said as I ran up. 'It's wet. I want to get into the car.'

'I know, I know. I just wanted to say I'm sorry.'

'Okay,' she said. 'Great.' Then she turned back and started walking.

'Wait!' I yelled. 'I haven't … I didn't get to say everything I wanted to say.'

'All right then,' she said. 'What did you want to say?'

'I shouldn't have acted like I did,' I said. 'It wasn't your fault. I was mad.'

'Okay.'

She had her arms crossed and she wasn't smiling. Somehow it didn't feel like it really was okay, even if she was saying it was. This was way harder than I thought.

'And my ankle wasn't really hurt, in case you were concerned.'

'I wasn't,' she said. 'See you at school.'

She turned away, and this time I didn't call her back. I just watched her walk off in the rain.

I moped the whole drive home. How come Thi, who'd always been so nice, had been the least nice? She hadn't even been concerned about my ankle. How come sorry wasn't enough even though I really meant it? What could I do to make it right? I'd always been a man of action. But I couldn't really kick my way out of this one, even if I tried really hard to figure out a way that I could.

When I woke up the next morning, it was obvious. If I couldn't talk my way out of this, I had to find another thing I was good at. I had to make her something to wear.

Mum and Dad were down in the kitchen, talking tactics for next week's game. 'You've seen Alice and Estelle, those sisters, and how they just hone in on someone,' Dad was saying to her. 'What are you going to do if they choose you?'

'Weave,' Mum said. 'Isla's been watching their technique and said they're bad at changing direction. I'm just going to dart around. I'll practise darting through the house and avoiding Homer.'

'I can hear you,' I said, coming up behind her.

'No, you can't!' she shrieked, leaping up and rushing off into the lounge.

'I'm heading off soon,' Dad said. 'The cheapest flight today is at midday. Mum says you guys will drive me to the airport.'

I got ready and we bundled into the car. On the way in, Mum said, 'So we were thinking that maybe you need to really visualise the amount we're saving for you two to see each other. So we'll open a bank account and deposit money in each week towards it so you can see that amount going up, okay? We're both going to put twenty dollars a week in, no matter what, and more if we can. Like, if my son asks me for less snacks at the supermarket, for example.'

'Would that make you feel better?' Dad asked.

'Actually,' I said, 'yeah. Can I put money in too?'

'Sure,' Mum said. 'But nobody expects you to, okay?'

I did feel better after that. Even while we watched the plane take off, and I got all choked up, it still didn't make me feel like this was forever. It'd be fine.

If I needed him, he'd be there. Just like he'd been on Thursday.

When we got home, I went into the garage and pulled out

the old dressmaker dummy that Pa had given me after he'd got a nicer one and took it into my room. I changed its measurements so that it was Thi-sized, and then searched through the material drawer to see if we had anything right. When I imagined Thi, it was hard to think of what she liked, since I only ever saw her in school uniform or footy jerseys.

Which meant that she liked comfortable fabrics. Ones that breathed. And short sleeves, too, since even in winter she wore t-shirts as much as she could.

I found this fabric I'd picked up once from Pa's shop floor. It was blue-and-white, her team colours, and all washy, like water. It was light, like a jersey.

I could do this.

QUALIFIYING FINAL

On Monday, I got in to school early, hoping to catch Thi before class started. She wasn't at the oval kicking with anyone, or at the stumps, which were empty. Maybe she was late. I guessed I could give it to her later.

Then I remembered what I'd spent days trying to push out of my mind: the jersey competition.

The library.

She was sitting at a desk there, under the air-conditioning, surrounded by pencils. When I sat opposite her, she looked up for a moment then back down again.

'Hi,' she said.

'Thi, I'm sorry,' I said. 'I really am. I had … there was stuff. I needed all that money to go visit my dad because I miss him. But then suddenly I couldn't win the jersey competition, and it was okay because I could make money off the shirts, but then Hien shut that down and all my ways to get money were suddenly gone, and I was mad. Madder than mad.' I took a breath. 'It wasn't you, it was me, but you were there, and I took it out on you. Anyway, I made you something.'

I took the brown paper package from under my arm and gave it to her.

She put her hand on it but didn't look up. 'You weren't going to win the jersey competition anyway.'

'What?'

'I'm going to win it,' she said. 'I need a football club membership so I can go to more games. I was always going to win it.'

She looked up at me, but she was smiling a little bit.

'You're not the only person who can draw,' she said.

She held up the picture she was working on. It was yellow and black and had a white cockatoo in the middle of the chest with wings stretching all the way up into the sleeves, like it could make anyone wearing it fly.

'Whoa,' I said, amazed. 'That is *great*.'

'Yep,' she said, putting it back down.

'It's okay that you're mad,' I said. And even though I didn't mean it, I said, 'And it's okay that you didn't care about my ankle being hurt.'

'Homer,' she said, sighing. 'I said I wasn't *concerned* about you. And I wasn't. I knew your ankle wasn't really hurt all along.'

I blinked at her. 'What?'

'When you were in PE you fell on your other foot.'

I stared. 'I did?'

'Yep.'

I sat back. She carefully started untying the ribbon on her parcel.

'Why didn't you say anything?'

She shrugged. 'I don't know. I guess I thought you had a reason for it.'

'I kind of did.'

'I heard you quit the team.'

'Yeah.'

She got through the paper and to the shirt. She gave a very quiet squeal and then lifted it up.

'Homer, what *is* this?'

'So, it's a t-shirt,' I said. 'I know I was adding a lot of things to everyone's shirts, but I didn't think yours really needed it. You kind of have everything under control already.' I pointed at the pocket. 'This is the exact right size for footy cards, though. And if you want, when you get your jersey numbers, I'll sew them on the back for you.'

She didn't say anything, but turned the whole thing inside out and started examining it up close.

'What are you doing?' I said nervously.

'Searching,' she said, then found what she was looking for and tore at the thread with her teeth.

'I didn't really mean for you—'

'May every kick be a goal,' she read out loud, showing me the not-curse I'd sewn into it.

'Yeah,' I said, feeling weird. Mario and Ng hadn't found their curses yet, and they probably never would. At the end of the year, they'd give their shirts to the uniform shop, and then some other kid would wear them instead until they graduated, and they wouldn't notice either. Maybe that was the point.

Thi disappeared into the bathroom and then reappeared a second later, wearing it. She held out her arms, then turned around, then sighed.

'Homer,' she said. 'It's like … it fits perfectly. It's the most comfortable thing ever.' She stretched her arms up. 'It doesn't pull. It's like wearing a soft cloud.' She looked at me. 'You are good at this.'

'I had your measurements,' I said. 'It was easy.'

'I don't think it was,' she said.

The bell rang, and she stuffed her school shirt in her bag and headed off.

'Aren't you going to change back?' I asked. 'You'll get in trouble.'

'Good,' she said. 'All these years and until last week I've never been in Hien's office. Why stop at just once?'

The bell rang, and she smiled, and I did too.

SEMIFINAL

Hien's office was hotter than usual. I mean, I couldn't think of any other reason I'd be sweating.

Hien was pretty good, for a principal. Aaron and Jerome from my team told me that their principal always picks students in the middle of assembly and asks them hard maths questions to show what they're learning, but then the kids always get too nervous to give the right answer, and once a kid just burst into tears instead. Bucky swears that *his* principal once ate a cockroach he'd picked up off the ground, but Bucky also said he beat his PE teacher in a fight once and we didn't believe that either. Anyway, what I'm saying is that Hien doesn't do those things and doesn't even give me as many detentions as I deserve.

But I'd never had to say sorry to her before. Or, at least, not when I meant it.

It was recess, and I had a sandwich bag full of all the money I needed to pay back. I'd had to take some out of the Christmas money I'd been given towards orange-and-silver LaFontaines, and the whole amount was there. I handed it over to her, along with the rest of the unfixed shirts, and said, 'So the other day, I didn't speak to you … good.'

Maybe I should've actually practised what I was going to say. I went on, 'I mean. I need to apologise.'

'You sure do,' she said.

'Wasn't that my apology?'

She gave me a hard stare.

Not the time for a joke, then. 'I'm sorry I was rude,' I said. 'I was mad, but that's not an excuse. I shouldn't have spoken to you like that. And you were right that there are rules about uniforms, and I get it. Having those extra things that could maybe hurt someone when we're doing sport … it makes sense that you don't want that.'

'I'm glad to hear it, Homer. Thank you. And thank you for paying the money back so promptly.'

'I don't want you to worry about me needing the money either. I'm not … we don't *need* it. I was just saving because I missed my Dad and wanted to see him.'

'I guessed it was something like that,' she said. 'Which is why I didn't give you seven detentions for shouting at me last week.'

I nodded and went to the door. 'I really do have something to say about the PE shirts, though. Can I make, like, an appointment so I can talk to you about it?'

She looked around. 'I really appreciate that you're separating your apology from your excuse. However, I am free now, and I accept your apology. What's up?'

'The shirts really are uncomfortable,' I said. 'I don't think it's fair to make students wear a shirt that makes it harder to do sports than our normal school clothes.'

'They're genuinely more uncomfortable than your normal uniform?'

I nodded.

'Hmm.' She wrote something down on a piece of paper in front of her. 'You're not the only person who thinks that?'

'No way. Ask anyone.'

'I might very well do that. Well, Homer, since you've always got a lot to say: what should I do about it?'

'Oh. Uh.' I stopped for a moment and thought while she waited with that Patient Hien-face she always had. 'I would fix the shirts. I mean, that's what I was doing.'

'I think you'll understand if we don't hire a student to do the fixing, though.'

'My grandpa could do it,' I said. 'He's a professional tailor.'

'Noted,' she said, but she didn't actually note anything down. 'Any other ideas?'

I shrugged.

'Hmm. I think I'm going to speak to the uniform supplier about it, and then have a chat with the senior teaching team. Does your teacher know how you all feel about the shirts?'

'Oh yeah, Mr Skia tells us off for whining about it all the time.'

'Interesting,' she said. 'And Miss Honeybone?'

'She says they don't stop the Olympics for a bad shirt.'

'Well, she's probably not wrong.' She stood up. 'Okay, then. Well, thank you for sharing that information with me, Homer. And maybe next time something like this happens, you could consider sharing it with me before you go defacing every single PE shirt in the school?'

'Sorry, Hien.'

'Thank you. You can go back to class now. And Homer?'

'Yeah?'

'You did a good job on those shirts.'

I went back to Ng's house after school while Mum was at training. We played Lego Hot Wheels Ponies with his little brother and sister, and it kind of felt normal, and nice, and like there was nothing else in my head. I stayed for dinner, and afterwards we played video games until Mum came to get me. I'd been so busy these past few weeks it was like I'd forgotten how to be a person. How you went to school, then hung out with your friends, and just, like, lived.

On Tuesday, instead of going to footy training, Mum took me to a basketball court and we shot some hoops. On Wednesday, I went to Mario's house and helped him dry out some tomato seeds. On Thursday, Mum and I rode our bikes all along the creek and stopped at the taco truck on the way back and got all messy from the salsa.

While she wiped her hands on a tree, she said, 'How are you feeling?'

'Sticky.'

'I don't mean your hands,' she said. 'I mean in your brains. How's it going up there?'

I looked around. The clouds were streaking the sky in long thin lines, like the corduroy pants that were Nanna's favourite kind to wear. It had been an okay day at school. I'd hung out with K. and Ava for a bit, and stopped by to sign one of Zara's petitions. (When I'd apologised to her on Monday, she'd said she would only forgive me if I signed every single petition for a year, which also meant the one she wrote on Wednesday called 'Petition to Stop Homer From Existing' after I accidentally stepped on Avery's sandwich.) At lunch, I'd played handball with Mario and Ng and we'd tried and failed to come up with evil plans for The Bad Corner.

'I'm okay, Mum,' I said.

'Hmm,' she said, watching me closely.

'I mean it.'

'You said you were okay a lot when you weren't before, though.'

'I know.'

'Why didn't you say anything to me about how you were feeling?'

I looked up at her. She was wearing the t-shirt Pa had made her last year, and her hair was out and wild.

'You had a lot on,' I said. 'And it wasn't like you could help.'

'What do you mean?'

'Like, you can't sew. No offence.'

'Is that a thing that mums have to do to be helpful?'

'I mean, it was with this.'

'But mums who can't sew can be helpful in other ways, right? Like, we can listen. And help you understand things.'

'We've already talked about you guys splitting up *so much*, though. There was so much talking. So …' I fell to the ground, '… much …' I held my hand up to the sky, '… talking.' I fell limp, my tongue rolling out the side of my mouth, definitely dead.

'All right, you're not wrong,' she said, laughing. 'There really was a lot of talking, wasn't there. I guess sometimes you've got to solve things by talking about them instead of kicking a football at them. And Homer, this was one of those times. No, I couldn't sew a shirt for you. But I probably could've helped in other ways. At the very least, if you'd talked to me about the jersey competition instead of running off to your room and ignoring me, I could've saved you some of the brain space you used up working on that. And maybe I would've remembered the rule about not being able to embellish your school shirts if you'd spoken about it more with me.'

'You're telling me you've read the school handbook?'

'Well, hmm. Once, probably, when you were in prep. Maybe. The point,' she said, yanking me off the ground, 'is that I could've tried to work out more times for you to talk to your dad if I'd known you were getting so messed up about it. Though I guess I should've just known without you having to point it out.' She sighed. 'Mate, it's hard.'

'I didn't want to add to all your football stuff. You were busy changing the world. And that's important.'

'It is,' she said, 'you're right. But you're important too. And I promise I have room in this brain for football *and* making sure my kid feels okay, just like you have room in your brain for making clothes *and* eating tacos. So,' she said, stretching out, '*are* you okay?'

'I miss Dad,' I said.

'I know. I'm sorry.'

'But I feel better after seeing him the other day.'

'Good. And there will be more times. We're working towards it, both of us. I promise.'

'Then I am okay,' I said.

'You're better than okay,' she said. 'You're the best.'

On Friday, I went to watch Mum train.

While I sat on the sidelines eating pasta salad out of a plastic container in my lap, I kept getting distracted by two kids nearby who just absolutely could not kick. They'd drop the ball, stare at it on the ground, kick it, then cheer themselves. It was cute, but it was also totally unbearable.

When they accidentally kicked it to me, I picked it up ready to handball back. It was a full-size ball they could barely lift, and as I held it in my hands I was surprised at how it felt, well, good.

'Hey, pals,' I said, getting off my camping chair. 'You know, it works a bit better if you start kicking while you're dropping it, like this.' I kicked the ball to one of them, very gently, and they ran forward and immediately fell face-first onto it.

'Good luck,' the grown-up behind them called out. 'I've been trying to show them for ages.'

'It's hard,' the smaller kid complained.

'And boring,' the bigger one said, but quietly.

'Why boring?'

The big one pointed at the goals. 'If they wanted to get the balls through the posts so quick, why don't they get on a bike?'

'That's a good question,' I said. 'I guess it's because you can't kick when you're on a bike. And the feeling you get when you make a really great kick … it's like nothing else.'

'The best feeling is jam,' the small kid said.

'It's even better than jam.'

'Nope.'

'Here, I'll show you.'

I helped them practise, first without the ball, miming dropping and kicking at the same time. The smaller one fell over about every five times. The bigger one concentrated, hard. I added the ball back into the mix, and the little one just looked at it, threw their arms up in the air and went off to get snacks. The bigger one had a go, missed, and said, 'Jam is way better.'

'Just wait.'

We kept practising. After a while, Mum jogged up and draped her arms over the fence.

'You got a future player there, huh?'

'I reckon,' I said. 'Good determination.'

'Nobody got good by giving up,' she said, and headed off.

When I turned back to the kid, they were staring. 'Do you know her?'

'Yeah, that's my mum.'

'Your *mum* is a player?'

'Yep.'

'Are you?'

'Nah.'

'But you're good.'

'Sometimes.'

'Show me.'

They passed the ball to me, and I held it in my hands, spun it, then kicked it over. They ran over to the ball, picked it up, then tried to do the spin, and dropped it. 'That's hard!'

'Oh, that's not important. You don't have to do that.'

'Then why do you do it?'

'I don't know,' I said, looking at my hands.

'It's because his mama does it,' the other kid said, pointing.

I turned to see Mum out there on the ground, lining up for a goal. She spun the ball forwards, then backwards, took four big strides, then four smaller steps, and booted it square through the goalposts.

Spin forward, spin back, walk four, jog four.

I hadn't realised until just then, but I did exactly the same thing. Before a goal, when I had time, I'd spin it just like she did. I'd take the same amount of steps. I didn't even realise I *had* an amount of steps until just then, but it had sunk in, that way she had when her confidence was high and her focus was needle-sharp. The way I'd starting doing it too, after Dad moved away, when it was only me and Mum and football and each other.

'It's true,' I said to the bigger kid. 'I do it just like her. Because she's a champion.'

'Can you show me?'

We practised. Forward, backward. Over and over, until they got it, with a big beam on their face.

'Amazing,' I said. 'Now try to kick again.'

They held the ball in front of them, dropped it, and kicked out. The ball was too big for their little foot, but they connected anyway, made a satisfying *whump* noise and watched the ball roll a solid twenty centimetres away. 'I did it!' they yelled.

'You sure did,' I said, beaming back.

'I'm the best,' they whispered, then aloud. 'You're good too, mister.' They looked up, eyes shining. 'You should be a player. That really did feel better than jam.'

PRELIMINARY FINAL

When I headed into school on Monday, wearing a pair of shorts I'd made out of blue scraps over the weekend, K. was waiting at The Bad Corner with Mario.

'Sorry about your mum not playing on the weekend,' they said when I pulled up on my bike.

'It's all good. Her shoulder was a bit sore after the last game, so they thought they'd give her an extra week of physio to make sure she was okay. She was super mad that they won without her, though.'

'If she'd been on the ground, they would've won by *too* much,' Mario said encouragingly. 'She's just making sure the losing team wasn't, like, completely humiliated.'

'Why are you at The Bad Corner anyway?' I asked K. 'You're only allowed here if you're willing to get up to huge trouble.'

'Like what?'

Me and Mario looked at each other.

'That's not the point,' Mario said. 'You just have to be totally up for it if it happens.'

'Then sure,' K. said. 'But I'm actually here because I think something's up at school. I was walking past the office and I saw Hien talking to some real fancy guy and I swear I heard them say your name, Homer.'

I started to sweat.

'Not in an angry way,' K. said, holding out their hands. 'Just in, like, a way.'

I looked nervously over at the school. Maybe I was in trouble? I'd been pretty good last week, at least if you didn't count when I kept sneaking Thi's erasers in Mr Skia's jacket pockets and yelling 'Thief!' every time he reached into one for a whiteboard marker and came out with an eraser instead.

Unless, of course, I was getting some kind of historical punishment for other things I'd done and gotten away with, like when I put the hand sanitiser label on the clear glue, or when I replaced Mr Skia's picture of his kids on his desk with a picture of border collies in hats and it took him five days to notice.

In class, after Skia took the roll, he said, 'Homer, you've got a meeting with Hien at nine-thirty, okay?'

The whole class gasped.

'What did you do?' Thi whispered.

'Nothing! I'm innocent! Make sure you tell everybody I said that after I'm arrested.'

At half past nine, I headed to Hien's office. Like K. said, there was somebody else in there with her, and K. was also right that the dude was fancy. He was wearing a really sharp brown suit with a moss green-and-white tie that was the same colour as both the lining of his vest and his pocket square – something I'd never seen on anyone who wasn't Pa or a footballer at an awards ceremony – and he even had a watch chain.

'Homer,' Hien said cheerfully, 'this is Fergus Samms. He's part of the company that makes the school uniforms.'

'Er, hi,' I said. He reached out to shake my hand and in a slight panic I shook his hand super hard back. Fergus laughed.

'I see why you're the one they turn to for sports advice,' he said. 'Nearly took my arm off there, you did.'

'Homer,' Hien said, 'Fergus is here because I contacted his company about the PE shirts. You were right,' she went on, raising her eyebrows. 'They did not fit correctly.'

'It was a batch problem,' Fergus said. 'Complete error on our behalf. We're resupplying your school with new shirts. They'll be ready in a couple of weeks.'

I gaped. 'We're getting new shirts?'

'You sure are! Thank you for bringing it to our attention. I also heard that you first attempted to take it upon yourself to solve the problem.' Fergus grinned. 'That's an entrepreneurial spirit if I ever saw one. I did also hear that you took it maybe a wee bit too far.'

I coughed.

'Even so, I was wondering if you could perhaps talk me through the fixes you made, maybe give me some advice for what you'd do to improve the shirts beyond just the shoulders?'

'But no bells,' Hien said.

'No bells,' Fergus agreed. 'Hien here – by the way, I can't believe you're allowed to call your principal by their first name, it would've been my neck if I'd dared say my principal's first name – says that we can have a corner of the staffroom for half an hour to talk about it? If that's okay with you?'

I turned and stared at Hien.

'Fergus, I'd just like to say that I've never actually seen him speechless before,' Hien said. 'I think it's a yes, but I'd like to know for sure.'

'Yes please,' I said, in my Polite Young Man voice.

'Grand,' he said. 'And don't be afraid to tell me everything I got wrong. I can take it on the chin. Not literally, though.' He looked me up and down. 'I'm pretty sure you could beat me in a fight.'

'You really want my opinion?' I said, finally getting some more interesting words out.

'I know the opinion of every adult in my company on these shirts,' he said. 'Probably about time I reminded myself what the kids who actually wear them think of them too. So, little man,' he went on, gathering a pen and a paper. 'Shoot.'

GRAND FINAL

On Wednesday, I went to Mum's training. Thi was there too, kicking a football repeatedly to herself and doing all the training things the team was doing while I sat on my butt with a needle and thread.

'What've you got there?' Thi said, jogging on the spot.

I held up the shorts I was making.

'Teenage Mutant Ninja Turtles?'

'They're for my Dad,' I said. 'He said he always wanted Ninja Turtle shorts when he was a kid and he never got any, so he asked me to make him some.'

'Radical,' she said, falling to the ground and doing some push-ups.

'You played footy all recess and lunch today,' I told her. 'Don't you want to sit down and, you know, chill out?'

'Nope,' she said. 'I'm too buzzed.'

'Why?'

'NOTHING,' she said, too loudly.

I stared at her.

'I can't say,' she wailed. 'I'm just excited, okay?'

I put out my hands. 'All right, jeez. Just don't sprain any of your muscles from overuse.'

'Oh my god,' she said, sitting down next to me in alarm. 'What if I already did? What if I'm working too hard?'

'I was joking,' I said, laughing. 'You're acting super weird.'

'You are!' she yelled.

It was too distracting to have a sharp needle in my hand while she was being all bizarre nearby, so I packed up my stuff and stopped talking to her. I searched around for the most oval-shaped rock I could find, stuck two sticks into the ground, and started flicking the rock between them. After a while, Thi shuffled over and said, 'Can I have a go?'

'Only if you promise not to win.'

'I am definitely going to win,' she said.

She did, but it was okay, since at least it had calmed her down. When training ended, Mum ran over to the fence and said, 'You two should go wait in the foyer, yeah?'

'OKAY,' Thi said.

We hung around with a few other people I half-recognised, like Bucky's older brother Big Bucky, the Cockatoos' leading goalkicker, Abby, and some other players I was good at nodding at as if I remembered their names. Thi stood there getting more and more nervous, while I was just confused why all these players from my old football team were around and hoped this wasn't going to turn into some kind of convince-Homer-to-come-back party, which I both definitely didn't want to happen and was also kind of offended that nobody had even tried to do yet.

When the team came out, Doug turned up in front of the crowd and said, 'Well, it's good to see you, everyone. We're here to talk about the winner of the jersey design competition for the Eastern Cockatoos, the footy club we sponsor. We've invited the designers of our shortlisted entries to be here with us today.'

So *that* was why Thi was here, and nervous. I looked at her hand and thought about how it was really comforting that time when I fell and somebody held mine, and thought that maybe it would be helpful if I held hers. Helpful for her, I mean. And that also it would be helpful for me, maybe, if I held her hand, because then maybe someday soon I could ask her if she wanted to hang out some weekend, and do something that wasn't about footy, so she knew that I knew that she wasn't all about footy.

I took her hand and squeezed it, gently. She squeezed mine back, hard, and I squeaked.

'Now, I'm not one for a lot of chitchat,' Doug said. 'The designs were great, and they'll all be up on the Cockatoos' website for you to see. I'd like to give a special runners-up prize, which is a poster signed by all our players, to the senior team's Donovan Kemp!'

'YES!' Donovan roared, leaping over, grabbing the poster, unrolling it and waving it above his head. I let go of Thi's hand and we clapped.

'Right. Yes.' Doug glared at him. 'Might want to look after that.'

'I will treasure it for eternity,' Donovan said seriously.

'And our winner today is somebody who'd been inspired by a player on our very own team. They'd heard one of our newer players – our star Angela Falzon – say that she was so happy to join that it was like she grew wings.'

Thi's hand was suddenly in mine again, squeezing even harder than before while I mustered up all my power not to yelp.

'And that winner is Thi Pham!'

She squealed, I squealed, her parents squealed, Mum squealed, Doug sighed, and then Thi was up there next to him while everyone applauded and Doug unrolled a blown-up picture of Thi's design. It was an improved version of the one she'd shown me, with the wings going up into the arms and the cockatoo so vibrant on the chest of the jersey it looked like it could've leapt right out of the picture.

'What are you going to use your two-hundred-dollar prize on?' Doug asked.

'Footy membership,' she said without blinking. 'The expensive one, where you can attend a footy clinic as well. And then,' she added, 'I'm going to spend the change on doughnuts.'

'You're amazing!' I said, when the applause died down and everyone started talking to each other again. 'You said you'd win, and you were right.'

'I'm always right,' she said smugly, but then she stopped talking completely. I looked around, confused, until I realised Polly Rocket was coming up to her.

'Great job on the poster,' Polly said, grinning. 'Can't wait to see all you kids wearing it when you're getting recruited in a few years.'

Thi made a sound that was probably supposed to be some kind of human word. I translated, 'She can't wait either.'

Polly reached out for a fist bump, and Thi woke from her shock enough to bump back. Polly walked off, and Thi said, 'She spoke to me. She spoke to me and I said nothing.'

'You definitely said something,' I said. 'But it wasn't a word. You'll meet her again one day anyway when you make the team in six years.'

She looked at me, and her eyes shone.

After everybody else had finished congratulating her too, we walked back outside together. Thi handballed a Sherrin to herself as she walked and we listened to Mum insisting she didn't have anything to do with the voting since she knew she'd be too biased. 'Everyone else loved it because of what it was,' she said proudly. 'Of course, we all know that you'd never have won without me being very inspiring. So, you know, just saying, you owe me a doughnut.'

'And me too!' I yelled. 'I told Thi her drawing was good.'

'You're lucky I even finished it around all the helping you I was doing,' Thi said, rolling her eyes. 'You should owe *me* a doughnut.'

'How about I just bring doughnuts for everyone to the next Cockatoos training session, and we're all square?' Thi's dad said.

'Homer's not at training anymore, remember?' Thi said. 'He quit.'

'Oh no,' Thi's mum said. 'For good?'

The sun was shining in just that right way, and the light was bright and yellow. It caught the ball in Thi's hands and lit it up like gold.

I thought about all the times over the past week since I'd said no to football and I'd just done it anyway. How I'd made my shirt into a ball and kicked it into the laundry basket. How I always imagined the world as goalposts I needed to get between. How I used to be just like Thi, so full of football that everything in my world was all about it, and then I'd gotten mad that everybody thought you could only be Football and you couldn't also be Shirts, and then somehow I'd convinced myself that if you wanted to be Shirts then you couldn't be Football anymore.

When really, you could be anything you wanted.

'No,' I said. 'I don't think it is for good.'

Acknowledgements

It's a very strange experience, writing a book in a pandemic. Especially when you're writing about football and then the whole season closes down so you can't go to any games for a year! So really, the first thing I should thank is my television, for showing matches and replays. Thank you, television, you wonderful thing. I couldn't have done this without you.

There is, of course, a bigger team than just me and a screen in my lounge room. As always, endless thanks to my editor, Meg Whelan, who is always full of excellent advice, logical conclusions and kind but firm suggestions to try and keep the word count from spiralling into thousand-page territory. Every book, there are words I use up to three times in a sentence, and this time it was 'just' and 'gonna'. Without her, these books would be pretty excruciating, and I'm so glad I have her on my squad. And extra thanks to Coral Huckstep as well, who caught the 986 times I wrote 'I mean' when I needed to just start a sentence already. Thanks to Martin, Keiran, Tash, Rosanna, Laura, Susie and Sasha, as well, and Jess Racklyeft, who knocks me out with her covers every time.

Enormous thanks to everybody who helps on the journey to get books into hands – it's a big undertaking, and it involves printers and couriers and warehouse staff and data entry. Then there's the booksellers and librarians, who know just the right book for the right person. Biggest thanks of all goes to the kids who read Movie and Soundtrack and liked them and told their friends or their teachers or told me – I hope you liked this one too!

Huge high-fives to Aaron, Jerome and Fiona Loo for their help on the world of junior football teams. On the clothes-making front, a massive hug to Lian Hingee for answering my frequent texts asking for help trying to work out clothes metaphors that made actual sense, instead of just sounding cool. Squeezy, grateful thanks to Ella Falzon, Matt Falzon, and Nina Silkenbeumer, for their help with language, culture, sport and general know-how – you're wonderful! Any mistakes you read in this book are my fault and not on my epic support team at all.

For their help when I was in need of a variety of knowledge, I want to thank those much smarter than me on many topics: my agent Danielle Binks, Martin & Elliot Shaw, Stephanie Lai, Toby Chan, Giselle Au-Nhien Nguyen, Liah Clark, Tye Cattanach, Kealy Siryj, Cassie Murphy and Andrew McNicol. Also, shout out to Lou and everyone at Little Things for letting me take up a lot of space and eat all your toast, and to all my encouraging, lovely pals at Readings.

As always, endless appreciation to a core group of endlessly helpful friends who do a lot for me in a kind of 'help, I'm stressed about my book being terrible, please reassure me but no you can't read it' kind of way: Dani Solomon, Lian Hingee, Stephanie Lai, Sarah Kennedy, Rachael Mays and Liz McShane.

Huge, massive hugs to my family, who do things like put my books face out to boost my sales (sorry, other booksellers!) or send me jokes, or just pat me on the head when I need it. And to Natalie and Chris, of course, who were the best lockdown company, and who answered my constant questions about things like what it's like to be a kid nowadays, or how cranky I could make Skia before I offended teachers everywhere.

I'm forever grateful for the mountains of times my dad took me to football games when I was a kid, filling me with a deep love for the game and yet only a vague understanding of the rules. It was always a blast, and it was fun to revisit all those memories for Homer. Finally, of course, to all the women who fought to start a league of their own and play Australian Rules so that I could have a kid that will grow up in a world where there's always been AFLW. Thank you. You've changed everything.

About the Author

Fiona Hardy knew she wanted to be a writer when she was in Grade One and got too many compliments for an underwhelming retelling of *Alice in Wonderland*. She loves books so much that she sells them, writes them, and has published reviews for them too. Her first book, *How to Make a Movie in 12 Days*, was a CBCA Notable book and shortlisted for the Speech Pathology Book of the Year Award. Her second book, *How to Write the Soundtrack to Your Life*, won the 2021 Children's Peace Literature Award.

Fiona became a Geelong supporter after her family adopted a cat when she was a kid, which was fine with everyone because the more teams your family barracks for, the more games you can watch. When she was at school, she was terrible at tennis and pretty good at netball. Now, Fiona is mostly just really fast at typing. She lives in Melbourne with her partner and daughter.